Dear Mary,

Happy Christmas

CU00921806

?

24

JOANNA PRICE

A MEANS OF ESCAPE

ASTON BAY

Published in the United Kingdom by Aston Bay Press in 2011

First Edition

Copyright © Joanna Price, 2011

ISBN 978-0-9569830-0-8

www.astonbay.co.uk
www.joannaprice.co.uk

www.facebook.com/AMeansOfEscape
#AMeansOfEscape, @JoPrice3, @AstonBayPress

Cover Design by GB Print
Typeset by Daniel Goldsmith Associates, Cheshire
Printed and bound in the UK by the MPG Books Group, Bodmin and King's Lynn

This book is printed on Vancouver Book Wove, a mixed sources paper, approved by the Forest Stewardship Council (FSC)

"Home is not where you live, but where they understand you"
Christian Morgenstern

"My first plan of escape having failed, I now determined upon another"
Buffalo Bill

For my Mum and Dad

PART ONE

THE
DISCOVERY

ONE

FRIDAY, 20TH OF NOVEMBER

An American couple found it on top of Glastonbury Tor. Despite the cold and misty morning they were picking their way around sheep droppings, determined to watch the sun rise behind the ruined tower. According to their guidebook King Arthur was buried on the hilltop but there was nothing mythical about what they stumbled upon.

Less than an hour later, Detective Sergeant Kate Linton was clambering up the same steep mound, trying to work out how many years it was since she'd been up there. Four, five? Probably more than that. It was certainly the quickest she'd ever climbed it, in spite of the cumbersome overalls and over-shoes she'd changed into at the bottom. She'd jogged most of the route – some of it steps, much of it muddy path – and arrived at the top clutching her left side.

"Stitch," she gasped, in answer to Detective Inspector Rob Brown's raised eyebrows.

He was standing legs astride, one hand on his hip, the other stroking his stubbly chin: a parody of masculinity.

"Less than five minutes it took me," he said. "Sprinted all the way. Hardly broke into a sweat."

"You're amazing. So where is it then?"

"The body?"

"No. Your special medal for being the fastest tosser up the Tor."

"You're in a good mood."

"It's six o'clock in the morning and I'm freezing."

"All right, keep your thong on. It's over by the tower. I'll show you." He turned abruptly and strode across the uneven ground towards the ruined structure. Linton followed, struggling to keep up with his long strides. As she leant into the biting wind, he shouted something. She strained to hear him over the howl of rushing air but couldn't make it out.

"What?" she yelled back.

He shouted again but all she caught was, ". . . we won't need the pathologist to tell us that."

"Shit," she said as, a moment later, they knelt on the damp, uneven ground. A small, sharp stone dug into her knee. She shifted her leg.

"Look at the neck," said Brown, unnecessarily. It was the first thing she'd noticed. Running its length was a deep furrow. It was a dark red. Raw. Linton winced, imagining how much it must've hurt.

"Have we got a name yet?"

"Angel Kingsley." Brown put his gloved hand inside an evidence bag, pulled out a driving licence and passed it to her. "Twenty-five years old. She's from Glastonbury. Windmill Hill. A bit of a looker."

Linton studied the photograph. The woman had shoulder-length chestnut hair, similar to her own. Hazel, almond-shaped eyes. A freckled nose. Pretty.

Not the adjective she'd use to describe her now, she thought, looking back at the body. Angel's face was blue and swollen; the whites of her staring eyes streaked with blood.

"He put so much pressure on her neck, it shot into her capillaries," said Brown. "You can see where they've ruptured and leaked."

"Petechial haemorrhage," she replied under her breath. It was a common feature of strangulation. "Can you smell that?"

Brown sniffed. "What?"

"Patchouli oil."

"I don't know how people can wear that shite."

"We've smelt worse things."

"True. There's the ligature." He pointed to the leather necklace lying limply across the woman's mangled throat. A small crystal pendant hung from it, the same shade of green as Linton's eyes. "It doesn't look sexually motivated."

She shook her head in agreement.

Of course, without a post-mortem they couldn't be certain, but the body had none of the hallmarks of a sex crime. The woman was fully clothed and there was no sign that anyone had disturbed her garments. Every button on her coat was fastened and her grey skinny jeans were still tucked inside the black, calf-length sheepskin boots. Linton had a pair just like them at home.

"Where was the licence?"

"In there." Brown nodded towards the leather handbag lying on the ground nearby. It was zipped. "It was like that when I got here. I took the licence out. And yes, I photographed it first."

Linton moved over to the bag and looked more closely.

"What're you thinking?" Brown asked.

That she'd spent ages looking for one just like it. And that for a split second she wished the woman was still alive so she could ask her where she'd bought it.

"Only that it doesn't look like theft," she said instead. *Unless you counted the taking of someone's life.* She kept that thought to herself as well; Brown wasn't much of a philosopher. "What the hell was she doing up here?"

"Sorry, guys," a voice boomed out behind them.

They turned to see Andy Wallis, the local police surgeon, striding towards them. He was large and hairy, with a stomach that looked like he'd swallowed a barrel. "Apologies for the delay," he bellowed. "I've been at a nasty accident on the Butleigh Road."

They moved away, leaving him with his job of verifying the death, taking the body's temperature and searching for signs of rigor mortis. Brown yanked his mobile from his pocket, pressed some buttons and put it to his ear. He turned away so his back was to the wind. Linton caught a muffled, "All right?", but the rest of his words were lost to the elements. She shivered: a mix of cold and unease. It was eerie in the half-light with a dead body lying a few feet away. For once she missed the annoying drivel of the tourists: the healers and the meditators, the grail theorists and the ley line enthusiasts.

Why had the woman come up here? she wondered again. *On a Thursday night in November?*

"OK," Wallis called out a few moments later.

Brown mumbled a quick "Cheers," and clicked his phone shut. They hurried over, huddling together to hear him better over the noisy gusts.

"The body's lost about sixteen degrees Celsius," said Wallis, as Linton held her hair back from her forehead, trying to stop it from blowing in her eyes. "Rigor hasn't completely set in and lividity isn't fixed yet. My best guess is somewhere between ten p.m. and two a.m."

Brown raised his eyebrows.

"Sorry, mate. That's the best I can do for now."

"All right," Brown sighed, "I'll get SOCO started."

A minute later and the Scene of Crime Officers began their foraging, looking like a bunch of overdressed nit-nurses as they combed and picked at the grass, searching for residues of hair and blood, fibres and scraps of clothing.

Linton's attention was caught by a sudden movement to her left. She looked around. *Shit!* It was Simon Talbot of all people, come to do some foraging of his own. She turned away, anxious not to make eye contact, thinking how ridiculous it was that she still felt embarrassed after all this time. She wasn't surprised to see him here so quickly, although this had to be a record. His sister-in-law worked in the central control room, logging the emergency calls and dispatching them to patrol vehicles for action. Once again she'd obviously done some dispatching closer to home.

Linton nudged Brown. He looked up from his notebook.

"We've got company." She nodded in Talbot's direction, hoping Brown wouldn't notice she was blushing.

"It's that wanker from the *Daily*," he said. "How did he get through? Keen's meant to have closed the paths. Where is he?"

"How should I know?"

"He can't be too close or we'd have smelt him. Ring him. Tell him to get his arse in gear. I'll deal with Talbot."

Linton watched him striding purposely towards Talbot and reached for her phone inside the pocket of her overalls. She dialled Keen's number, hearing the familiar ring tone of 'I Should Be So Lucky' nearby.

The music stopped as he picked up. "I'm just below you," he said. "Look down. I'm waving at you."

She peered through the curling mist. She could see a shadowy figure, one arm outstretched towards her. Maybe she was imagining it, but she thought she could smell the scent of sweaty beef he carried permanently around with him.

"What's up?" he asked.

"Brown wants to know if everything's cordoned off. A journalist's managed to slip through."

"Nearly there. And tell him we've done a thorough search and no sign of anyone suspicious. You know how these sickos like to stick around at the crime scene."

Linton hung up, wondering as she did what her mum would make of this. A murder on her precious landmark, her favourite place, her *inspiration*.

"It's so steeped in myth and legend," she'd say to visitors to the gallery where she displayed her work. "When I recreate it on a canvas, I can feel its immense power being channelled through my brushes. It's as though, by painting it, I'm being linked to ancient times."

Her sales patter had always made Linton cringe.

But this morning, she thought grudgingly, she understood what her mum meant. Watching the SOCO team move slowly round the body, kneeling gently at the victim's head and feet, she felt she was witnessing a strange and primitive ritual.

Just beyond the tower, Brown was talking to one of the SOCO team. He looked animated, waving his arms around, tipping his head back as he laughed. After a minute it dawned on Linton that the SOCO was a woman.

"Unbelievable," she muttered, shaking her head.

As she turned away, she spotted Simon Talbot again. He was now standing behind the phosphorescent tape that whirled and flapped against his thighs, banging his gloved hands together in an effort to keep warm. He looked expectant, as though waiting for further instruction. He must've sensed Linton watching him, because he suddenly looked up and waved. She nodded back in what she hoped was a casual manner, feeling herself redden again. It was fifteen years since that awkward hour spent in his bedroom, but she still felt humiliated.

"The head of SOCO seems to know what she's doing." She jumped. It was Brown.

"What's the verdict?"

"She seems all right. It's hard to tell with all that stuff on."

"I meant that." She tutted and waved her hand in the direction of the body.

"I know what you meant, Linton. I was joking."

"Let me know next time and I'll make sure I laugh."

"What's up with you?"

"Nothing," she snapped, wondering why she suddenly felt so irritable. "Do they think she was killed in situ?"

"They're almost certain. There's no sign of her being dragged. No grass or mud stains on her jeans or boots. Not that anyone could haul a dead body up here."

"True." Lugging her crime scene bag up the steep path had been hard enough.

"D'you think she knew him?"

Brown shrugged. He didn't correct her use of the pronoun. He obviously assumed it was a man as well. Of course talking to the media, they'd be careful to say "him or her", but with something like this, it was bound to be a bloke. It nearly always was.

"I know an outdoors murder means it's more likely to be random," he said, "but not up here."

She nodded her agreement. "It's a bit far-fetched: coming up alone in the dark and then being attacked by a stranger. It's more likely she was here with someone she knew."

"No wedding ring," said Brown.

"A lovers' tiff that got out of hand?"

"Maybe."

"Rob?" They both turned in the direction of the voice. It was the SOCO he'd been chatting up; she was walking towards them.

"I expect she wants to give me her phone number," he murmured. Linton rolled her eyes. "Joke," he mouthed, as the SOCO reached them.

"We've found something," she said, breathlessly. "I'm not sure if it's significant. Can you come and take a look?"

TWO

For the second time that day, Linton was straining to hear what Brown was saying. She'd been listening in on his phone call for the last couple of minutes, ever since he'd punched his fist in the air and shouted, "Bingo!" He was mumbling into the receiver now, swinging from side to side in his chair and it was impossible to make out what he was saying.

She went back to her notes. She was supposed to be compiling a list of what she'd found out about the murdered woman, Angel Kingsley.

Since graduating from Plymouth three years ago with a degree in Drama, the twenty-five-year-old had lived with her mum in Glastonbury. She had no siblings. Her dad had re-married and emigrated to Vancouver seven years ago. He was currently touring Canada with his blues band.

Keen was the first Detective Sergeant at the scene, so it was his duty to break the news to Angel's mum. Mrs Kingsley told him her daughter was currently unemployed, but her last job was with All's Well, a local theatre company. She'd left them four months ago.

"Poor cow," Brown had said, out of earshot. "It's bad enough being told your daughter's dead without being on the receiving end of Keen's halitosis."

Linton had rung the theatre company earlier. She was greeted by an answerphone message so she'd left one of her own, asking someone to call her back. So far, nobody had.

As she reached for the phone to try again, Brown slammed his down. "Who's the daddy!" he called out.

She glanced up. He was looking over with a self-satisfied grin. She shook her head and looked back down again. *Who's the daddy?* What a prick.

Faking a yawn, she stared at her computer, studying the screensaver with intensity. She swore she could hear Brown begging, *Go on then, ask me, ask me what I know*, and wondered why recently she got so much pleasure from winding him up.

"That was the NCC lot," he said finally, in a loud enough voice to ensure Hooper, who was working on a desk across from them, looked up. "Guess what?" He paused dramatically, making sure he'd got the trainee detective's attention. "We've got a definite match with another murder. An unsolved in Wiltshire. He's killed before."

"When?" asked Hooper, eager as ever. Out of the corner of her eye, Linton saw Detective Chief Inspector Hargreaves through the glass window of his office, rising slowly out of his seat. His eyes bulged as he pushed down on his short arms, struggling to propel himself up. It amazed her: his unnerving ability to sense when anything major was happening. Sometimes she wondered if their office was bugged.

"It'll have to wait," Brown said, nodding towards Hargreaves. "I better tell The Toad first. Don't want him thinking he was the last to know."

Arselicker, Linton thought as he grinned at her and strode towards the DCI's office.

•••

A couple of hours earlier, Linton had heard Brown give instructions for four words to be run through the National Crime Computer to see if the particulars of Angel Kingsley's murder matched any others on the database.

The first three words entered into the system were obvious ones, FEMALE, STRANGLED, OUTDOORS.

The fourth, however, was a word she doubted the operator had used before and came about thanks to the discovery Brown's new SOCO 'friend' had made. She'd spotted a circle in the earth close to Angel Kingsley's body, roughly three metres in circumference and made up of twelve small holes. The holes were approximately six centimetres deep and around each one was a tiny lump of hardened wax in red, yellow, orange or green.

"What d'you think?" she'd asked Brown.

"Garden flares," he'd announced confidently, pushing himself back up from the dewy grass. The SOCO had looked confused. "Outdoor candles," he explained. "People have them at barbecues and garden parties."

Linton knew exactly what he meant. She'd once policed Glastonbury Festival as a PC and watched a drunken partygoer stagger forward onto one, setting the front of his t-shirt alight.

"Judging by the amount of wax deposit, I shouldn't think they were burning for long before someone took them away."

"Do you think it's connected to the death?"

"It's got to be worth a go. I'll get the NCC to add it to the search terms – see if it matches any other crimes."

WAX. The fourth word.

Such a small, simple one, but it got them a result. An unsolved murder in Wiltshire. And right now Brown was in Hargreaves' office no doubt boasting it was down to him they'd thought of using the search term.

Linton wondered how long he'd be in with The Toad. Despite pretending not to be interested, she wanted to know what Brown had found out. Who else had Angel's killer murdered? Where in Wiltshire? And when? She hated being left out of the loop and Brown knew it. God, he was such a dickhead.

Then she remembered he'd been scrawling on an A4 pad while he was on the phone. Perhaps she'd be able work it out from his notes?

She sent Hooper off to make some tea and moved round to Brown's desk, sweeping crumbs off his swivel chair before sitting down. She shuddered involuntarily at the mess. As usual, it was covered with paperwork and tatty Post-it notes. Four mugs, their insides brown and stained, were arranged haphazardly among his wallet, iPhone and a heavy bunch of keys. His keyboard was coated with crumbs and a half-eaten muffin lay discarded next to his mouse. As always, she was baffled. How could someone so fastidious about his appearance be happy to sit in such squalor?

She found the notepad next to his phone and pulled it towards her. He'd written *WILTSHIRE* in capital letters and drawn a couple of thick, black rings around it. Next to it he'd jotted down the initials *AS*. What did they stand for? Asphyxiation? No. That didn't make sense. It must mean something else.

He'd scribbled down two other words – *wax* and *circle* – along with two names – *Hannah James* and *Sadie Carter*. That didn't make sense either. He said it was a direct match. An unsolved in Wiltshire. He didn't say anything about *two* matches.

Her phone started ringing so she moved round to her own desk, relieved to be back in the land of hygiene.

"Hello? DS Linton speaking."

The woman on the other end introduced herself as the manager of All's Well, the theatre company Angel had worked for.

"I . . . I've just got your message," she stammered. "I turned on the news to check . . . I just can't believe it . . ."

"I understand Angel Kingsley was a member of your company," Linton interrupted.

"Well, she *was*, until about four months ago. She had a part in our current production, *One Flew over the Cuckoo's Nest*." There was an obvious tremor in the woman's voice, whether from nerves or excitement Linton couldn't be sure.

"Why did she leave? Did she have another job lined up?"

"As far as I know, she hasn't worked since she left."

Linton glanced up to see Hooper advancing towards her with a mug of tea. She smiled and put her thumb up as he left it on her desk. She watched him lollop back to his own then took a quick sip and winced.

"Did she fall out with someone?"

"Nothing like that. To be honest, I think we were too small for her."

"Too local?"

"I wouldn't say that, we tour all over the country. We were in Lincoln yesterday. That's why I hadn't heard. The radio in the minibus doesn't work and we've only just got back. The roads were a nightmare. It took us over five hours . . ."

"What do you mean by 'too small'?" Linton interrupted again, sensing she'd been about to get an insight into Angel's personality.

"Put it this way, we're never going to be on telly. And Angel was obsessed with being famous. Most of the younger ones are. She didn't have a very big part. She played one of the nurses. But, like I say, everyone's got to start somewhere."

"So you stayed the night in Lincoln?"

"The whole company did. We didn't come off stage until eleven."

"And was it the same cast as when Angel was with you?"

"Exactly the same. Oh, except for Elisa of course, the girl we got to replace her."

Nothing there, then. No falling out with anyone in the theatre company and, besides, they were miles away when she was killed. Linton thanked her and hung up.

It was another five minutes before Brown came sauntering out of The Toad's office. He sat down and started making an annoying clicking noise with his tongue. Linton pretended he wasn't there and carried on typing.

"The direct match," he said finally, "you'll never guess where in Wiltshire it was."

She looked up and shrugged. "Salisbury?" she replied, hoping she'd at least got the right county.

"Come on!" he said, reaching for the muffin and pulling off a chunk. "What's Wiltshire got in common with Glastonbury Tor?"

She shook her head.

"Think ancient sites," he mumbled, his mouth full of cake.

"Stonehenge?"

"Guess again."

"Brown, stop being such a tosser and tell me."

"You know, I could have you up for insolence to a superior."

"Brown!"

"All right." He put his hand up in mock defence. "Our direct match was at Avebury Stones."

So that's what the initials AS stood for, she thought.

"I told The Toad it could be a sacrificial thing. A ritual killing. They're both ancient sites, the Tor and Avebury, running along the same ley lines and all that bollocks."

"What do we know about the case?"

"The victim was a twenty-one-year-old. Hannah James. Local to Avebury. She was strangled, but manually this time."

"When?"

"Back in January. And guess what they found near her body?"

"A circle of wax?"

He grinned. "Just like on the Tor."

She remembered what else she'd seen in his notebook. "Why did you write down two names?"

He raised his eyebrows.

"You ran off without telling me anything."

"I didn't think you were interested. Too busy studying the Avon and Somerset screensaver. What? Don't look so surprised. I can see your computer screen reflected in the window behind you. I know everything you're up to."

She flushed, hoping he hadn't seen the website link Lisa had sent yesterday, the one she'd clicked on before she realised what it was. She'd hit the back button as soon as she saw the montage of photos and its caption: *Somerset singles latest members! Could your perfect partner be online now?* But perhaps she hadn't been quick enough.

"Why the two names?" she said, trying to hide her embarrassment by leaning over and picking up her handbag from the floor, hoping he'd credit the colour in her cheeks to her bending down.

"The NCC also threw up a partial match. Another link to a separate death."

"What d'you mean by a 'partial match'?" she asked, confused, as she found the packet of tissues she didn't need and pulled them out of her bag.

"Another woman was found dead a few weeks later. Sadie Carter. Same place, Avebury Stones, but this time the flares were left in the ground at the crime scene." He paused. "Except it wasn't technically a crime scene. Hence the partial match."

"What are you saying? Was it suicide?"

"No. But she wasn't murdered either. Not as such."

"Hang on. You've lost me now. We've got one murder and one not exactly a murder."

"Apparently when we read the police report, it'll all become clear."

"Brown!" It was The Toad, advancing towards them at a pace considerable considering the stumpiness of his legs.

"I've got authorisation from Wiltshire," he croaked. "Permission to dial into their files. Chop-chop."

"I'll get on with it now, Sir." With that, The Toad turned and stomped back towards his lair.

Linton glanced at her watch. It was gone six o'clock. She'd already done twelve hours and she was knackered.

"You go home," said Brown. "No point both of us being here. We're going to be flat out for the next few days."

"You sure?" she said, gratefully. She started to reach for her handbag again and stopped. "Hang on. Why are you being nice to me all of a sudden?"

"Don't sound so suspicious. You look like shit, that's all."

"Thanks."

"You're bright red. Like you've got a temperature." He nodded at the packet of tissues, still in her hand. "I don't want you ringing in sick; not with all this going on."

"I'm fine . . ."

"Anyway, I'm meeting Matt at eight and I can't be arsed to go home first. What about you? Fancy coming out later? It might perk you up. I expect we'll end up at Joker's."

Joker's. The local nightclub, if you could call it a nightclub. Well, there was music playing and you could have a drink, but then the same could be said about her front room. It was funny for about five minutes, taking the piss out of the decor and the DJ, but then it just felt desperate.

"My ideal night out: watching you two ponce around in your tight jeans, full of testosterone and making idiots of yourselves. I can stay at home and watch *Top Gear* if I want to see that."

"Worried about bumping into Ben, are you?"

Linton felt a tight squeeze in her chest. "I couldn't care less," she said, looking down at her desk to avoid eye contact.

"You know he'd have you back in an instant."

"After what he did? He can get stuffed."

Brown shook his head slowly and said, "I still can't believe he was such a twat."

"Finally," she said, triumphantly, "You agree with me."

"I meant for telling you. Why didn't he just keep his mouth shut?" She looked up. Brown was smirking. "Oh come on," he said, "you've got to admit. It is quite funny."

"You know what?" she said, "I think he was more of a twat for telling *you*."

"He'd had a skinful. And not only that," he said, in response to her look of disdain, "I think he wanted someone to talk to."

"Boast to, you mean," she said bitterly. "Of everyone, he knows you'd be the most impressed."

•••

Sam Jenkins could feel the irritation creeping up on her. Jittery legs, a clenched jaw, the urge to scream at the driver to *hurry up*.

She recognised the symptoms. It was the beginning of a hypo. She'd check her blood sugar with her testing kit as soon as she got to the Star and Garter, but for now some Lucozade should do the trick.

She pulled the bottle out of her handbag, undid the lid and took a sip, pleased with herself that, for once, she'd been organised and bought some from the newsagents before getting on the bus. She'd lost count of the number of times she'd been caught short, having to send a mate off to buy glucose tablets or a carton of orange juice, anything sugary to stop the sweating and the heart palpitations and the agitation from taking a more dangerous turn, like loss of consciousness or, God forbid, a coma.

Her phone rang. It was Claire, her sister.

"Where are you?"

"Still on the bus," she groaned. "We've just gone past that place where mum goes for acupuncture."

"I wanted to check you're all right for tomorrow."

"I'm looking forward to it."

"Are you still staying at Abby's tonight?"

"Yeah. I reckon it's going to be a late one."

"I was hoping you might change your mind," said Claire, disappointment evident in her voice. "It's lonely here without mum."

"I won't get in until late and you'll be in bed by then."

"I s'pose," Claire conceded. "Go careful, won't you? Have you got all your stuff with you?"

"Yes! You can tell you're living with mum again. You're starting to sound like her!"

"It's just I know what you're like."

Bugger, Sam thought as she hung up. Had she packed her diabetes kit? She pulled open her overnight bag and rooted around. No. She frigging well hadn't. *Fuck, fuck, fuckety-fuck.* No monitor, no insulin, no syringes. Luckily she kept a spare at their mum's, who, thank God, was on holiday, so she could pick it up without getting the 'Oh, Sam, you need to start being more responsible' lecture. Of course she'd have to ring Claire later, suffer the humiliation of her older sister's 'So I was right to be worried' lecture instead. But then, *she* could hardly lecture her on irresponsibility, could she?

Perhaps Claire wouldn't mind popping up to the pub with it? On second thoughts, it probably wasn't fair to ask her, not under the circumstances. No, she'd meet her friends as planned, have a couple of drinks, nip down and pick up her spare kit, and walk back up to the pub again.

She sighed loudly and shifted in her seat, hoping the Lucozade would work soon. The chug and throb of the vibrating bus was getting to her now.

Wiping condensation from the window with the back of her sleeve, she peered out into the November gloom and saw the familiar road sign: WELCOME TO THE ANCIENT ISLE OF AVALON. Not long to go now. A few more minutes and they'd reach the high street: the gentle hill of New Age shops with their crystals and incense, tarot cards and essential oils, paintings and postcards of the Tor.

She thought of Angel. She still couldn't believe what had happened. She was never that friendly with her, but she seemed like a nice enough girl. It was a shock to hear it on the news; exciting to be honest, not that she'd ever admit it. Murders weren't uncommon in Bristol, but in Glastonbury . . . nothing like this had happened before. Everyone at work was impressed she knew the victim.

This frigging bus. It was so hot and stuffy and noisy. She put her headphones on and pressed shuffle, hoping for some respite from the annoying drone of the engine. Amy Winehouse's 'Rehab' started playing.

As she listened to the lyrics she couldn't help thinking of Claire again. She'd already made her decision; there was no backing out now. She'd tell her sister this weekend. About what had *really* happened the night their dad died. She'd had enough of lugging this guilt around with her for the last three years. She'd made excuse after excuse for not telling her and for the last couple of years Claire couldn't have handled it. But she was better now.

She'd tell her tomorrow. After they'd had the massage she'd booked at Aphrodite's.

She'd confess and finally get the weight of this guilt off her shoulders.

THREE

"Morning, everyone," Linton called out across the incident room, weaving her way in and out of desks. Nobody answered. As she reached the end of the obstacle course, she tried again. "Morning. Anyone?"

Brown managed a short grunt, but didn't look up. If she was in a better mood, she might've put the lack of response down to hard work and concentration. But she wasn't.

"Ignorant tossers," she muttered.

"What?" Brown asked, still not looking up.

Linton didn't bother answering. Instead she turned on her computer and sneaked a glance at him. A slight redness around his eyes was the only evidence of his night on the tiles, otherwise he looked his usual magazine-styled self.

How did he do it? Look so bloody polished? She knew his routine because she'd heard it often enough. The pub, the club and six pints of Stella. And then, if he pulled, which he always did, hardly any sleep. She thought how long it had taken her to look vaguely presentable this morning. And that was without a single drop of alcohol passing her lips the night before.

She felt like punching him.

"What time were you in?" *It must've been early*, she thought; the mug he'd chosen to pilfer today, *Elmtree School – 50 Years*, was nearly empty, and he always let his tea go cold before he drank it.

"About an hour ago. I made a bad choice," he said, leaning back in his seat and grinning. "She seemed like a good idea at the time. Anyway, I couldn't wait to get away this morning."

So she'd been right about him pulling someone. Linton pictured the scene in Joker's: a woman with her cleavage hanging out, shrieking and laughing at everything he said, her eyes glistening at the prospect of getting off with the good-looking detective.

"Bloody hell!" her friend Lisa had said when she first met Brown. "I wouldn't chuck him out of bed."

"He's a bit too chiselled for my liking," Linton had replied. "And besides, he's a womanising prick."

As for Brown, she often wondered if he had a type. Blonde, brunette, busty, slim? It didn't seem to matter as long as they were up for it. If last night's conquest was put in a line up, she doubted she'd be able to pick her out. Mind you, in future, he might not have as much choice. A lot of women would be scared to go out once they'd seen today's headlines: *"How long before he kills again?"*

"Have you seen the papers?" she asked. "They're saying it's a serial killer."

"They're probably right."

"We don't know for sure."

He looked up. "Come on, Linton. We've got a match on the NCC with another unsolved."

"Who told the media about the connection to Avebury?"

"The Toad."

"It's a bit premature, isn't it?"

"We know he's killed before and he hasn't been caught. That's enough. Hargreaves wants the public made aware of the possible danger. I s'pose he doesn't want egg on his warty face if another girl gets it." He ended the sentence with a long yawn.

"I presume you made it to Joker's then," she said. "How was the hottest venue in the South West? Did you throw some shapes on the dance floor?"

"Why? What did you get up to that was so exciting? In bed by nine with Charles Dickens and a cup of Horlicks?"

"I've never even read a Dickens novel."

"I thought you said your dad taught English Literature?"

"He did. That's why. And actually," she continued hurriedly, before he could ask what she meant, "I caught up with a couple of friends." She hadn't, of course. She went to bed with Patricia Cornwell – her newest Scarpetta novel was out. And it wasn't because she was a sad loser without a life, but because she'd got it back to herself. She could go to bed when she liked, keep her reading light on all night if she wanted without Ben grumbling that it was keeping him awake. But Brown wouldn't understand that.

Had he seen her ex last night, Linton wondered, clenching her fists until she realised her nails were digging into her palms. She wouldn't ask. She wouldn't know what to do with the answer anyway.

"In case you're interested," he said, "I went through the initial reports from the Avebury deaths."

"What's that meant to mean? Of course I'm interested."

"You're more concerned with what I got up to last night. I bet you're dying to ask if I saw Ben."

"No, I'm not." She felt her nails again.

He shrugged. "I printed the reports off." He rummaged around on his desk, until he found a pile of A4 sheets held together with a clip. "Have a look." He leant across his desk and handed them to her. He smelt of aftershave and washing powder and for a split second she wondered what the stubble on his chin would feel like.

"What?" he said, rubbing at his cheeks. "Have I got something on my face?"

She'd been about to ask how the second victim at Avebury died, but instead she grabbed the pile of paperwork from him, swallowing hard as she felt the familiar flush of embarrassment creeping up her neck. What was wrong with her?

She pulled the sheets of typed A4 sharply towards her and began to read.

WILTSHIRE POLICE

Report created: 3 January 2009 by PC Hopkins

Victim: Hannah James DOB: 13/07/1988

Place: Avebury Stones

Nature of Case: Homicide

At 7.45 a.m. on 2 January 2009, Sergeant Pritchard contacted myself and PC Merton and asked us to respond to a report that a dead body had been found at Avebury Stones. We arrived at the location at 7.51 a.m., where we were met by an elderly gentleman who'd discovered the body of a young woman whilst taking a shortcut across the field (see Appendix 1a for interview).

Initial observations:
Markings on the victim's neck led us to believe she was
strangled to death. This was backed up by the police surgeon
when he arrived ten minutes later. We also noticed a circle of
colourful waxy residue next to the victim's body and
mentioned this to the Scene of Crime Officers when they
arrived.

Appendix 1a, the interview with the elderly gentleman, was attached
to the report. Linton skim-read it, but didn't find anything particularly
illuminating; he'd discovered the body, he'd phoned the police. She
was much more interested in finding out about Sadie Carter, the
second woman to die at the stones; the one who wasn't killed or
committed suicide. She riffled through the pile until she found the
police report.

WILTSHIRE POLICE
Report created: 26 February 2009 by PC Mantel
Victim: Sadie Carter DOB: 22/05/1984
Place: Avebury Stones
Nature of Case: Suspicious Death
At 7.45 a.m. on Sunday 25 February 2009 PC Hammond and
I were asked to respond to a report of a body discovered at
Avebury Stones. It appeared to match the description of Sadie
Carter, a local woman reported missing two days earlier. We
arrived at the scene at 7.56 a.m. and were met by Mr Colin
Brine, the vicar. He said he was on his way to church to
rehearse his sermon when he spotted a man as he turned the
corner from Church Lane. Mr Brine said the man was
obviously in shock as he was running around, tripping over
his wellies and shouting, "It's not fair!" over and over again.
He took him to the church to calm him down, which is where
we later interviewed him (please refer to interview notes,
Appendix A). The man's name is Mr Richard Cooke. He has
been in Avebury for a week and is staying here temporarily
while he flat-sits for a friend. He found the body whilst
searching for his car keys, which he believes he dropped the
evening before whilst walking his friend's dog.

Observations:
My colleague and I concluded the most recent victim was
sexually assaulted and killed. Her coat was lying nearby. She
was wearing a black fitted top but it was pulled up over her
breasts to reveal a flesh-coloured, lace-trimmed bra. She was
curled up under an overhang of one of the larger stones. The
scraping on the back of her hands and elbows suggested a
struggle.
    We found a circle of twelve unlit wax garden flares in a
variety of colours next to Sadie Carter's body. We knew waxy
residue was found near the body of the woman who was
murdered at the same place seven weeks ago and thought the
cases may be linked.

"So the Wiltshire lot were wrong about Sadie Carter," she said to
Brown, when she reached the end of the second report.
    "What do you mean?"
    "They thought it was sexual assault and murder. But you said she
wasn't killed."
    "She wasn't. At least not according to the pathologist's report."
    "What did it say?"
He rummaged about on his desk again, pushing pieces of paper
around. "It's here somewhere." She had to fight the temptation to go
over and look for it herself. He finally found it, flicked over a couple of
pages and cleared his throat.
    "Despite circumstantial evidence and finding a large amount of
barbiturate in her system, I don't believe the victim was sexually
assaulted or murdered. In accordance with my findings I have stated
the cause of death was accidental . . ."
    "Accidental?" she interrupted. "What findings is he on about?"
He yawned and put the report down. "It goes on for pages. Basically,
it explains why Sadie's clothing was removed. And why they found her
huddled against one of the stones."
    "And?" she prompted.
    "It was due to 'paradoxical undressing' and 'hide and die'."
    "I've never heard of them."
    "Really?" He sounded genuinely surprised. "Don't you remember that
old woman who died last winter? The one in Yorkshire." Linton shook

her head. "Her son found her under her bed, half-naked and covered in blood. He thought she'd been sexually assaulted. It was in the papers."

"If you mean the *Sunday Sport*, then I wouldn't have seen it."

He ignored the dig. "She was worried about paying bills so she'd turned her heating off. Her body got so cold it shut down and her hypothalamus went haywire."

"Her what?"

He tutted. "Her body's thermostat. She thought she was boiling hot but she was freezing to death. Anyway, she took off her clothes to try and cool herself down. That's why they call it paradoxical undressing. Paradoxical means . . ."

"I know what it means, thank you."

"She died of hypothermia."

"That's horrible." The idea of old people in any distress upset her. "So what's 'hide and die'?"

"What animals do when they know they're going to die. They find somewhere to crawl under, out of sight. It's how the old lady got her scrapes and bruises: she tried to cram herself under her bed."

"And that's why they found Sadie half-naked, curled up under the stones?"

"Exactly."

She could almost picture it. A young woman shaking with cold as she pulled off her clothes, desperately trying to cool herself down despite the fact she was freezing to death, crawling across the icy ground, to cower under some rocks. She shuddered.

"What do you think happened to our candle man?"

"I reckon he must've heard something and ran off. Left her there to freeze to death. Don't forget, she was drugged up to her eyeballs, so she was probably only half-conscious. And then once the cold got to her that was it."

"It makes sense," she said. "About the killer being interrupted. That's obviously why the flares were still in the ground. He didn't get a chance to take them with him." She paused and then said, "Do they think he'd held her captive for the two days she was missing?"

"It's the most likely explanation."

"But why didn't he take her to the stones straight away?"

"Perhaps he couldn't. Or if it *was* some sort of sacrifice, maybe the date was significant."

"I suppose it's why he drugged her," she said, thoughtfully. "She was hardly going to go without a fight, was she? Not when she knew someone was killed there a few weeks before." She paused. "It's not a nice way to go, is it? Dying of hypothermia."

"And you think the alternative's better?" said Brown. "Being strangled?"

He was right. It's probably what would've happened to Sadie Carter if the killer hadn't been interrupted. The killer who throttled Hannah James and then went on to strangle Angel Kingsley.

How long before he kills again?

•••

Claire Jenkins felt queasy. She'd drunk too much tea on an empty stomach. And the Silk Cut hadn't helped. She was annoyed with herself for giving up so soon on her new 'no smoking before midday' rule. More than anything, she was pissed off at her sister, Sam. She was over an hour late now and *still* no sign of her. She wasn't answering her mobile either.

She checked her phone again. No messages. *Come on Sam, you lazy cow. Wake up.* She was used to her younger sibling being late, but this was taking the piss. She could've made the effort today; set the alarm on her phone or something. Especially today. *Today of all days.* Sam knew how much of a milestone this was for her.

She stared out of the window of the café, irritated by the number of people already lining the pavements of the high street despite the weather, baggsy-ing their places for the evening ahead. Hunched over, hoods up and faces defiant. *We will not be moved.*

"For God's sake," Claire wanted to shout, "it doesn't even start until seven o'clock."

There were another eight hours to go, probably even longer. She couldn't remember a year when it had begun on time. There was always a last-minute hitch. A generator would break down; a float would get stuck.

Glastonbury Carnival. The Mardi Gras of the Mendips. It wasn't as big or as famous as its summer cousin, the music festival, but it was just as popular with the locals.

She looked at her watch again. It wouldn't be long before they closed the roads but there was still no sign of her sister. On the other side of the street she could see Dick from the crystal and gem shop striding along the pavement, his dark ponytail whipping his lower back. Her friend Adam had nicknamed him 'Sunbeam', taking the piss out of the way he'd changed his name to Star because it sounded more cosmic. She and Sam were going to see him later, to buy a present for their mum's birthday before their pampering session at Aphrodite's. Sam wanted to get a bracelet to match the turquoise necklace her mum always wore. She'd spoken to Dick the day before and he'd promised to give them a discount.

Where was she? Sod it. She'd ring Abby. Surely she'd be up by now. She picked up her phone again. Sam's friend eventually answered, her voice throaty, slightly muffled.

"Hiya. It's Claire. I hope I didn't get you up . . . fine, thanks. Good time last night . . .? Great. I've been trying to get hold of Sam, but she's not answering. Listen, you couldn't do me a favour, could you, and wake her up? . . . Oh, that's weird. She was definitely in Glastonbury last night. I rang her. She was on the bus. She said she was going straight to the pub and staying at yours . . . maybe. I'll try her next."

Typical Sam. It wasn't enough to let one person down. No wonder their dad used to get so cross with her. Her constant lateness at college, the way she never took anything seriously. She sighed and scrolled down her numbers looking for the name Abby suggested.

Ten minutes later and she'd had enough of waking people up. She would give Sam five more minutes, she decided, and then go. She leant across to the table next to her and picked up the magazine left behind by its previous occupant. Becki Harvey, complete with trademark tan and scarlet lipstick, was smiling coyly on the front cover, accompanied by the headline: *"Reality star to publish autobiography."* Sam would definitely want to read this. *That's if she ever turned up.* She flicked through the glossy pages until she found the story:

COME ON, BECKI. TELL US WHO HE IS!

Not to be outdone by her fellow reality TV stars, Becki Harvey, winner of the hit television series *Working Girl*, has announced she's writing her autobiography at the tender age of 22. One critic has joked she should call it a 'short

story', but Becki says she's packed more into the last two years than most people do in a lifetime.

She promises her autobiography will be 'no holds barred' and she'll spill the beans on a relationship she's had with a yet unnamed prominent public figure – who happens to be a happily married father of four.

When she won *Working Girl* back in 2007, Becki was seldom out of the papers. Since splitting up with footballer Gavin Shanks at the end of last year, her fame has dwindled. She recently appeared in OK! magazine with an exclusive, claiming this mystery man threatened her when she told him she was going to reveal his identity, but many see this as a ploy to get her name into the headlines again.

Claire studied the picture of the skimpily clad Becki Harvey. If it weren't for the cold weather, she thought, her sister would be similarly dressed. It was funny how alike Becki and Sam were. Both self-centred, attention-seeking blondes. No wonder they got on so well when they worked together.

She tried her sister's phone again. It went straight to voicemail. For the first time, she felt a vague sense that something wasn't right. Her sister was unreliable, but she wasn't normally as bad as this.

Had she had a hypo? Perhaps she was lying somewhere in a coma. But that was crazy. She'd spoken to her moments before the bus was due to arrive in Glastonbury and she'd sounded fine, hadn't she? And anyway, she only had to walk from the bus stop to the pub. If she'd collapsed, it would've have been on the high street and someone would've found her.

There was another possibility of course, another reason for Sam not to answer her phone. But she didn't want to think about that. If the idea of her sister lying in a ditch somewhere filled her with panic, this was almost as bad.

It couldn't be that. Could it? She was being paranoid. Danny, Sam's ex-boyfriend, promised he wouldn't tell. He'd sworn on his life – said it'd only give Sam another excuse to hassle him.

But then, why else couldn't she get hold of her sister?

FOUR

Claire read the message before pressing 'Send'.

Hi mum,
Sorry I missed your call. I must've been on the phone to someone else. I tried ringing you back but your mobile was switched off (what a surprise!).

Just wondered if you'd heard from Sam. Probably not as your phone's not on! I've left a couple of messages, but she hasn't rung back. Don't start worrying! You know what she's like.

Thanks for what you said in your email. And for your support over the last few months. I couldn't have done it without you.

I hope you're enjoying your last day. Make the most of it. It's pouring with rain here.
Can't wait to see you tomorrow. Have a good flight!
Lots and lots of love, Claire

PS. If you do speak to Sam, can you ask her to ring me asap?

...

Everyone was squeezed into the already cramped incident room for a briefing. Bottoms were balanced precariously on the edge of desks, hierarchies ignored when it came to chairs.

Thanks to the offer of help from neighbouring forces, their number had increased by two. Linton let her gaze roam over the new recruits, allowing first impressions and stereotyping to do the work.

Bald, overweight bloke. Red-raw face, like a big chilblain. Lives in tracksuits on his days off, loves football but never plays it, thinks Kormas are for poofs, drinks too much coffee and real ale.

Girly-looking woman with painted nails. Blonde hair pulled up into a high ponytail. Loves children and baby animals. Bedroom painted in Dulux's 'Sexy Pink'. Probably says "ahh" and "bless" a lot. No ring on her finger. Perfect fodder for Brown's ever ravenous ego. Nice boots though . . .

The Toad's mobile rang.

"I need to take this," he said, moving towards the door and ending the no-nonsense ringtone with a deft jab of his thumb. "Brown," he ordered, "you can start without me." He pulled his phone to his ear and left the room.

Brown jumped up and strode to the middle of the room, standing in the spot The Toad had occupied seconds before.

"Morning everyone," he said, confidently. "Hargreaves has asked me to put together a short summary of what we've gleaned so far from going through the two unsolved Avebury cases. I'll start with the first body, discovered back in January. Twenty-one-year-old Hannah James. She was manually strangled . . ."

God, he loves himself, Linton thought, tuning out. Anyone watching could see how much he was relishing his moment in front of a captive audience, the intensity of his eyes heightened by his cornflower-blue shirt. She wondered if he was vain enough to have worn it for that reason, and watched him flash his celebrity-white grin at the new girly blonde woman, deciding that, yes, he definitely was.

Hargreaves returned a few minutes later, as Brown's monologue was drawing to a close.

" . . . so we need to cross-check every name we collect from Angel Kingsley's case against those gathered during the Avebury investigation."

Hargreaves gestured to Brown to sit down and then turned to address the rest of them. Not for the first time, Linton was taken aback by his sheer ugliness. His skin looked particularly dry and bumpy, his hooded eyes more bulging and watery than ever. The combination of a brown suit with a bright purple tie didn't help.

When he spoke, she could hear the sticky tackiness of his mouth as he carefully pronounced his words. She could tell he was stressed. A case like this was bound to attract lots of media attention: a young woman murdered, the possibility of a serial killer. He was under extra pressure to get it solved quickly.

"Right then," he said, looking over at Fat Bloke and Blonde Ponytail. "For the benefit of colleagues who've recently joined us, I'll go over what we've got so far. We're waiting for results from forensics but in the meantime we need to assume the deaths of the two Avebury women, Hannah James and Sadie Carter, are connected to the murder of Angel Kingsley. The NCC matched the crimes. Similar location, similar MO, outdoors, strangulation, and, above all, evidence of wax flares placed in a circle at each of the crime scenes."

"It's definitely a serial killer then, Sir?" It was Hooper, sounding excited.

"Why? Would you like it to be? Bit of a thrill for you?" The trainee DC looked away and Linton felt a stab of pity for him. It wasn't that long ago she was in a similar position, desperate to please and impress the boss. There were some days when she *still* felt like that.

She put up her hand, not sure what she was going to say, but anxious to take the heat off Hooper. The Toad turned his rheumy glare to her.

"Yes, yes?" he said.

Recognising the repetition of words as a sign of his impatience, she spoke quickly.

"Sir, is there any chance Angel's murder is the work of a copycat? Someone who knew about the flares?"

The Toad shook his balding head, the bony ridge on the top looking even more prominent than usual. "That particular detail was deliberately kept from the media so we can rule it out," he said impatiently. "Now. Locations. We've got flares laid out in a circle, at two so-called spiritual sites. This suggests we may be dealing with a ritual or sacrificial murder. What have you come up with?" Linton realised with a start that Hargreaves was still looking at her. "Come on, come on. What have you got?"

Nothing. She'd spent the last few hours ploughing through the Avebury cases. She felt the familiar heat creeping up her neck.

"Sir, I'm using the Internet to find out what I can about religions or cults that are into that kind of thing . . ."

"I want a report by the end of play tomorrow," he interrupted, slowly scanning the room, as though searching for his next prey. "Keen!" he bellowed suddenly, as his glare came to rest on the rumpled figure of the DS. "The wax flares. Where did he get them?"

"It's a bit of a nightmare, Sir," he answered.

"Hard cheddar. That's your job, isn't it? Come on, what have you got? Chop-chop."

"There's five shops in Glastonbury High Street alone that stock them. Plus a couple of the local garden centres. And then there's the online shops. There's dozens of them."

The Toad nodded, his jowls continued to wobble long after his head was still. It reminded Linton of those nodding dogs you see in the back of cars.

"Anything more on Angel's last movements?" he asked, turning to Brown.

"Only what we already know, Sir."

Which isn't much, she thought, as The Toad went over it for the "benefit of newcomers".

Angel Kingsley had arrived at The Rifleman's Arms, a pub near the bottom of the Tor, just after 8 p.m. She'd arranged to meet a friend from one of the neighbouring villages. The evening was a standard one. She talked to lots of different people and drank three halves of weak lager, made one phone call to a girlfriend and sent a short text to another. She looked well and seemed her usual outgoing self.

Her friend arranged to get a taxi back to West Pennard at 10.30 p.m. Angel left the pub at the same time to walk home. It was only ten minutes away on foot and it was a journey she often made. She hugged and kissed her friend goodbye outside the pub and, according to the taxi driver, waited on the pavement for him to pull away before crossing the road that led towards the top of the high street. That was the last time anyone *definitely* saw her, though a man rang after hearing about the murder on the news. He was driving home in his van at around 10.40 p.m. and reported seeing a young woman along the road from the pub, who *may* have been Angel. She was talking to a man. However, it was dark and his sighting fleeting. His descriptions were vague.

"If it *was* Angel talking to her killer," Hargreaves said, "it's likely they went up the Tor from there. We've got no further sightings after that. Not surprising, considering the cold weather and the time of night. Most people would've been tucked up indoors."

As he finished speaking, a skinny arm shot up. It was Hooper again. He cleared his throat nervously.

"Actually, Sir, there is something else."

"Chop-chop."

"I was looking through this afternoon's call sheet. Just before the briefing. We've got another possible sighting of Angel. After she left the pub. Sort of."

"What do you mean, 'sort of'?"

Hooper cleared his throat again. "The man who rang is registered blind, Sir." Linton heard sniggering coming from the back of the room. Hargreaves' face remained impassive.

"And what did he say?"

Hooper grabbed at the piece of paper in front of him, his long, bony fingers wrestling with the sheet.

"Come on! Chop-chop."

"Err, just before midnight on Thursday, Mr Woods was walking up Glastonbury High Street when a man and a woman overtook him on foot. He remembers them because they were the only other people he saw – I mean, um, encountered – on his way home. He says he can tell from the way they spoke they were in their twenties, possibly early thirties. He's certain the woman was wearing flat footwear otherwise he'd have heard her heels. He also says he smelt perfume oil, like the stuff those hippies wear – his words, not mine. It had a sweet, sickly smell."

Brown put up his hand. "Patchouli oil. It's what you smelt on Angel Kingsley's body, isn't it?" he said, directing his question at Linton.

She shrugged. "But it doesn't mean it was definitely them. Half of Glastonbury wears it."

"But it fits her description. Angel's in her twenties. She was wearing flat boots when she was killed. And if they were walking *up* the high street, then there's every chance they were heading for the Tor."

"Or to a house at the top of town," she said. "Maybe it was a couple going home from one of the pubs at the bottom." She didn't know why she was being so difficult. She sounded like a petulant teenager.

Hargreaves put up his right hand to intervene. He turned to Hooper again. "Was he able to hear anything they were saying?"

"Apparently the woman called her companion a dickhead. Or something like that. And then he replied, 'Don't call me that'."

"So they were arguing?"

"He said the man sounded annoyed. Irritated."

"Anything else?"

"He thinks the woman said something like, 'I don't want you to get your hopes up. It only happened once before and I was off my head.' He assumed she was talking about, um, sex."

"Hmmm," said The Toad. "This could be significant." His chins were wobbling again. "Let's say this *was* Angel and her killer. According to our witness, it was after midnight. Angel left the pub at 10.30. Where had she been for the last hour and a half? And why was she walking *up* the high street?"

Brown put up his hand again. "Sir, if we go back to the possible sighting of her near the Rifleman's with a man," he began.

"Yes?"

"If we assume this *was* Angel, and her killer, maybe they didn't go straight up the Tor. Perhaps she died later, in the early hours of the morning. It would still fit the estimated time of death. Maybe, initially, he took her back to his place and they went up the Tor much later."

"It doesn't make sense. Why not go straight up the Tor from the pub?" Linton asked. "They were so close to it."

"Angel may've needed persuading. Or perhaps it wasn't pre-planned. Maybe the killer didn't have the flares with him so he took Angel back to his house to get them."

"If that's the case," said Hargreaves, "and they went back to his place and were walking *up* the high street, logic would suggest he lives or he's staying somewhere at the bottom of town. What have house-to-house come up with around that area?"

"Not a lot, Sir. They've been concentrating on the top of town because we assumed Angel went up the Tor straight from the pub."

"CCTV?"

"Nothing significant, Sir."

Linton waited for The Toad's rant about the *sodding* council and their lack of *sodding* funding and the need for more *sodding* close circuit cameras, but instead he said thoughtfully, "We could be looking for somebody who lives in town as opposed to a transient. Possibly someone who's moved here from the Avebury area."

"That's if it *was* her that the van passenger saw talking to a bloke," she said.

"It's pretty likely it was," Fat Bloke piped up. "I mean, you've asked for this man to come forward and nobody has. Which makes it likely he's the killer. If he was innocent he'd have contacted us by now."

"Unless he's worried he may be in trouble. Or maybe he was up to something else," she replied.

"Like what?" asked Brown.

"He could be a dealer talking to his client. Someone completely unconnected to Angel's death but afraid to come forward . . ."

"The most likely explanation is the killer was someone who was drinking in the pub that night," interrupted Brown. "He probably followed her outside and that was who the van driver saw Angel talking to. Then they went back to his house, collected the flares and walked back up town to the Tor where he strangled her."

"How far have we got with people who were in the pub?" asked Hargreaves.

"Hooper's about to start working his way through the list, but it's a long one," said Brown.

"Hard cheddar."

"What I mean, Sir, is there's bound to be people left off it. They have live music on Thursday nights, so it was packed. The staff've done their best to come up with names, but they couldn't remember everyone."

"What I want to know is how he convinced her to go up the sodding Tor."

"It must be someone she knew," Linton said, "or trusted."

"Or fancied," Brown added.

"So. They walk down the high street to his place to collect the flares," said Hargreaves, as though neither of them had spoken. "Then at around midnight, they walked back *up* the high street to the Tor and they passed our blind bloke. Why? Why the Tor? How the hell did he persuade her to go up there on a freezing night in November?"

"It's exciting, isn't it? Something different to do." The Toad looked at Brown blankly. "Don't you remember being that age, Sir? I expect he made it sound romantic. He probably spouted some stuff about how magical it is up there. How you can see the whole town below, just the two of you."

"Is that what you do?" asked Blonde Ponytail.

Brown winked at her. "Works every time."

"What about drugs?" Keen asked.

"That's what he uses when they say no," someone shouted. A couple of people laughed.

"What about them?" Hargreaves asked.

"Perhaps he suggested they go up there to take something. There's always people up the Tor tripping their nuts off."

"We'll wait until we get the toxicology report back, but it does sound like a possibility," said Hargreaves, "especially as we've got her saying she was off her head the last time. Whatever the last time means."

"But why kill her?" asked Fat Bloke. *The million dollar question.* "The murders don't appear to be sexually motivated, at least not overtly."

"Or crimes of passion," said Brown.

"Hmmm. Quite," Hargreaves replied, seeming to shudder at the mention of the word. Linton tried to imagine him in the throes of passion. His dry, warty face bending down to embrace her. It didn't bear thinking about. "I'm convinced it's some sort of sacrifice – a ritual killing," he said. "That's our best bet. It all fits. Avebury Stones, the Tor, wax flares set out in a circle."

"Sir, going back to what I said before, about the possibility of it being a copycat," she said. "What if we're dealing with a cult? Maybe we've got different members in different places carrying out these killings."

"Hmmm. Let's see what we get back from the FSS." He stopped abruptly, looked at his watch and then clapped his hands together. "Right then," he bellowed. "Let's get on with it. Chop-chop." Chatter broke out as chairs were scraped and notebooks closed. "One more thing," he shouted, over the noise, "for those of you who are interested, there's a copy of Angel Kingsley's autopsy on the shared drive."

•••

Linton wanted to open the file as soon as she got back to her desk. Brown, however, had other ideas.

"Have a quick look at this, will you?" he grinned, passing her a sheet of paper.

"What is it?" she asked suspiciously.

"The *Forum's* asked me to appear on their celebrity page."

He was talking about a monthly 'What's On' guide one of the cafés produced and delivered free to Glastonbury residents. Every month they focused on a well-known person in the community.

"Why've they asked you?"

"I'd have thought it was obvious, wasn't it? Clever, talented, dynamic *and* good-looking." She rolled her eyes. "Anyway, what do you reckon?"

She looked down at the typewritten sheet.

"'Do you have any hobbies?'" Linton read aloud. "'Drinking, women and water sports.' Water sports? Since when were you into water sports?" He smirked and she realised what he meant. She shook her head and pulled her face into an expression of disgust. "God, you're so childish. 'What is your favourite film? *Misadventures at Megaboob Manor.* What is your favourite book? *The Joy of Sex.* What do you hate more than anything? Dog shit.'" She'd already known the answer to *that* one. Brown's dislike of canine faeces was intense to the point of being phobic. "'What is your most embarrassing moment? Being mistaken for David Beckham by a group of Japanese tourists.' Yeah, right."

"I was. That night I went out in Bath, on Nick's stag do. You ask him."

"'What is your biggest ambition? To have a three-in-a-bed with Cameron Diaz and Kelly Brook.' You can't send this in."

"I'm not. I was messing about. I'm going to change the answers." He tutted. "God, Linton, where's your sense of humour?"

"I'm finding it hard to see the funny side of anything at the moment," she said.

"Just because I'm not walking round looking like a wet weekend doesn't mean I'm not affected. I've got different ways of dealing with the job."

Actually, it wasn't the case that was getting her down; she was still obsessing over what her ex, Ben, had done, but she wasn't about to admit it. How shallow would *that* make her look? Instead, she shoved the piece of paper back onto Brown's jumbled desk, pulled her keyboard towards her and grabbed her mouse. She clicked on the shared drive, found Angel Kingsley's autopsy file and opened it.

Whoever had typed those words hadn't been joking. As she skim-read the report, she imagined Angel's body laid out, smelling of fresh lamb and chemicals, her hands covered by paper bags to protect any evidence that might be hiding under her nails.

She read quickly, picking out the important sentences:

Asphyxia due to ligature strangulation . . . the ligature mark on her neck is dark red and encircles the anterior midline just below the laryngeal prominence . . . visible injuries . . . parallel markings which are deep and vicious and run vertically down the front of her neck, most likely from the victim's fingernails as a defensive manoeuvre.

She continued down the page, until she reached a sentence that brought it all home – the sheer bloody waste of it all: *The hyoid bone is still intact.*

The hyoid. The small bone in the neck, shaped like a horseshoe, which supports the tongue. Ligature marks on the neck were normally a clue the hyoid bone was broken. In Angel's case, this hadn't happened.

A pathologist once explained to her that in younger victims it was common for them not to break. "The two halves of the hyoid won't have fused," she'd said. "It doesn't happen until you're at least thirty."

Angel was only twenty-five when she died. There were so many things, least of all the fusing of her hyoid bone, which her body would never have the chance to do. Get pregnant. Give birth . . .

But perhaps Angel wasn't the only one. Maybe *she'd* never have the chance to have a baby either. A few weeks ago having a family of her own was a given. Until Ben had gone and fucked it all up.

Stop it! She had to stop getting so angry about what he'd done. Stop being so self-absorbed and concentrate on her job. Focus on finding this maniac.

How long before he kills again?

FIVE

Claire had been looking out of her living room window for over two hours now, searching the lively crowd below in the hope she might spot Sam. The carnival had eventually begun its slow and noisy progress up the high street, but she wasn't exactly in the mood for watching it. She'd spoken to everyone she could think of. Everyone, that is, except the one person she *needed* to speak to. But Danny wouldn't reply to her texts, let alone answer his phone.

She was going to have to face up to it. There was only one explanation for why Sam was ignoring her calls. Danny had broken his promise. If only she'd been honest and told her sister before he had.

She pulled up the sash window, stuck her head out and lit a cigarette. The cold, damp air was thick with the sound of cheering and clapping, with the smell of burgers and frying onions. A couple of teenage girls were rolling around drunkenly on the pavement in front of a group of horrified pensioners. She felt ashamed as she remembered the time she'd watched the procession from the Abbey wall, sharing a box of wine with her friends. She'd drunk far more than her fair share and slipped off backwards into a bush behind. She'd ended up in hospital having her stomach pumped and a broken arm put into plaster.

"Oi!" a familiar voice shouted up. "I've been ringing your doorbell for the last five minutes."

"Sorry!" she called back. "I didn't hear it. Hang on. Two secs. I'll come down."

"Flowers," she said, as she opened the door a minute later. The drooping heads and browning petals had the local corner shop stamped all over them. Behind them was the grinning face of a tall, dark-haired man. His coat was open and she saw the badge on his sweatshirt: Adam Brooks – Warehouse Operative.

"Congratulations! You did it." Claire nodded and forced a smile. "These are for you. Well done, sweetheart. I'm proud of you." He bent down and kissed her cheek. He smelt of spearmint chewing gum.

"Thanks," she said, taking the flowers and stepping back into the small hallway. "They're lovely."

"You don't have to lie. I was going to get some nice ones on my way to work this morning but I overslept. Have you heard from Sam yet?" Adam slammed the front door behind him, the loud bang making Claire wince.

"Not yet," she replied, climbing the stairs.

"What did the police say?" He was right behind her and she was conscious of her backside only inches from his face.

"Hang on a sec. I'll tell you in a minute."

She led him into the kitchen, placing the flowers on the nearest worktop and pushed the switch on the kettle. "Coffee?" she asked.

"Please." Adam sat down at the table and pulled his gloves off. "So, what did they say?" he asked again.

"Nothing," she replied, reaching for two mugs from the wooden shelf above the sink.

"What do you mean, nothing?"

"I didn't bother in the end."

"But I thought you were going to ring them after I spoke to you at lunchtime."

"I know. But then I thought about what you said. It's only been a day."

"Like I said, she's probably with a bloke and hasn't bothered getting out of bed yet. You know what she's like."

"I was more worried about her diabetes," she said, opening a cupboard and pulling out a jar of instant coffee. "But I rang her flatmate to check she'd taken her kit. She's looked everywhere and can't find it, so Sam must have it with her." She paused to tip a heaped spoonful of granules into each mug, and said, "Anyway, mum's home number is on Sam's ID bracelet. Someone would've rung here if anything had happened to her."

"It's pretty unlikely. She was only walking to the pub from the bus stop. If she'd collapsed, it would've been on the high street. Someone would've seen her."

Claire nodded her agreement as the kettle made a loud click and turned itself off. She picked it up and poured the water into the mugs, briefly comforted by the smell of coffee.

Maybe she should tell him the *real* reason why she thought Sam wasn't answering her phone. He was a good listener, non-judgemental. Perhaps he'd understand.

"The thing is," she said, warily, "I think she might be avoiding me."

"How come?"

"Maybe she's pissed off with me."

"Why?" he asked, suspiciously. "What have you done?"

She'd been asking herself the same question since it happened.

"I don't know." She turned to reach for the sugar jar, the urge to confess suddenly quashed by the thought of having to say it out loud.

"Look," he said, pulling a tissue from his pocket and spitting his chewing gum into it. "I like Sam, but she always puts herself first. I've heard you say it yourself. She probably didn't meet you today because she found something better to do."

"Thanks a lot," she said, setting the steaming mugs onto the kitchen table and sitting down.

"You know what I mean."

"The thing is, Adam," she said, pausing to blow on her drink, "she knows how much today meant to me. I mean even *she's* not that thoughtless. We'd planned to spend the whole day together. We'd booked a massage and a facial. Why would she want to ruin it for me? Why didn't she ring to say she couldn't make it unless she's pissed off with me? She's not even answering her phone."

Just as she uttered the word, her mobile rang. She looked at the number. "It's her flatmate."

"Perhaps Sam's back in Bristol."

"Hello?" she said, breathlessly. "Have you heard from her? Oh . . . shit."

What? Adam mouthed.

She shook her head impatiently. "I mean, she's got a spare one here but . . . no, I know. Oh God. Listen. If you hear from her, ring me. Even if it's the middle of the night."

She clicked her phone off. "I don't believe it."

"What's happened?"

"She found Sam's diabetic kit. It was under a coat in their hallway, which means she hasn't got any insulin with her."

"Shit."

"Adam. I don't understand. I've rung the hospitals. No one's seen her. What's going on?"

Her mobile bleeped. She clicked on her messages, half expecting it to be a text from Sam's flatmate, telling her not to worry. But it wasn't. It was from Danny.

I haven't told her but if u dont leave me alone I will.

She stared at the message. Thinking through the implications of the words. If he hadn't told Sam, then that meant she wasn't avoiding her.

And if that was the case, then where was she?

And why the hell wasn't she answering her phone?

"I know you think I'm mad, but I've suddenly got a bad feeling about this. I'm ringing the police."

•••

The carnival was over. The pulsating music and the dense hum of generators was replaced by other noise: men shouting and hooting, girls shrieking with laughter, the shattering of glass as a bottle slipped through someone's hand or was smashed deliberately on the pavement below.

The room was in darkness. Sam could make out the shadowy outline of the bedroom door. She stared at it, both willing and dreading its opening. She hadn't seen him since her breakfast of two capsules washed down with a cup of tepid water.

"I'm going to work," he'd said. "There's a bucket if you need to use it."

Whatever drug he'd given her had worn off hours ago leaving her scared again. And ashamed, conscious of her semi-nudity, of the contents in the black bucket. She'd promised herself she wouldn't use it, but when she woke from the black hole of sleep she'd been plunged into, she was desperate, knowing if she didn't, she'd wet herself.

It wasn't easy, not with her hands bound behind her back, but she managed to use her thumbs to pull her jeans and knickers down over her hips.

Pulling them up had proved impossible so she left them resting on the tops of her thighs. The only way she could move around the icy room was by shuffling.

She'd tried opening the door by reversing into it, twisting the cold, porcelain handle with her numb hands. It was locked, of course. She'd thumped her back against it for a while, trying to call out. The only noise she could make was a low, throaty groan, thanks to the duct tape he'd stuck across her mouth. It was hopeless. No one would hear her over the din of the carnival.

Hobbling over to the window, she'd nudged open the thick velvet curtains with her head but, instead of glass, found a piece of plywood nailed into the wooden surrounds.

Now, lying on the bare mattress, she thought about the insane things he'd said to her. She'd kept telling him he'd got it all wrong – that she hadn't meant what she'd said all that time ago – that she'd forgotten all about it until now.

She flinched. It was the sound she'd been waiting for. The clatter of the letterbox and a dull thud as the front door shut.

She could make out a jangle of keys being tossed onto a hard surface followed by tuneful whistling. 'Singin' in the Rain'. She'd heard it playing earlier, on one of the carnival floats. She listened to the thump of footsteps coming closer to the room, felt her heartbeat quicken and her stomach constrict. Flinching at the rattle of the key in the door, she watched it swing open. Light from the hallway spilt into the room, stinging her eyes. She felt sick.

"Hello, Sam." He moved quickly towards the bed. She couldn't help recoiling as he crouched down and leant over the mattress. "Don't worry. I'm not going to do anything like *that*."

He took hold of the top of her knickers and jeans and began to gently ease them up. She lifted her hips instinctively off the bed, wriggling into them until they were pulled firmly up.

"Now I'm going to take the tape off your mouth again. You have to promise not to scream."

She nodded her head in agreement. He lent down and she felt his hot, minty breath against her face. He peeled back the edge of the strip and quickly yanked it across her mouth. The intense stinging of her lips and skin made her yelp.

"Sorry," she whispered.

He twisted around and pulled something from his back pocket. The pills. He popped two tablets from the foil packet, shaking them into his large hand.

"Please," she said, frightened by how dry her tongue and throat felt. "I need insulin."

"Samantha. You're not going to start this again, are you?"

"If I don't have it soon, I'll be really ill. I've got all the symptoms already: drowsy and thirsty, blurred vision."

"It's probably down to these," he said. "Side effects. I've had the same thing. Now open wide. Come on, Sam, it's for your own good."

"What are they?"

"I told you. Nothing harmful. Temazepam. I take them for insomnia. They help you relax, stop you feeling anxious. I'm not a horrible person, Sam, you know I'm not. I don't want you getting upset. It wouldn't be fair, would it? Not when you're here to help me."

"Please. You don't understand. I could die."

"I don't know why you keep saying the same thing, Sam. You know I don't believe you. You never had diabetes before."

"I wasn't diagnosed until three years ago. They think I caught a virus. It did something to my pancreas, stopped it from working. You've got to believe me." *The bracelet,* she thought. Why didn't she think of it before? "Look at my left wrist. I've got my MedicAlert bracelet on. It's got my family's contact details, in case I collapse."

"Come on Sam. I looked through your bags. I didn't see any insulin in there. Or syringes. I know what diabetics need, I'm not stupid."

"I left my kit in Bristol. But there's a spare one. At my mum's," she jabbered, tripping over the words, in her hurry to get them out. "There's a key in my handbag. You could go and get it."

"Great idea!" he said coldly. "Oh, hello, Sally. I've got Sam in my flat. Mind if I pop in and get her medication?"

"But she's not even there. She's in Australia, on holiday and Claire's at work all day. At the bookshop."

"It's Sunday tomorrow."

"Monday then. But you need to get it soon. Please. Without insulin I'll die."

"Aren't they amazing?" he said suddenly, as though she hadn't spoken.

"Who?"

He laughed, then stopped abruptly. "You know exactly who I mean,

Sam. Don't pretend you don't. Aren't they clever getting us together like this? It shows they're always watching."

"Please," she begged. "I've told you before. You've got it all wrong."

"Or maybe you really don't remember anything from before. Perhaps it's their way of protecting you from people who wouldn't understand. But don't worry. As long as you do what you're told, you'll be home soon. We both will. And then, I promise you, you'll remember everything."

•••

It was after ten when Linton got in. She was light-headed with tiredness and hunger. Driving home, she promised herself she'd cook something decent to eat and check her emails. Instead, she lay on the sofa eating a banana and picking at the dry skin on the back of her heels, determined not to think about what Ben had done but failing.

She rolled over and flicked the empty banana skin onto the coffee table, confronted once again by the unopened parcel, with its Malaysian postmark, sitting there accusingly. It was from her Dad – the latest instalment of the crime novel he was writing. He'd originally emailed it and she thought she'd got out of reading it, firstly telling him it was difficult to follow on screen, then that she couldn't print off a copy because her printer was on the blink. And so he'd put the bloody thing in the post.

She thought of him now, experiencing the heavy sensation she felt in the pit of her stomach whenever she contemplated either of her parents; not a singular emotion she could name, but a mix of resentment, embarrassment and guilt.

It's funny; part of her was desperate to tell him she was working on the case of a serial killer, the part that, despite everything, still craved his approval. She knew he'd love it, especially now it was useful to him. But the other part of her thought, *Stuff it, why should I tell him?* Up until a few months ago, he hadn't taken any interest in her job. In fact, if anything, he was embarrassed his daughter's job was so establishment.

Then, of course, everything had changed after he retired and moved to Malaysia and decided he was going to use his talents to make his millions writing crime novels. Exactly like the ones she loved reading, the ones that he, the esteemed university lecturer in English Literature, had spent years taking the piss out of. Suddenly he wouldn't leave her alone, emailing her questions, sending her bits of manuscript to check for accuracy.

She sighed. She didn't want to read it. He didn't deserve her help. Yet, despite the way he was happy to trample over other people's feelings, she still hated upsetting him. She reached for the package, groaning as she unpicked the thick duct tape he'd used to seal it. Pulling out the small bundle of typewritten sheets, she read the opening.

> "Kate,
> I have decided to change the DI's name from Summers to
> Stone. I think you'll agree it makes him sound much tougher.
> Don't you think?"

Where was '*Dear Kate*' and the '*how are you*'? God, he was so self-obsessed.

She dumped the pile of paper back onto the coffee table and lay back on the sofa, remembering the email she'd sent him in response to his questions about tracking serial killers, thinking how relevant it was to the Angel Kingsley case.

"They can create real problems," she'd written. "Often they don't have any connection to the victims, selecting them at random. With most murders, there are easily identifiable motives – revenge, jealously, financial gain – and you start by focusing on the people the victims knew and who will gain by their death. But often a serial killer will prey on strangers and his personal motives may appear completely irrational to anyone but himself."

She jumped at the sound of her mobile. Maybe it was her dad, ringing to find out what she thought of his latest offering. She reached for the phone and checked the number.

Even worse. It was Ben.

What the hell did he want? Did he really think she was going to talk to him? After what he'd done?

She let it go straight to answerphone.

SIX

It was a cold, wet Sunday morning: perfect for lounging in bed with the newspaper and a mug of tea. *No such luck*, Linton thought, as she made her sluggish way along the fluorescent-lit corridor towards the incident room.

The second she stepped into the office, she sensed it. Something had happened.

Hooper leapt up from his desk as soon as he saw her.

"A local woman's gone missing! She got off the bus at the Town Hall on Friday evening and no one's seen her since. Her sister reported it last night."

"Anyone we know?" Linton asked, looking around the office to see who else was in.

"Samantha Jenkins. She's twenty-six."

"I recognise the name." She nodded at Keen who was on the phone, his pock-marked forehead glistening with sweat. "They're a local family, aren't they?"

"Her mum and older sister live in High Street," Hooper replied, nodding vigorously. "Above that hippy shop."

"Which one?"

"The Psychic Piglet."

"What about Samantha?"

"She lives in Bristol. She was back for the carnival and was meant to meet her sister yesterday morning but didn't show up."

Linton sat down and switched on her computer. "Any history of depression?"

Hooper shook his head. "Her sister doesn't think so. She split up with her boyfriend, but that was a while ago."

"Has she been in any trouble?"

"I don't know, but the thing is she's diabetic and she hasn't got any insulin with her."

"Maybe she's collapsed somewhere."

"Nothing's been reported and we've checked the hospitals. Besides, she was headed for the Star and Garter and it's only a minute's walk from the town hall bus stop."

"Who's taking it on?"

"Rumour is we are."

She stopped halfway through typing her password and looked up. "Are you sure?"

"That's what I heard. Well, overheard," he said, sheepishly. "Milne was talking to The Toad out in the corridor. That's how I know."

"It makes sense," she said thoughtfully, "if her disappearance is connected to Angel's death."

"It's got to be, hasn't it? It's a mirror of what happened in Avebury. One girl got killed and then another went missing."

Linton looked across at the pictures of the three women, Angel, Hannah and Sadie in their various poses, grinning down at her from the whiteboard. *How long before he kills again?*

It looked like they might have their answer.

"Where's Brown?"

"Here."

She turned to see him striding through the door, shrugging off his leather jacket and shaking rain from his tousled hair. He glanced over at Blonde Ponytail who was photocopying something in the corner of the room. She looked up and smiled.

"What's up?" he said, turning back to address Linton.

"A woman's gone missing," said Hooper, before she could answer. "Samantha Jenkins. Hasn't been seen since Friday."

Brown narrowed his eyes. "A cup of tea would be nice."

Hooper reddened. "No problem," he said, spinning round and scuttling across the room, resembling a daddy-long-legs.

"What was that about?" she asked, when he was out of earshot.

"I'm not having some trainee fill me in, thanks very much. And what's he doing in anyway? Doesn't he ever go home?"

"He's eager, that's all."

Brown grunted. "Come on then. Let's hear it."

She repeated what Hooper had told her. Brown didn't say a word, just sat back in his chair frowning and rubbing his bottom lip with his index finger.

"What d'you think?" she asked, when he'd finished. "It's too much of a coincidence for it not to be connected to Angel Kingsley's murder. I reckon he's abducted Samantha Jenkins, like he did with the second woman at Avebury."

Brown didn't reply. Instead he leant forward and switched on his computer.

"So?"

"What?"

"Do you think her disappearance is connected?"

He shrugged.

"What's up with you?"

"What d'you mean?"

"Why are being so quiet?"

"I'm thinking."

"About what?"

He looked up and she glimpsed a flicker of emotion in his eyes. It was so quick, it barely registered, but, if pressed, she'd say it was guilt.

She sighed and shook her head. "Clunk," she said.

"What?" Brown was frowning.

"That was the sound of the penny dropping. You've slept with her, haven't you?"

"Who?" Hooper asked, back in the room and carrying three mugs.

"None of your fucking business," Brown growled.

At the same time, Linton said, "Samantha Jenkins. The missing girl."

Hooper passed Brown the *I love my Guinea Pig* mug that another DC had left behind when she moved departments.

"You haven't, have you?" he said, with something approaching awe in his voice.

"Of course I haven't."

Linton raised her eyebrows at Hooper in a parody of disbelief.

"I don't even know her," he added quickly.

"He couldn't have done. We'd have heard all about it by now," Hooper said and walked off chuckling to himself.

"I don't like him. There's something a bit off. Don't you think?"

"Hooper? He's harmless."

"How come he knows so much about it?"

"He overheard Milne and The Toad talking."

He made another grunting sound. "It's not like being a detective on TV, is it? They always get rung up in the middle of the night and told what's going on."

"Is that what's bothering you? That Hooper knew something before you did?"

"I never said anything was bothering me. Stop going on, will you? Why don't you sort out your pens or something? Better still, see what you can find out about the missing woman."

I give up, she thought. If he didn't want to tell her what was wrong, that was his lookout. If it wasn't Samantha Jenkins, it was probably another woman. Perhaps he couldn't get rid of the one from Saturday night as easily as he'd hoped.

A minute later his phone rang. He snatched it up and belted out an unfriendly, "Yeah?" followed by an even more irritated, "Oh, it's you." *Simon Talbot*, he mouthed, making the wanker sign with his free hand. "Didn't you get enough titbits for your paper when you were sniffing around on the Tor the other night?"

Linton felt herself redden at the mention of his name, grateful he'd rung Brown to pester him for information and not her.

She'd been at sixth-form college with Talbot and they'd gone out with each other for a while. He was married now with two kids, but apart from looking older and a little bulkier, he hadn't changed much. When they'd first met up in their professional capacity, he'd joked about Linton being his ex-girlfriend. He hadn't mentioned it since and she was grateful; it wasn't something she needed reminding of.

Talbot hadn't just been a boyfriend; he'd been the first person she'd had sex with. Or, in fact, done *anything* with. Her friends were shocked when she'd told them. Not all of them had gone so far and everyone in their group would've voted Linton 'Least Likely to Lose her Virginity'. She was one of the quiet ones, a late developer and a 'goody-goody'; not the sort to have sex with someone while his mum popped down the road for a Neighbourhood Watch meeting.

She didn't still think about it because the event didn't hold any significance for her. She wasn't into attaching importance to what were considered life's landmarks. She hadn't even gone to her own graduation.

No, the reason she still dwelled on it was because she was annoyed. Annoyed she'd been so crap. She hadn't even intended going all the way. She knew he'd be more than happy doing other things. Once on top of his black duvet, the slam of the front door a cue to begin, she'd attempted to carry out the request he'd mumbled in her ear. She was acutely embarrassed when, after what felt like an eternity, his excitement literally shrank before her eyes. Never one to admit defeat, she'd embarked on another method but it didn't get a result either. So she'd suggested they have sex instead, partly as an apology for her poor performance, but mainly in the hope she'd redeem herself. She didn't.

What irked her most was that Talbot probably still thought of her as that fumbling teenager. She knew it was ridiculous – so what if he did? – but she knew that if she ever got the chance to sleep with him, she would, to show him how wrong he was.

"Briefing in half an hour," a loud voice barked, breaking her reverie. Good. That gave her enough time to look up Samantha Jenkins on Facebook.

•••

Detective Superintendent Milne looked stern and brooding when she marched into the incident room precisely thirty minutes later. Her ash-blonde fringe was pulled back from her face, held in place by a Kirby grip – a girlish accessory at odds with the rest of her appearance. As usual, she looked wrinkled. Not only her pale skin, but her light-grey suit – as though she'd gone bed in her clothes.

Milne was the archetypal Jekyll and Hyde figure. She could be sympathetic and considerate, sometimes even gentle, but there were plenty of times when Linton had gone home thinking she was a complete bitch.

"Quiet please." The room fell silent. Not even a whisper or an exchange of looks. Everyone knew from the rhythmic tapping of her fingers what sort of mood she was in.

"Thank you," she said, although Linton couldn't detect any gratitude in her tone. She took off her watch and laid it on the desk in front of her.

"We've got a lot on our plate, so I'll keep this quick," she said, her voice husky from years of menthol cigarettes. "As most of you will now be aware, a young woman's gone missing." She glanced down at her notebook. "Her name's Samantha Jenkins, known as Sam to family and friends. She's twenty-six years old and originally from Glastonbury, but now resides in the St Andrew's area of Bristol. Her mother and older sister both still live here. It was her sister, Claire Jenkins, who reported her as missing last night at half past ten; she was due to meet her yesterday morning, but didn't show. Sam's an insulin-dependent diabetic. Is there anybody who doesn't know what that means?"

Blonde Ponytail raised her hand. "Not exactly," she said, her accent a soft Devon burr.

"DC Turley, isn't it?" Blonde Ponytail nodded. "Basically her body doesn't produce insulin, so she has to inject it artificially, four times a day. If she injects too much she needs to counteract it by ingesting something sugary. If, on the other hand, she doesn't have enough, then sooner or later she'll fall unconscious and slip into a coma. Eventually she'll die."

"How long can someone survive without insulin?" Linton asked.

"Five days. Six at the most. And that's the thing; she doesn't have any with her. Sam's flatmate rang the sister to say she'd found her diabetic kit in Bristol." She stopped to cough the phlegmy hack of a smoker, before continuing. "From what we know of Sam's last movements, a work colleague saw her boarding the 376 bus from Bristol to Glastonbury on Friday evening at seventeen-oh-five. She was coming back for the weekend to watch the carnival and was meant to be meeting friends in the Star and Garter. She never showed. Her friend rang her mobile a couple of times, but it was turned off. Apparently she was annoyed rather than worried. Sam's known to be unreliable. She assumed she'd bumped into some other friends and changed her mind."

"Did she definitely get off the bus in Glastonbury, Ma'am?" asked Brown.

"Her sister thinks so. She spoke to her a few minutes before it was due at the Town Hall at eighteen-fifteen."

"We'll need to interview the driver then."

"And check CCTV footage. There's the camera at the Town Hall, and one further up opposite the war memorial. If she was walking to the Star and Garter, she should appear on both." She stopped to cough again. "We've contacted all the hospitals, but no admittances. Helicopter and uniform are searching the area and asking people for any sightings of her. Both operations will continue until dusk."

"What about Bristol?" It was Brown again.

"So far we've had no sightings of her in the city by her flatmate, friends or colleagues."

"Where does she work?"

"A small TV production company called About Face, at the top of Whiteladies Road. You'll need to pay them a visit. Find out what her job involves, whether it could've brought her in contact with her abductor." She paused to cough, holding up her hand to cover her mouth. Her crimson nail polish was flaky and chipped. "Any other questions?"

They all shook their heads; there were a couple of mumbled nos.

"Nobody's going to come out and ask why I'm giving this case to you lot?" *As if anyone would dare*, Linton thought. "Then presumably you've put two and two together. I strongly believe the man who murdered Angel Kingsley, and is probably responsible for the death of the two women in Avebury, has abducted Sam Jenkins. And in case any of you need persuading, I'll tell you why. It's simple. I don't believe in coincidences. A young woman going missing in Glastonbury so soon after a murder is too much of one. Can anyone tell me the last time we had a murder followed by an abduction in the same week?"

Silence.

"Precisely. In fact it's a whole year since we had a murder in Glastonbury and that was a domestic. It's not as though we're tripping over dead bodies or missing people."

You could hardly trip over a person if they were missing, thought Linton, although she wasn't about to bring this to Milne's attention.

"What's more, it's mimicking what happened in Avebury. A young woman was strangled and, shortly after, a second woman went missing. This second woman died, maybe not directly at the hands of this man, but certainly as a result of him abandoning her to the cold. Wiltshire police weren't as quick to react to reports of the missing woman as they could've been. Understandably so. She wasn't considered vulnerable. Plus they didn't have the benefit of hindsight. We *have* so we need to act quickly."

She paused and looked round the room, making sure she had everyone's attention then said, "This is a matter of absolute urgency. We've got to move fast. I strongly believe if we don't find the man responsible for the deaths of Hannah, Sadie and Angel, then Sam Jenkins is going to die."

Pausing again to let her words sink in, she turned to The Toad. He was wearing his purple tie again, but today he'd mismatched it with a navy double-breasted blazer.

"Hargreaves. What do we know about our man so far?"

The Toad cleared his throat. "At the moment, Ma'am, all we can do is hypothesise. My guess is he has the typical serial-killer profile; his victims are white, so it's likely he is too. Age? I'd say somewhere between twenty and forty-five. He's a charmer, or at least persuasive enough to have got the women to go to these particular locations in the middle of the night."

"Although Sadie Carter was drugged."

"True. But Hannah and Angel appear to have gone with him willingly enough. The tox report for Hannah was negative; we're still waiting for the one for Angel."

Keen raised his hand.

"Ma'am, do you think he's planning to take Sam Jenkins up the Tor? He must know we'll have surveillance set up."

"My guess is he's got a similar location in mind. It appears part of his MO is to kill women on sites that are considered spiritual."

"Should we be keeping a watch, Ma'am?" asked Keen. "On places like the Chalice Well and Glastonbury Abbey?'

"Or the Holy Thorn. Or Wearyall Hill. Or Gog and Magog." Milne shook her head impatiently. "We haven't got the manpower."

"Every hill and monument around here is sitting on a sodding ley line," said Hargreaves. He looked across at Milne. She nodded in agreement.

"Where do you think he's holding her?" asked Keen.

"Somewhere local, I'd imagine," said Milne. "If he lives here he could be hiding her in his home." She paused to glance at her watch. "Where do we go from here? I've already mentioned the bus driver and CCTV. We also need to look for connections to the other deaths. Find out if Sam Jenkins knew Angel Kingsley or if there's anything linking her to either of the cases in Avebury. We need to interview the sister, Claire

Jenkins; speak to other relatives, her friends and acquaintances. And I want someone to go and see Angel Kingsley's mother again. Same thing. Find out if there's anything or anyone linking Sam to her daughter." She turned to address Hunt, the Office Manager. He was sat on a desk, his short legs dangling down.

"Ma'am?"

"An appeal will go out later today on local TV and radio, so expect a lot of activity in the contact centre. One last thing," she said, turning back to Hargreaves. "I know you're looking into the possibility of these deaths being some sort of human sacrifice. What have you got so far?"

"Linton?" he said, turning to her. His eyes looked even more protruding than usual, the whites heavily bloodshot.

She shuddered involuntarily and grabbed at her notebook.

"At the moment, Ma'am, we're exploring various avenues. As you say, there's a possibility it's a religious cult at work. Or even some sort of satanic ritual. I'm looking into how likely it might be nowadays."

"Where are you getting the information from?"

"Mainly internet sites, Ma'am."

"Keep going with it." She paused, pursed her lips and then said thoughtfully, "What's the name of the chap who's always in the local paper? He wrote the book they've got featured in the window of A Helping Hand."

"Vine, Ma'am" said Brown.

Trust him to bloody know, thought Linton.

"That's the one. I heard him on Radio Bristol the other day. His book's called *Myths and Legends through the Ages* or something similar. Hargreaves. Get someone in your team to set up an interview with him. It sounds as though he's an expert on that sort of thing."

"Yes, Ma'am."

She looked at her watch again. "Has anybody got anything else they want to add before we bring this to a close?"

Linton raised her hand again. "Ma'am, I was looking at Sam Jenkins' Facebook profile just before we came in. To see if Angel, Hannah or Sadie are listed as her friends."

"And?"

"They're not."

Before Milne could answer, Brown turned to Linton and said sharply, "How did you get to see her profile? Are you her Facebook friend?"

"Of course not. But I thought that in itself was interesting."

"What do you mean?" asked Milne, putting her hand up to hush Brown before he said anything else.

"She didn't have a privacy setting on her page."

"Meaning?"

"There's a setting on your account you can alter, depending on who you want to see to your profile. Most people only let their Facebook friends have access. Either she's not Internet savvy – which I doubt – or she's an exhibitionist. She's happy for anyone to see what she's up to. Whether she knows them or not."

"And what's the significance of the three women not being her Facebook friends?"

"The fact they aren't makes me think she probably wasn't friends with them outside of cyberspace."

"Perhaps they didn't have Facebook accounts."

"They did. I checked."

"But they're dead."

"I guess no one's bothered to remove them, Ma'am. Presumably you'll want us to be following up the other friends Sam's got listed on there."

"How many are there?"

"Four hundred and eighty-six, Ma'am."

"Good grief!" There was a ripple of murmurs and sighs as everyone contemplated the amount of work involved in looking at the Facebook angle alone. "Well, do your best. And remember, this is all about attention to detail." She picked up her watch and slid it on to her slim wrist. "I don't need to stress the urgency of the situation. We need to find Angel Kingsley's killer if we're going to save Sam Jenkins. And we need to find him quickly."

How long before he kills again.

•••

"Let's have a look then," said Brown as the meeting broke up.

"At what?"

"Sam's profile. Have you still got it up on screen?"

"I think so."

Brown followed Linton back to her desk. As she sat down and clicked her mouse, the Avon and Somerset screensaver disappeared and was replaced by a picture of Sam Jenkins wearing a halter-neck top, bright pink lipstick and a gleaming white smile. To the right of the photo was her list of personal information.

Network: Bristol
Sex: Female
Interested in: Men
Relationship status: Single
Birthday: 28th July
Political views: Very Liberal

"She's got four hundred and eighty-six friends and a hundred and seventy-six photographs of herself," said Linton. "That's the next three years tied up."

"Have you looked through any of the pictures?"

"I skimmed through the first few. Just the usual stuff you'd expect: pictures of her with her friends out drinking; a few holiday snaps; a couple of photos of her holding someone's baby."

"You didn't look at all of them then?"

"Why? Are you worried you'll see yourself on there?"

"I never shagged her," he said impatiently. "Stop going on about it."

"Why are you so jumpy then?"

"I'm not. Did you look at the messages on her wall as well?"

"Some of them."

"And?"

"There's a message from a friend the day before she went missing, inviting her to a party in London, but nothing about going back to Glastonbury."

"I'll have a quick look through as well."

"Why waste your time? Get Hooper to do it. Unless you've got something to hide."

"Give it up, will you, Linton?" he said tersely. "You're pissing me off now."

An hour later, as Linton walked back to her desk from the photocopier, she glanced at Brown's computer screen. He quickly clicked into a word document, but he was too late. She saw what he was looking at – Sam Jenkins' Facebook profile.

•••

Sam twisted onto her side, and clutched at her stomach, asking herself for the hundredth time how could she have been so stupid?

The thing is, he'd sounded so genuine and she'd had no reason to doubt him. Even when she'd got inside the flat there was no gut reaction telling her to turn and run. And when she'd asked why it was so quiet, she'd believed his explanation.

She'd assumed she was walking into the front room, expecting to meet his girlfriend until she saw the single bed and, by the time it had registered, she was lying face down on it, his knees in her back, as he pulled her arms tightly behind her. He'd told her not to scream or he'd break them; said he wanted to go home and she was the only one who could help him.

He was so much stronger than he looked.

SEVEN

Why did it have to be PC Wells? Claire Jenkins thought, as she opened her front door to be met by heavy rain and two solemn police officers. Why couldn't they have sent someone anonymous? Someone who didn't know, in quite so much detail, about her almighty balls-up just over a year ago?

"Hello, Miss Jenkins," he said, his face impassive.

"You don't have to call me that any more. Claire will do."

"Habit. This is PC Turley." The pretty blonde woman offered her hand for Claire to shake.

"It was me who rang this morning," she said, in a soft West Country accent.

"Come in." Claire stood back and gestured them in. They pushed their way through the small doorway, rubbing their wet shoes vigorously on the doormat. "I'm presuming you haven't heard anything since you rang."

"Sorry," the policewoman replied, shutting the door behind her and shaking herself like a puppy, so droplets of rain sprayed from her high ponytail.

"Hang your coats there if you like," Claire said, nodding towards the already heavily laden pegs. She waited while they heaved their way out of their dripping garments, then turned and mounted the stairs. The officers followed.

"How's Darren getting on?" she asked PC Wells, over her shoulder. "He must be at St Ben's now."

"Fine, thanks."

"He's a lovely boy," replied Claire, lowering her voice as they reached the top. "He was a pleasure to teach."

"He takes after me."

"We'll go up the other end if that's OK," she whispered. "I'm hoping mum's asleep."

She led them down the hallway and through the open doorway into the large modern kitchen. "She was in a state earlier, so I persuaded her to take a couple of sleeping pills," she continued, talking at a more normal level. "She didn't sleep on the plane coming home. You know what it's like. She's jet-lagged and now with all of this on top of it . . ." She realised she was babbling. She stopped and took a deep, shuddering breath. "I've finished the list you asked me to do. I've put down everyone I can think of."

She picked up a piece of lined A4 paper from the sideboard and handed it to Wells.

"What's the celebration?" asked the policewoman, nodding towards the vase of flowers and the three greeting cards displayed next to it, two of them emblazoned with the word *Congratulations*.

"Nothing, really." Claire felt herself flushing. "Just something I, um, passed." Her reply was greeted with silence. She realised she was expected to fill it with an explanation, but she didn't want to, not with PC Wells looking at her like that. She felt humiliated enough as it was. "Do you want a cup of tea or coffee?" she said hurriedly instead. "I've got orange juice if you'd prefer a cold drink." She waited for the policewoman to ask about the cards again, but she didn't.

"We're fine, thanks. Why don't we sit down?"

Claire took a seat opposite them, feeling as though she was about to be interrogated. Their faces were expressionless, not giving anything away. It was a look she remembered from before and wondered if it was something they practised.

"We want to know if you've thought of anything since last night," said PC Wells.

She shook her head.

"Has she had an argument with someone? One of her mates? Her boyfriend?"

"She hasn't got one. And anyway," she added hastily, "she's not the type to run off because she's upset."

He paused. "I'm curious. Why did it take you so long to report Sam as missing?"

"I was confused. I was thinking all kinds of things. That she'd overslept or she was annoyed with me . . ."

"Annoyed with you?" Wells interrupted. "Why?"

Claire looked away. "I don't know. I only started to worry when her flatmate rang and said she'd found her diabetes kit. And then when Danny texted me to say he hadn't spoken to her." She stopped.

"Danny?"

"Hicks. Her ex."

"Why would you have expected him to have spoken to her?"

"I don't know." There was a short silence as PC Wells wrote in his notebook.

Claire took a deep breath. "Can I ask you something?"

He looked up and smiled. "Of course."

"Do you think it's that bloke? The one who killed Angel. And those other women. Do you think he's got Sam?"

It was the policewoman who answered. "Look," she said, gently. "The link to Angel Kingsley's death is one angle we're exploring among many others."

"But I've read about it in the papers. They said he abducted the second girl who died at Avebury. That's what's happened here, isn't it?"

"There are other possibilities. Maybe she went to a party and met someone and hasn't got round to contacting you."

"But she'd have rung me to say she hasn't got her diabetes kit."

"Perhaps she's managed to get hold of some insulin from somewhere else."

"How? She'd need a prescription. And Glastonbury surgery is closed on a Saturday."

"She must have repeat prescriptions. Perhaps she took one to a chemist round here." Claire watched Wells make a note in his book, presumably to remind himself to follow it up later.

"Maybe. If it wasn't for the diabetes kit, then I'd assume she'd met a bloke but . . ." She felt herself trailing off, as an image of Sam came into her mind. The one that had haunted her dreams last night; her sister curled up in a whimpering ball, frightened and ill.

"Did your sister know Angel Kingsley?" Wells asked.

"Just to say hello to. Our mums used to be friendly. You *do* think that bloke's got her. Or you wouldn't be asking me these questions."

The policewoman put her hand gently on Claire's arm.

"What about mutual friends?" Wells continued. "Does Sam know anyone who's friends with Angel?"

"Probably. But round here everyone's linked to each other in some way. You know what it's like."

"What about the two women from Avebury? The ones who died at the beginning of the year?"

Claire put a hand over her mouth and shook her head. "She never mentioned them."

"Not even when it was in the news?"

"I vaguely remember hearing about it, but it was more the place that registered than the names of the women. And Sam definitely never said anything about knowing them and I'm sure she would've done."

"What about any links to Avebury? Any friends who live or come from there?"

"None I can think of."

"Has she ever lived there?"

"No."

"And Danny?"

Claire shook her head. "He's lived in Bristol all his life."

"Perhaps she went there recently?"

"Not that I know of." She felt a hot tear slither down her cheek and realised with a start she was crying.

The policewoman reached across the table and gave her hand a gentle squeeze. "Look, I can see this is hard for you. Why don't we leave it for now and give you a chance to have another think?"

"Don't worry about seeing us out," said Wells, as Claire pushed herself up from the table. "We'll make sure we're quiet so we don't wake your mum."

Claire sniffed and nodded her goodbye. She listened to them treading quietly along the hall and then down the stairs. She got up and walked over to the kettle, hearing the faint clack as they pushed the front door shut. The kitchen window was open and from below Claire heard the distinctive voice of the policewoman.

"You know what, Wells, if you hadn't told me about her arrest, I'd have never believed it. She doesn't seem the type. And her being a teacher."

"*Was* a teacher."

"What happened exactly?"

Their voices become fainter, as they walked off, much to Claire's relief. She didn't need reminding. She'd been living with the aftermath for the last year. She shuddered. Seeing Wells again had taken her back to the time of the court case. To all the whispering and nudging, the expressions on people's faces as she hurried past them in the high street. She couldn't bear to be judged again.

Ignoring the click of the kettle as it finished boiling, she went into the living room and picked up her phone from the mantelpiece where it had lain all night charging. Catching a glimpse of her face in the mirror above, she was shocked at how white and pinched she looked.

She checked the words of the text before sending it to Danny:

> Dont tell police about u no what or I'll tell them what I no about u.

•••

Linton drove to Mrs Kingsley's house with a sense of dread. Questioning people about their dead relatives was one of the things she hated most about her job.

"Can't I speak to her on the phone?" she'd begged Brown.

"I want her to look at the photos of the Avebury women."

"But she's already said she didn't know them."

"She said she hadn't *heard* of them. But she might recognise them from their pictures. They could've been friends with Angel for all you know."

It took a while for Mrs Kingsley to come to her door. Someone had set up a skate ramp at the end of the cul-de-sac and a small boy, despite the rain, cycled up and down the wooden slope a dozen times before the door to number nine was reluctantly edged open.

The skin beneath the hooded nose of the woman that greeted Linton looked raw, as if she'd scrubbed it with a scouring pad. Behind the crescent-shaped frames of her glasses, her red-rimmed eyes had the look of an animal caught in headlights. The frightened gaze reminded Linton of her brother Michael, on one of his bad days.

"Mrs Kingsley? DS Kate Linton," she said, holding out her card. "I know this is probably the last thing . . ." She tailed off as the woman opened the door wider, gesturing her inside with a slight nod of her head.

"We'll sit in the kitchen, shall we, love? It's warmer in there."

She stepped into a narrow hallway. She smelt the sickly, sweet scent of cannabis and wondered whether that was reason for the delay in the front door being opened. She wasn't about to say anything. If it helped

Angel's mum cope then let her get on with it. They had bigger things to worry about.

At the end of the passageway was a beaded door curtain, decorated with multi-coloured hearts. Mrs Kingsley held up a handful of the strings, making enough space for her to clamber through. Linton followed behind.

The beads clicked and clattered as they fell back into place and Linton found herself in a kitchen that looked remarkably similar to the one she'd grown up in. Its walls were painted lilac, the same colour as the loosely belted cotton bathrobe Mrs Kingsley wore. Every surface was covered; it was a mishmash of plant pots, jars and vases, joss stick holders and half-used candles, tins, pots, picture frames, papier-mâché sculptures and a large collection of oil burners. She pictured her own kitchen, its gleaming surfaces free from any objects or clutter, cold and pretentious in comparison.

"I haven't got any milk, love," Mrs Kingsley said, collapsing onto one of the wooden chairs surrounding the table in the centre of the room. "Otherwise I'd make some tea."

"It's fine." Linton placed her briefcase on the table and clicked it open. She sat down and pulled out the photographs of Hannah James and Sadie Carter. "Mrs Kingsley . . ."

"Please. Call me Liz, will you?"

"OK." Linton pushed a copy of the local paper to one side and gently placed the photos on the table. "Would you mind having a look at these and telling me whether you think your daughter knew either of the women?"

Mrs Kingsley pulled the pictures towards her, nudging her glasses down her nose with her other hand. Linton watched her closely as she studied them, but there was no sign of any recognition. She shook her head, pushing the glossy prints back across the table.

"Not that I know of. At least *I've* never met them," she said.

"And what about Sam Jenkins – the woman who went missing from Glastonbury on Friday night? Did Angel know her?"

"Oh yes. We both know Sam. But then she's local, isn't she? Not like those other two."

"But she wasn't friends with her on Facebook," she said.

"I wouldn't know," she shrugged. "To be honest I don't think she went on it much; only to keep in touch with her mates from Uni. We don't have a computer in the house, you see. Angel used to moan because she had to go to the library, but I didn't want one. Wi-Fi makes you ill."

"How well did they know each other?"

"I wouldn't say they were good friends. I mean Angel never talked about her," she paused, running her hands through her uncombed hair. It was dyed the colour of raspberries, the same shade of lipstick Linton wore when she could be bothered. "She only knew Sam because I used to be friendly with her mum. Before her husband died in that awful crash. Poor woman. She must be beside herself with worry."

So Sam and Angel knew each other. But was that information significant? Possibly not. It was as likely the killer was choosing his victims at random in which case it wouldn't make any difference to the investigation.

"Can you think why Angel might have a connection to the women in Avebury? Did she belong to any groups?"

"Groups? No."

"Liz, I know we've asked you this already, but was she interested or involved in any sort of spiritual activities?"

"You mean was she part of a cult? Or into wacky religions? That's what the other officer asked me. And I told him, no . . . not Angel. She hated anything like that."

"We thought if you'd had a chance to think you might've remembered something."

"Like I said before, love, that's more my thing. I'm into it all: astrology, crystals, hands on healing. Anything Angel would've called *Glastonburyfied*. She was very cynical. Used to take the mickey a lot . . ." She paused to take her glasses off, pushing her fingers into the dark hollows beneath her eyes, as though trying to stop her tears. "She's one of those who like to have proof. The only time she ever admitted believing in anything was that time she saw a UFO." She stopped suddenly. "There is one thing though, that's odd."

"What?"

She shook her head. "It's probably nothing."

"You never know. It could be important."

"I found something in her room." She stopped.

"What?" Linton asked, leaning forward.

"A painting."

"Why is that odd?"

"It was under her bed. It's of the Tor. She hates anything like that."

"Even the Tor?"

"Especially the Tor. It winds her up how people go on about it being all sacred and magical. 'It's just a hill, mum,' she was always saying."

"Do you think she had more of an interest in, how can I put it, New Age things than you think? Perhaps she hid it because she felt embarrassed about going back on what she'd said to you in the past." *Or maybe whoever took her up the Tor gave it to her. Perhaps it was a present? A way of coaxing her into some cult?*

"Do you think the painting might be important?"

"I'm not sure," said Linton, "but I'll need to take it away. Get it checked for trace evidence."

"What? Fingerprints and the like?" Linton nodded. "Why? Do you think the bloke who killed her gave it to her? That doesn't make sense."

"Can you think of any reason for Angel to go up the Tor?"

She shook her head. "She hadn't gone up there for years."

"Are you sure?"

"She wasn't the sort to keep things to herself. That's why it's odd that she hid the painting."

"Did she take drugs?"

Mrs Kingsley shifted in her seat. "Depends on what you mean by drugs. Caffeine's a drug. So's alcohol."

"Illegal drugs. There's a suggestion she may have gone up there to take something."

"She's no drug addict. But they experiment, don't they? It's part of being young."

And old, Linton thought, glancing at the blue Rizla packet next to the empty ashtray.

"You said she didn't like anything Glastonbury-ish, but she was wearing patchouli oil when we found her. We smelt it on her. That's about as Glastonbury a smell as you can get."

"Patchouli oil?" She shook her head adamantly. Her dangly earrings gently tapped the sides of her jaw. "Not Angel. She hates the smell of the stuff. I use it all the time. It's got amazing antiseptic properties . . ." she stopped. "Sorry. I'm rambling."

"Perhaps she put it on that night."

"I was with her when she stormed out the house. We'd had an argument, you see. I'd have smelt it on her."

"Well, maybe she put some on after she went out?"

"Why would she do that?"

Linton paused. There was something else, she thought. Something she didn't want to mention, but knew she had to. "What about the necklace she was wearing? The one with the green gemstone." She didn't need to say the one that was used to strangle her; it was obvious what Mrs Kingsley was thinking from the way she flinched. "Is that the sort of thing she'd normally wear?"

"I don't know. I assumed it was the latest fashion." She paused and said thoughtfully, "But, now you mention it, it was quite hippy-ish."

"How long has she had it?"

"She's been wearing it for a couple of weeks."

"Do you know if she bought it herself?"

"I didn't ask."

"Perhaps it was a present from someone."

"Maybe."

They sat in silence for a moment and then Mrs Kingsley said, "You know, last night I lay awake on the sofa, going over and over it in my head, trying to make some sense out of it all. But I came to the conclusion there isn't any. It probably exists inside some lunatic's head. I'm not sure if it makes it better or worse."

"Whoever's done this, and for whatever reason, we're going to do everything in our power to find him." Linton winced at how scripted she sounded. She glanced at her watch surreptitiously, knowing she was going to have to get back soon. But she didn't want to look callous, like she was buggering off now she'd got the information she wanted. She'd give it another five minutes; remind Angel's mum that the family liaison officer would be in later today and then she'd go.

"Do you have any children?" asked Mrs Kingsley suddenly.

Linton shook her head.

"Do you think you ever will?"

"It's not looking too hopeful at the moment."

"Before all this I'd have felt sorry for you. Thought you were missing out. But now, do you know what? I envy you. That you won't have to feel this pain." She brought both hands inwards pointing briefly at her chest. "I keep thinking what it must have been like for her. How scared she would've been."

"I know this is no consolation, but she'd have died quickly," Linton said.

Mrs Kingsley was crying now, bulbous tears she didn't bother to wipe off dripping onto her resigned hands.

"I miss her so much. And I keep thinking of all the things I should've said to her." She paused then said, "That's one thing I've learnt. You should tell the people you love what they mean to you. Don't put it off because you never know what's around the corner." She stopped to catch her breath. "She told me she hated me, the night she was killed."

"I'm sure she didn't mean it."

"I deserved it. I was interfering again. Telling her how to live her life."

"What did you argue about?"

"She wanted to audition for *Second Chance* – that dreadful reality show. I said I didn't want her to. All she wanted was to be famous. It's her dad's fault, putting silly ideas in her head. He's a musician. He's well known in Canada."

"She knew you had her best interests at heart."

"I don't expect she did."

She stopped, unable to control her tears.

"What if she was meant to be famous, but didn't get the chance?" she added quietly. Then she turned slowly in her chair and yanked open the top right-hand drawer in the dresser behind her. She pulled out a framed photograph and passed it to Linton.

"It was on the wall at the bottom of the stairs. I had to put it in here. I'd never get past the bottom step otherwise."

Linton looked down at the picture of a radiant woman, holding a baby wrapped in a soft white blanket.

"You look beautiful," she said, looking up from the young Mrs Kingsley to the worn-out version sitting opposite her.

"It was taken on the day I had her. My mum said I looked like I'd been given the world. And you know what, that's how I felt. I'll never forget what she wrote in the card she gave me: 'The overwhelming love you feel for your daughter is how I feel about you.'"

Linton tried to imagine her own mum saying something like that. She couldn't. She handed the framed photograph back.

"I expect they'll blame the mother."

"Sorry?"

"Whoever this nutter is that did it to her," said Mrs Kingsley. "I expect they'll blame the mother, say it's all her fault. That's the way she brought him up."

"And what do you think?"

"I'm not sure what to think about anything anymore. I'll get that painting." She pulled herself up from the table and left the room.

A few seconds later Linton heard footsteps above her. She jumped as a cat leapt onto her lap. Its fur was so dark, it made her black trousers look grey. It settled down and started to purr.

A minute later Mrs Kingsley returned with the painting, carrying it so the picture-side was turned away from Linton.

"I see Grimalkin found you," she said.

"That's an unusual name."

"That's what Nostradamus called his cat. Angel called him Grim for short."

She turned the painting round and laid it on the table.

Linton stared at it for a couple of seconds. Mrs Kingsley must've sensed her surprise because she said, "What? Do you think it's important?"

Linton shook her head, quickly recovering herself.

"I'll need something to protect it," she said, nodding toward the kitchen window. "It's still pouring out there. A bin bag will do."

And on the way out, she thought, *perhaps I'll chuck it in the dustbin where it belongs.*

•••

Linton didn't recognise the woman behind the counter in Glastonbury, but she recognised her type.

"Yee-ess?" she drawled, only raising her head from the glossy book she was flicking languidly through after Linton cleared her throat and coughed a couple of times. She reminded her of a cat, with her slanted eyes thickly lined with black kohl and high, razor-sharp cheekbones. She was wearing a necklace with a jade pendant the size of a small frying pan.

She let the covered canvas rest against the side of the counter and took out her ID.

"I need to ask you some questions about a painting. It's got the gallery's name stuck to the back of it, so I'm assuming it was bought from here."

"OK," replied Cat Woman, drawing out the word so it lasted a few seconds. She pulled the picture out of the black bin bag and held it up for her to see.

"Ahhh," she said, as though Linton was showing off a kitten or a newborn baby. "One of my favourites. I've always loved this one. The way she's, like, captured the, uhh, exhilarating freshness of Glastonbury Tor in the spring."

"Do you have any idea who bought it?"

"Who bought it?" She shook her head at the speed a hypnotist might swing his watch. "I've got no idea."

"Do you keep records of your buyers?"

"No, but I can tell you who sold it." She stared at Linton for a few moments and then ducked down behind the counter reappearing a couple of seconds later with a notebook in her hand. She flicked slowly through it, humming discordantly under her breath. "Ah, here we go," she said eventually.

"And?"

She looked up and stared at Linton, cocking her head to one side, as if noticing her for the first time. "Oh. Yes. Um, Mikey."

"Is he here?"

"Mikey?" *No, Mickey Mouse, who d'you think?*

"I'd like to ask him if he remembers who bought the painting."

"Oh. Right. He's travelling. He's in India for like . . . three months." The woman yawned, covering her mouth with a hand that looked too heavy for its skinny wrists. Linton was surprised by her nails. She'd expected them to be manicured, but instead they were bitten to the quick, the skin around them bloodied and sore-looking.

"Have you got a mobile number for him?"

"Mikey?"

Linton was getting exasperated now. "So I can contact him."

"He doesn't have a mobile."

"Everyone has a mobile."

"Not Mikey. He's, like, worried it might give him a brain tumour."

"Have you got *any* contact details for him?"

"He's travelling."

"He must be staying somewhere." Cat Woman shrugged. "Did he mention if a man or woman bought it?"

"Mikey? No. He never said."

"Well, if you do hear from him, ask him to ring Glastonbury Police station. As a matter of urgency."

As Linton turned to leave, Cat Woman said, "Whoever bought that painting made a good choice, you know. It's a Tessa Linton and one of the very few ones we've got left. Sadly the artist doesn't, like, paint the Tor much anymore."

No, Linton thought. *That's because she was living in Holland; shacked up with a Dutch woman two years younger than her eldest daughter. A woman who Linton hated almost as much as Ben.*

EIGHT

B rown was in a foul mood when Linton got back to the station. He seemed unimpressed by anything she had to report. "Angel knew Sam. So what," he said, his tone scornful. "They're about the same age and both from round here."

"What about the picture her mother found under her bed?"

"Your mum painted it. Big deal."

"I didn't mean that," although it was weird, seeing her signature on something that might end up as evidence in a murder trial. "Don't you think it's odd she'd hidden it?"

"You said Mrs Kingsley liked the painting."

"So?"

"Well, perhaps Angel bought it for her as a present. Maybe that's why she didn't want her to see it."

"It's a bit of a coincidence though. Don't you think?"

"What is?" he said bluntly.

"The fact that the painting she's got hidden under her bed turns out to be the place where she ends up getting murdered."

He shrugged, "Like you said. A coincidence."

"So you don't think whoever took her up the Tor gave it to her?"

"No. Which is lucky seeing as you've dragged it halfway round town. Any trace evidence will be destroyed."

"We might still get fingerprints off it."

"Yeah, well, it wouldn't hurt," he conceded. "But I'm not convinced it's got anything to do with this."

"What about the patchouli oil? Don't you think it's strange? Her mum said she never wore it."

Another shrug. "Perhaps he put some on her. It might be part of his MO."

"The smell of patchouli wasn't mentioned in the Avebury reports."

"They might not have seen it as being significant. And even if it is, what are we meant to do? Arrest anyone in Glastonbury who happens to have a bottle of the stuff in the house? That's half the bloody town."

Lunch was a bag of cola bottles Linton found in her handbag that she'd forgotten to give her nephew. Popping the last sweet in her mouth she typed 'human sacrifice' into Google, sighing when the search engine came back with almost three million results. She glanced at the computer clock. *Shit*. She didn't have time for this.

She decided to limit herself to the first two pages of results and raced through them hoping she hadn't missed anything important. There was all the stuff she'd expected; how human sacrifice was practised in ancient cultures as payment to please or appease the gods. The Celtic Druids favoured hanging and drowning; the Vikings, strangulation and stabbing, while the Aztecs preferred to pin their victims to an altar and cut out their beating hearts.

But what about nowadays? Did stuff like this still go on? Linton typed 'modern human sacrifice' and discovered that apparently it did.

"You won't believe some of this," she said, after a few minutes of reading.

"What?" Brown said abruptly.

"Listen to this. On August 11, 1999, a Finnish court jailed a man for murdering his friend in a satanic ritual involving torture, cannibalism and necrophilia. A document released after the verdict stated that the defendant had strong leanings towards Satanism. After attacking his friend, he ate parts of him, sexually abused his body, sawed it into small pieces and left them on a rubbish tip."

"What's your point?"

"It's a lot more violent than anything our killer's done, isn't it?"

"I s'pose."

"This one's as bad," she said, continuing to read. "A Welsh teenager was found guilty of the savage murder of a ninety-year-old widow. The seventeen-year-old, who was once her paperboy, removed her heart and drank her blood in a macabre ritual." She paused, "I'm pretty certain we're not dealing with a satanic ritual. What d'you think?"

"What about the locations?" Brown said, tersely. "They've got to be significant."

"So maybe it's religiously motivated rather than satanic. Perhaps Angel got lured into a cult that practises sacrifice by strangulation. It might explain why she had a picture of the Tor under her bed. And why she put on patchouli oil."

"Hang on a minute. Why would having one of your mum's paintings or wearing perfume oil mean you were part of a cult?"

"It might do." Linton paused, thinking about what she'd read. "Or maybe it was a Druid sacrifice: a modern-day one. If such a thing exists."

"We'll find out tomorrow, when we meet Mr Vine."

"Who?"

"The bloke who wrote the book," he said impatiently. "The one Milne was on about. *Myths and Legends through the Ages* or whatever-the-crap it's called. We've got an appointment at half nine."

"He might not know about modern-day Druids though."

"Yes, he will."

"How do you know?"

"Because he is one. A Druid. I found out when I spoke to him."

"What?" she said indignantly, "You never told me."

"I'm telling you now," he said. "You know, this whole sacrificial thing might turn out to be a red herring."

"But, like you said, what about Avebury Stones and Tor Hill? They must mean something. And the flares. Why else would the killer have placed them there?"

"Perhaps he had them for another reason."

"Like what?"

"To help him see better? To attract someone's attention? Maybe they were used as some sort of signal."

"Why? Do you think somebody else is involved?"

"We don't even know who the killer is yet. Let alone whether anyone else is involved."

"What's up with you?"

He sighed and shook his head. "I'm fed up with all this fucking about." He picked up a wad of paper and waved it at her. "Look at this. The reports from yesterday's house-to-house enquires. I've spent the last two hours going through them. Nothing. We're just picking through bits of paper and waiting around for the FSS results. We should be out there looking for Sam."

"What else can we do? We've got helicopters searching fields. Most of Avon and Somerset are knocking on people's doors. You know what Milne says. Cases like this are most likely to be solved by desk work."

He grunted and turned back to the pile of paperwork in front of him. *Fine,* Linton thought. *Be like that.*

They sat in silence for a minute and then Brown said, "By the way it's not Tor Hill."

"What?"

"You said Tor Hill."

"So? That's what it's called."

He shook his head. "Tor is an old Celtic word. It means conical hill. So when you say Tor Hill that's like saying Hill Hill."

God, he is a wanker. "I'll try and remember that in the future, Professor Pedantic."

"You know just because I'm gorgeous doesn't mean I'm a complete airhead."

"Dickhead more like," she said under her breath, but loud enough for him to hear.

They sat mostly in silence for the next hour; Linton typed up her findings for The Toad's report, Brown appeared to be reading. The only time he spoke was to remind her to make an appointment with Sam's boss at About Face, the production company she worked for in Bristol.

Just after half-past three, Hargreaves stuck his head out of his office.

"We've got some results back from the FSS. Briefing in two."

"Thank fuck for that," mumbled Brown. "Now we might be getting somewhere."

•••

Claire could hear her mum out in the kitchen clattering around. She'd tried to persuade her to go back to bed, but she'd refused.

"What's the point?" she said. "I didn't sleep. I can't. Not until they find her."

Why was her laptop being so slow? Perhaps it only seemed slow because everything else was speeded up – her heartbeat, her breathing, the tapping of her fingers as she waited for the page to download.

Finally. She typed in the name and password – the password she'd guessed first time when she tried a few months ago. *Marmalade.* The name of their family cat that had to be put down. Typical of Sam to go against advice not to use anything obvious like a pet's name.

There were five new messages in her sister's inbox. She clicked on the open box and glanced down at them. It was the usual offers and incentives: triple points; free postage and packaging on any orders over seventy-five pounds; ten per cent off everything if you buy today. There was nothing personal, no messages from Facebook, nothing that wasn't sitting in millions of other Hotmail inboxes. Even so, it still felt wrong.

What did she expect? Danny wouldn't email Sam, not now. He hadn't for weeks, not since he'd finished with her, saying he was fed up with her selfish, shallow ways.

She looked in the Sent folder and found an email to Abby dated Thursday, 19th November. The day before Sam disappeared. She clicked on it.

"Hi Abs. Hope it's still OK to stay at yours at the weekend. I'm planning to get shitfaced, so I don't want to stay at mum's. Not fair on Claire. Especially as it's . . ."

She jumped as her mum walked into the room, fighting the urge to pull the laptop shut.

"Sorry, love. I didn't mean to startle you. I thought you might like a cup of tea," she said, placing it gently on the table next to the mouse. "What are you looking at?"

"Just checking my emails again. You never know. I thought there may be a message from Sam."

Her mum nodded. Claire looked at her exhausted face, her eyes puffy from too much crying and too little sleep. Her kind, comfortable, trusting face. She wished she were a little girl again so she could climb onto her mum's lap and tell her everything. Tell her she was sorry. Sorry for being a bad daughter and an even worse sister. Instead, she clicked on the little cross on the top right hand of the computer screen, shutting the program down, making it all go away.

Wishing it was that easy.

•••

Somebody needed to say something, Linton thought, as they gathered round for the briefing. It couldn't go on like this. That purple tie and maroon shirt. Still, she wasn't about to volunteer to be the messenger.

The Toad's bizarre colour combinations had coincided precisely with his wife leaving him. They'd all concluded it was the beginning of a nervous breakdown, until Brown overheard him telling someone he was colour blind. Sandra Hargreaves had obviously dressed him for the previous twenty-odd years.

"Right then," he bellowed, rocking back and forth on his tiny feet. "FSS results. First up, the patchouli oil. Traces of the perfume were found on the sleeve of Angel's jumper, not her skin."

Linton raised her hand and The Toad turned his bulbous eyes to stare at her.

"Sir. Angel's mum said she didn't smell of if when she left the house."

He nodded brusquely. "So at some point during the course of the evening she managed to get patchouli oil on the sleeve of her jumper. At this stage we have no idea if it's got any significant bearing on the case." The tune of 'I Should Be So Lucky' suddenly rang out.

"Switch that sodding thing off!" shouted Hargreaves.

"Sorry, Sir," DS Keen mumbled, groping around in his pocket.

The Toad turned back to address the rest of them. "As I was saying . . ." he was interrupted by the sound of his own mobile ringing. He grabbed it off the desk, glaring at it as though it had insulted him before prodding it with a stumpy finger and smacking it back down on the table.

"It turns out," he continued, still looking fiercely at his phone, "that the FSS have got sod all." There was a universal groan. "No semen. No saliva. No fingerprints."

"Nothing on the leather thong of the necklace?" asked Keen.

"Sweet Fanny Adams."

"Does it mean he was wearing gloves?" It was Hooper.

Hargreaves whipped his head round at surprising speed. "You're like a sodding dog, aren't you? One of those jumpy buggers that get overexcited. Yes, Hooper. So it would seem."

"Which means it might have been premeditated," said Brown.

"Or he was cold," Linton ventured.

"Blokes don't wear gloves," Brown scoffed. "Not unless they're skiing. Or on a motorbike."

"I'm talking about your *average* bloke," she said. Brown flicked her the finger. It was subtle, but not enough for her to miss the gesture. "Hands up which men wear gloves in the winter," she asked, looking round the room to capture the response. One man gingerly raised his. "See?" she said.

"Linton. If you've finished with your market research, then perhaps I can move on to the second lot of results."

"Sir."

"We've got footprints. Big uns. Size fourteens, to be precise. It turns out the Wiltshire lot found the same size ones close to the body of Sadie Carter." Linton felt a trickle of excitement ripple through the room. "According to the FSS, only three per cent of the male population takes that size. It could be a coincidence, but I think it's unlikely."

"So it's definitely the same man," Hooper ventured.

"Give the dog a bone." Hargreaves clapped his hands slowly together in mock applause.

"They must grow them big in Avebury then," Brown said thoughtfully.

"What do you mean?" barked The Toad, his stumpy arms dropping back down by his side.

"They also found size fifteen footprints. I remember seeing it in one of the reports. It was at the same crime scene . . ."

"What about Hannah James' murder scene?" Keen interrupted. "Did they find size fourteen prints there?"

Brown shook his head. "Apparently the footprints were compromised. They couldn't lift any decent ones, due to the condition of the ground."

"Did the footprints come from the same shoes, Sir?" Linton asked.

"The FSS tried to trace the origins of both pairs. The footprints in Avebury were left by a Timberland boot. That particular style is only available in the US in a size fourteen, which gives rise to a number of possibilities. The killer could have purchased them online or bought them when he was in the States himself . . ."

"Or maybe someone he knew brought them back," said Brown.

"Or he could be American," Keen chipped in.

"The size fourteen prints found on the Tor," said The Toad, ignoring both of them, "belong to footwear resembling some sort of desert boot. The soles are marked with the initials WT. The FSS looked for a match on the Cinderella database of shoes and sole patterns, but couldn't find one. Apparently the larger manufacturers update it at regular intervals, so they've concluded a smaller company must've made the footwear." He stopped and looked at Brown. "You need to find the company."

•••

Sam woke to the sound of the front door slamming, the letterbox fluttering shut. She could hear him banging around the flat, the noise of the toilet flushing, whistling. Twice he came into the room: once to bring her tablets and empty the bucket, the other to read some passages aloud from a book.

He was definitely mad, but he was right about the tablets though. They helped. Once they kicked in, it felt as if this was happening to somebody else. Now though, they were beginning to wear off; fear and doubt were creeping in again. He kept saying he wasn't going to hurt her, that he needed her help. She wondered if he'd said the same thing to Angel Kingsley.

Her stomach was killing her and she felt nauseous. She was certain if she could smell her breath, it would reek of nail polish. Hyperglycaemia. She had all the symptoms. If she didn't inject herself with insulin soon, she'd slip into a coma. She *had* to make him believe her.

If only she still had that card. The one with all her medical details on it. The one that said she had diabetes. But after they'd given her the bracelet, she'd taken it out of her purse and chucked it away.

Her purse! She'd forgotten all about it. The repeat prescription she'd picked up from the doctor's. She'd stuffed it in there. If he saw it was for insulin, he'd believe her and then maybe she could persuade him to let himself into her mum's house and get the spare kit. It was in the kitchen, in the drawer next to the oven. He could be in and out in less than a minute.

She felt another sharp stabbing pain in her stomach. She rolled over onto her side, pulling up her knees to her abdomen, wincing as the ligature dug into the raw furrows on her wrists. From somewhere in the flat she heard the low rumble of the radio. She wondered if he was listening to the news. Maybe he'd come back in. Read some more passages from that freaky book.

If she couldn't persuade him to get her insulin, she was going to die. It was as simple as that. Then she'd never get the chance to tell Claire the truth. And she had to. She needed to confess: to clear her conscience so she could be forgiven.

•••

Linton and Brown sat hunched in front of the monitor, sleeves rolled up, chins in their hands, elbows resting on the desk. The surface felt sticky against Linton's bare skin, probably the remnants of a spillage from the nearby can of coke.

PC Broughton stood behind them. He'd seen the footage countless times before and was only there to point out the highlights. The three of them watched in silence as the 376 pulled up outside Glastonbury Town Hall. The windows were steamed up so despite the brightness inside the bus, it was impossible to make out who was in the queue forming in the aisle. Then the door opened and a steady stream of people got off. Two old ladies holding on to one another's arm, a man with dreadlocks and an unlit roll-up hanging from his mouth, three teenage boys with skateboards, a group of five teenage girls giggling and clutching shopping bags and a pretty blonde woman carrying a handbag and a small holdall.

"There she is," Linton said, instinctively leaning forward towards the screen. She waited for the customary response from Brown, but the "niiiiice" followed by a low whistle under his breath didn't come. It wasn't like him. His bad mood was making her oddly unsettled, as though she was somehow responsible for it, although she couldn't think how.

"Pretty, isn't she?" she said, as they watched her march confidently past the stationary bus, along the pavement which eventually curved round the corner onto the hill forming the main stretch of the High Street. Her verbal nudge brought no response. "Don't you think?" she tried again.

"I s'pose," said Brown. He folded his arms. The movement brought with it a not-unpleasant aroma of aftershave and fresh sweat. She shifted in her seat.

"What d'you think?" Broughton asked, as Sam moved out of sight of the camera.

"Not much to go on, is there? She was alone and she didn't speak to anyone. Nobody on the bus took any notice of her. Nobody followed her."

The man with the dreadlocks had already ambled off in the other direction and they watched as a middle-aged woman helped the two old ladies into a waiting car. The teenage skateboarders and shoppers crossed at the zebra crossing and disappeared down Benedict Street. Two other passengers got off the bus. A young woman with a toddler, struggling to open her pushchair and keep her child from running off into the road and an old man with a walking stick.

"Is that it?" asked Brown.

"I'm afraid so," said Broughton.

"And nothing from any of the other cameras in town?"

"Believe me, I've watched hours and hours of this stuff and she doesn't appear anywhere else. The next logical place you'd expect to see her is halfway up the High Street, on the camera trained on the war memorial. She'd need to pass it to get to the pub. I'd estimate it takes less than a minute to reach that point from the bus stop. But you don't ever see her. Either she didn't get as far as that or, for some reason, she crossed over so the camera didn't pick her up."

"Why, though? The pub's on the side of street she was already on."

"Perhaps she crossed over to speak to someone?" Linton suggested.

"Could she have got into another vehicle?"

"Nothing came past this camera for another thirty seconds."

"Then what?"

"A Ford Fiesta. Registered to a Mrs Best. A seventy-two-year-old widow. We've checked. It was her driving the car that night and she doesn't remember seeing Sam Jenkins, let alone anything suspicious."

"Anyone else?"

"I carried on looking for another ten minutes. A total of twenty-one cars in that time. We're tracking them down, one by one, and questioning the drivers. Nothing of interest so far."

"What about the other camera? The one further up the High Street, on the other side of the road?"

"A motorbike and nineteen cars. None of them stopped to pick anyone up. We're tracking them down and questioning drivers, same as the others."

There was silence for a few seconds. Linton wondered if the other two were thinking the same thing as her. That Sam might already be dead and this could be the last time anyone, apart from her killer, saw her alive. Brown was the first to break it.

"Sod it. There's nothing more we can do today. I'm off to the pub." He turned to Linton and said tersely, "Coming?"

"Actually, I will." *A small vodka and tonic might help me sleep*, she thought. And maybe she'd find out what was bothering Brown so much.

NINE

Linton was woken by the sound of her front door slamming shut. She opened her eyes and quickly closed them. Her first thought was that he'd gone; her second, that she wanted to die. It took a moment for her to locate the source of her nausea. It was in her head, rather than her body, spinning and swirling and making her giddy. Her chest felt tight and she could taste something alien at the back of her throat. *What the fuck happened?*

Rolling slowly onto her side, she cautiously pulled her knees up to her stomach. Perhaps if she stayed like this, she wouldn't be sick. She'd do anything to avoid it; lie like this for hours if that's what it took. But she knew it was only a matter of time before she felt the dry mouth, followed by the retching and the stagger to the toilet. Black and red figures curled and twisted behind her aching eyelids. The movement made her more nauseated. She needed to open her eyes again. It took all her effort.

Wondering what the time was, she searched for a thin, dull line of light at the bottom of the blackout blind that would tell her if she was late for work. No, it was still dark.

Thank God for that.

She gingerly rolled her eyeballs so she could check the time on her bedside table. The movement was enough. She was out of bed, stumbling and retching, clutching her pounding head. A moment later and she was hanging over the toilet.

As she pulled the flush, she realised she was shivering. It was freezing in the bathroom, especially with no clothes on. She wanted water. She needed it to get rid of the taste in her mouth, but knew from experience that it wouldn't stay down. A teaspoon of water every five minutes. Isn't that what they recommended with alcohol poisoning? Is that was this was?

She crawled back into bed, wondering how long a reprise before the next lurch to the bathroom. She closed her eyes and found herself tormented by a rerun of the night before.

•••

She was only going to have one drink. Perhaps it was the combination of talking to Angel's mum earlier in the day and the unsettling phone conversation she'd had with her brother before following Brown through the doors of the Albert. Still, she was amazed she'd got so drunk, although the handful of sweets she'd had for lunch hadn't exactly lined her stomach.

She remembered the beginning of the evening clearly. It was a chance meeting. She'd never seen Simon Talbot in there before, but they ended up sitting at tables next to each other. He introduced her to his colleagues as his ex-girlfriend and she laughed, praying he wouldn't go into details, especially in front of Brown, who was sitting next to her. They chatted for a while and, when she turned back to say something to Brown, she discovered he'd gone.

Gradually other people followed. Wives and husbands, dinner and *Midsomer Murders* to get back to. Soon it was only the two of them. They mentioned getting something to eat and then forgot about it. They talked about work for a while and then, inevitably, he brought up the case.

"I know it's awful, but at least it makes a change from all the usual stuff," he said. "How about an exclusive, for old time's sake?"

"I'm not that drunk."

"I'd better get you another one then," he said, nodding at her empty glass. As he walked to the bar, she glanced up at the clock, astonished by how late it was.

"What about your wife?" she asked, when he finally returned to the table. "Won't she wonder where you are?"

"Haven't you heard?" She shook her head. "I moved out. I'm staying at a mate's flat at the bottom of town until I get sorted. He's working away, so I'm doing him a favour. We've told the kids it's a temporary thing, to let them get used to the idea. But it's not . . . and, before you ask, there isn't anyone else."

"I wasn't going to."

"Can I ask *you* something?" He leant forward and Linton had a sudden flashback of him lying on his teenage bed.

"OK," she said, hesitatingly.

"Have you got any suspects?"

She laughed. "You don't give up, do you?"

"Have you had a profiler in?"

"No!"

"Don't bother paying for one. I'll do it for you." He cleared his throat and put on a deep, gravelly voice. "I believe without doubt we're looking at what's known in the trade as a serial killer. The suspect is probably male, white, in his late twenties or thirties, and someone who has a particular issue with women. He may have been abused or abandoned by his mother or been badly let down by a woman in the past. There's a good chance it's motivated by religion. Perhaps he's on a Christian mission, clearing the world of women who've led men astray and corrupted mankind. What do you think? Do I get the job?"

"Very good," she laughed. "Sorry to disappoint you, but we're more likely to solve it using house-to-house and police records than anything as glamorous as a profiler."

"I could tell you a thing or two about the Avebury murders."

"What d'you mean?"

"My mum moved back to Marlborough about five years ago, after my dad died. It's only ten miles from Avebury, and I always read the local when I'm there. The paper was full of it when they happened."

"It's OK, thanks. Funnily enough, we've managed to gather some information about them all by ourselves."

He grinned then took a sip of lager. "Tell me this though and I'll shut up. Do you think it *is* some sort of sacrificial killing? The fact the women were killed on ley lines?"

"Sadie Carter wasn't killed. She died of hypothermia."

"Come on, you know what I mean. Stop avoiding the question."

"You're not into all that, are you?"

"What? Ley lines?" he said. He paused and took another sip. "I think it's a load of bollocks. And you're still avoiding the question. Is it a sacrificial killing?"

"We're not certain. That's all I can say, I'm afraid."

"What about you?"

"What *about* me?"

"Do you get off on all the Glastonbury stuff? Ley lines and crystals and tarot cards."

"Not at all."

"But when you were at college, you were a bit of a hippy if I remember rightly."

"And you were a DJ and called yourself Talbotski if *I* remember rightly."

He laughed. "You won't believe how many people still call me that now. Although I wish they bloody wouldn't. Winds me up to be honest."

"What is it they say? Nicknames stick to people and the most ridiculous are the most adhesive."

"Mind you, there's a lot round here with stranger names. What is it with this place? You hear it all the time don't you? Marks calling themselves Merlin. Sharons changing their name to Shambala. Like this bloke I interviewed the other day, who calls himself Star Child. They all think they're being so individual, but they're as concerned about fitting in as everybody else."

"I wonder if people thought that about Angel?"

"But that was her real name."

"Did you know her then?"

He shrugged. "Only from around."

Then her memory of the evening changed. From something fluid to something more jerky. Until it was a series of split-second moments. Like watching a sequence of five-second video stills on her phone. Short snapshots of time that became more and more blurred and out of focus.

The back of a taxi driver's head. Giggling and slurring her address. Fumbling in her bag for her keys and purse. Spilling coffee granules all over the kitchen worktop. Sitting astride him on the sofa with one leg on the floor for balance. And then astride him in bed, her hands letting go of the headboard as she sensed defeat. She remembered the frustration in his voice as he apologised.

And then nothing. Why couldn't she remember anything else? She hoped it was because she'd fallen asleep. Remembering was bad enough. Not remembering was worse. Did they do anything after that? What did she say to him?

The red and black images were back again. Spinning and swirling. She was stumbling and retching, clutching her head. How could she have been so irresponsible? She had such a busy day ahead. What is it they were doing again? *Think, think* . . . They had an interview with that author lined up. The Druid, who'd written the book about myths and legends. And then they were driving to Bristol to interview Sam Jenkins' boss. Oh, God. The thought of sitting in a stuffy car, all the way to Bristol.

How the hell am I even going to make the journey into work?

Five minutes later, she was crawling back into bed, vowing she'd never drink again.

•••

Andrew Chubb glanced at his watch. Becki Harvey's constant hair-twiddling and foot-tapping was getting on his nerves. For some reason she seemed as anxious to get this over with as he was. If she just stopped being so bloody coy, he could get out and get on with writing the damned thing.

"The thing is, Andrew, if I tell you his name, how do I know you're not going to tell everyone else?"

He'd often used the phrase 'talking through gritted teeth' in his writing. Now, as he spoke, he experienced the sensation first hand.

"Becki. The whole point of this exercise is for you to tell me everything so I can put it in the book. It's your revelation about the affair that's going to make people go out and buy it."

"It could be dangerous though, he's a very important man. He might have links to the Mafia or the FBI. He might have me bumped off if it gets out."

Give me strength, thought Chubb. As a ghostwriter, he was used to working with difficult clients: celebrities who were arrogant or insecure or so strung out on prescription drugs they could barely get a sentence out, let alone one that made sense. But he'd never dealt with anyone quite as stupid as Becki Harvey. That the public believed she could write a book was laughable.

"Unless you've slept with the Prime Minister or a member of the royal family, I think that's pretty unlikely. I'm sorry to be blunt, but if you don't tell me who it is, this book's going be worth bugger all."

There was a short pause.

"What about the girl that's gone missing in Glastonbury?" she said, suddenly. "She's all over the papers. Can't we put something in about her instead?"

Chubb looked at her blankly. *What the hell was she on about now?* "Which girl?"

"Sam Jenkins. The one who's been abducted. She was on *Working Girl* with me. She was a researcher. We were good friends."

"I'm surprised you haven't gone to the papers with that story already," Chubb said caustically.

"My agent's going to approach them today," she said, his tone completely lost on her. "But I was thinking more about the book. Perhaps instead of the revelation."

He took a deep breath. "Look, Becki, it's probably worth a line or two, but it's not why people are going to buy it. They want to know *your* secrets. The fact you know someone who's been abducted is interesting, but it's more about *her*. I don't mean to sound callous, but if she gets out of this alive, it's her story they'll want to read. This book is about you. That's the whole point of an autobiography."

He could feel himself getting agitated. He paused, took another deep breath and spoke as calmly as he could. "Basically Becki, if you don't come up with the goods, this book isn't going to print. And your life as a celebrity will be over."

•••

Somehow Linton made it into work. She was unsure which line to adopt. Should she announce the hangover upfront and admit she felt like shit, or pretend she was fine and hope it would go away? She decided on the latter, but was soon forced into a rethink when Brown saw her.

"You look like crap. Big night in the end, was it? Hooper said you were still in the pub when he left."

Hooper? Had he been there? God. She must've been drunker than she thought.

"Don't you remember? He said he went in just before last orders. By that time you were dribbling on the table."

She sunk into her chair giving Brown the finger.

"Look at you. You've got the shakes."

"I've got a bit of a hangover, that's all."

"Not the best time to go out drinking, was it? Right in the middle of a case." She looked at him open-mouthed. "I can handle my booze," he said, rebutting the implicit accusation.

"Well, for your information, I didn't drink much."

"Dirty glass, was it?"

"An empty stomach. Anyway, I'm fine."

"Glad to hear it because we've got a busy day. We're off to Bristol later . . ."

"I know. I haven't forgotten."

" . . . and we're meeting Mr Vine, that mythology author, in half an hour. Which reminds me. Have you seen the papers? They're calling him the *ley line strangler* now. At least the nationals are. I expect it'll take the local a couple of weeks to catch on."

"What happened to you last night?" she asked, anxious to steer the conversation away from anything connected to Simon Talbot. "You didn't stay long. You don't normally leave until you've found someone to take home with you."

"I'm off women at the moment."

So she was right about the girl from Saturday. She probably turned out to be one of the bunny boilers he attracted. It served him right. She knew from his tone he wanted to talk about it, but it was his sordid bed – let him lie in it. Switching on her computer, she glanced over at him. He'd picked up the latest copy of the *Forum* and was reading it, his forehead creased in concentration.

"What?" he asked, when he realised she was looking at him. "I'm taking a break. Some of us were in early this morning."

"Is your interview in there?"

"That's the next edition. I'm seeing what the person wrote for this month."

"And?"

"Load of crap. Have a look for yourself," he said, leaning over and handing it to her.

Neither of them spoke as she read an interview with the man who ran the olive stall in Glastonbury's market.

Brown was the first to break the silence. "Simon Talbot, all right?"

"Here we go," she said, sighing loudly, "I wondered when that was going to start."

"You were getting very friendly last night. I wouldn't have thought he was your type."

"What's that meant to mean?"

"He's a bit beneath you, isn't he? I thought you liked clever blokes. Academics, like Ben."

"Ben's not *that* clever."

"Depends how you define it," he smirked. "I mean, look what he did in Amsterdam. It's not every day a bloke manages to . . ."

"Shut up, Brown," she said, putting her hand up before he went any further. "I don't even know why we're having this conversation. Nothing happened with Talbot."

They were silent again as she flicked through the rest of the *Forum*. Why didn't she tell him the truth and get the jibbing over with? He was bound to find out eventually. Simon was the sort to tell people and it wouldn't take long to get back to Brown. She flicked to the end of magazine. There was an advert on the inside cover.

"Oh my God," she said.

Brown glanced up. "What?"

"Look." She tried to frisbee the magazine across to his desk, but her aim was off and it landed on the floor beside his chair. "There's an ad on the inside back cover."

"So?" he said, bending down to retrieve it.

"It's for a shoe company in Glastonbury that specialises in large sizes for men. Look what they're called."

He rifled through the magazine and then stopped. "Walktall." It took a moment for it to sink in. "Shit. WT."

"Exactly. The initials on the size fourteens. I think we might have found the company that made the killer's shoes."

•••

What am I doing here? Claire asked herself for the twentieth time that morning. Perhaps she should've accepted her boss's offer to cover for her, but then what difference would it have made? There was no escape from the thoughts scurrying around her head, gnawing away like rats. Well, there was one, albeit a temporary one and she'd be lying if she said she wasn't tempted. But what good would that do?

If she was at home, she couldn't do anything to help. She'd already given the police a list of everyone she could think of. They'd been round yet again, asking if Sam had mentioned anything that might be significant. Had she noticed anyone acting differently, suspiciously? Had Sam fallen out with anybody, had she met someone new?

When would they talk to Danny? she wondered. And what would he tell them? It was bad enough imagining what the police *already* thought of her, without him telling them what she'd done.

The shop had been painfully quiet. She was grateful to the woman with the purple highlights who'd kept her occupied for a while. She came in clutching a long list of books, a spiritual pick-and-mix, from *Harnessing your Psychic Powers* to *Divining for Health*. She'd recently moved to the area, she said, and was displaying all the mannerisms of what Claire called the 'born-again Glastonbury'. The coloured hair, the flowing dress, the purple boots complete with hand-painted suns and moons; throwing herself into the town's culture with a fervour and enthusiasm that only a newcomer could muster, leaving Claire feeling jaded and cynical.

Other than her, she'd only had two paying customers. Most of their business was online now. Claire couldn't see the shop lasting much longer, not with rent and rates the way they were.

She looked around for something to do. Something to take her mind off it. They were low on bookmarks, the ones they gave away free with every sale as a way of getting people to remember their name. Not that Claire liked it much. A Helping Hand. She could see why her boss came up with it. Their speciality was self-help books, but it made Claire think of the sticks old people used to pick things up when they couldn't bend down. Perhaps she should ring the printers and find out when they were going to deliver them.

She reached for the phone, but changed her mind as a wave of tiredness and despair swept over her. She couldn't face it. Couldn't face talking to their account manager, who was bound to answer the phone. He was nosy at the best of times. She didn't want to have to go through it all again. Listen to the same things she'd heard for the last couple of days.

Last night she'd trudged up and down the High Street knocking on every door, asking people if they'd seen her sister the night she went missing. Nobody had. Someone had obviously told the police what she was up to because when she got home she found a message waiting for her from Detective Chief Inspector Hargreaves. She was to stop this activity immediately as it could hamper the investigation and put her sister's life in danger. She couldn't see how, but it wasn't worth risking it.

A man was waving at her now through the shop window. She waved back, recognising the striking face and long, dark ponytail. It was Dick from the crystal and gem shop. He was one of the people she'd called on last night. He'd been very sweet, saying how sorry he was that he couldn't help, how he'd thought it was odd when she and Sam hadn't come into the shop to buy the bracelet on Saturday. Now his smile of encouragement made her feel claustrophobic. It reminded her of what she'd gone through before. Having to put up with the furtive glances, with people not knowing what to say. Firstly when her dad died and then, of course, that other time.

"Hi, Claire," he said gently, as he pushed open the door. "I've got something for you." He shut the door behind him and walked towards the counter, pulling out a small velvet bag from the pocket of his long, sheepskin coat. "It's that bracelet you wanted for your mum's birthday. The one Sam asked me to put back." He pulled it out of the bag and handed it to her. "I want you to have it."

She couldn't care less about it and she doubted her mum would either. But despite everything, she didn't want to offend him. He'd always struck her as the sensitive type.

"Hang on a sec," she said. "I'll get my handbag. How much do I owe you?"

"I meant for free. I spoke to my uncle and he said it was fine. He owes me a favour anyway."

"Are you sure?"

"Yes, honestly. I'm not sure why, but it makes me feel like I'm doing something."

Claire noticed a movement out of the corner of her eye. It was Adam, waving at her through the shop window, just as Dick had only moments before. He was wearing a black beanie and clutching a paper bag from the bakers.

"Thanks, um, Star," she said to Dick, embarrassed at using the name he'd recently adopted. "It's beautiful and it's really kind of you."

He smiled sadly before turning and walking back towards the door. Meanwhile, Adam pushed it open, bending instinctively as he entered the shop. The two men nodded as they passed one another.

"How's Sunbeam, or whatever he calls himself now?" he asked, as Dick shut the door behind him.

"Fine," she said.

"You know, I'm thinking of changing my name to Incense Stick. Unless you've got a better one."

It was a running joke, taking the piss out of Dick for changing his name by deed poll. He'd think of a name and Claire would come back with her usual retort. "I've got a good one. How about wanker?" Today however, she wasn't in the mood.

"I don't know what you've got against him. He's sweet."

"He's full of shit. Did you know he tells people he's a traveller? He's gone all round England apparently. Big deal. So has my granny and she's in her eighties."

"She goes on coach tours. It's not the same thing."

He pulled a face. "He's a fruit loop. I saw him putting up a poster earlier. He's organised some stupid UFO convention. Hungry?" he asked. She shook her head. "I got you your favourite – cherry bakewell," he said, waving a Sarah's Bakery bag in her face.

"No, thanks. You have it."

"I can't believe you're even at work today."

"I didn't know what else to do. I feel like I'm going mad. Every time the phone goes, I'm scared to pick it up in case they've found her." She paused, running a finger over the bracelet. "Like they did with Angel," she said quietly.

"I've asked around," he said. "Nobody knows anything. It's mad, isn't it? Normally you can't fart at the bottom of the high street without someone at the top saying they can smell it."

Claire pulled another face.

"Sorry. But you'd think someone would have seen something on Friday night."

"It was a shame you didn't walk home from work that night," she said. "You'd have passed the town hall around the time the bus came in. You'd have probably seen her."

"I know. I can't remember the last time I got a lift home. I think Dave only offered so he could show off his new car."

The shop door opened again and they both looked up. It was a customer head to toe in cerise tie-dye, whose fashion sense, if nothing else, was clearly in need of a helping hand.

"I'll leave you to it," said Adam, brushing sausage-roll crumbs off his top and onto the floor. He winked and smiled. It was another sad smile. She was starting to get used to them again.

•••

Brown was also brushing crumbs off his top, his other hand clutching the steering wheel. He'd bought a pasty and eaten it with relish, even though Linton had begged him to get rid of it.

"It smells like Keen's armpits," she'd moaned.

Their appointment with Mr Vine, Druid and author of *Myths and Legends through the Ages*, was arranged for nine-thirty. He'd invited them to his house out on the moors. That was fine with them; they were always happy to find an excuse to get out. It helped break up the day.

Linton had left the station with the vague hope she'd feel better away from her desk. But who was she kidding? It didn't matter where she was – she had the hangover from hell and it was going wherever she went.

"Where exactly does he live?" she asked, wondering how long she was likely to be cooped up in the car.

"Shapwick Heath. Just down the road from the entrance to the Sweet Track."

They'd been late leaving. Linton had rung Walktall a couple of times, but their lines were busy and she didn't want to hold.

Then Brown had insisted on stopping to buy his stupid pasty. He drove quickly now, trying to make up time, splashing and jolting through puddle-filled potholes as the rain lashed at the car windows. The bumpy Mendip roads were uncomfortable at the best of times but feeling the way Linton did that morning it was akin to torture.

"Try Walktall again," said Brown.

"I will in a sec."

"Still feeling sick, are you?"

"I'm fine."

"Ring them then."

Linton felt her mouth turning dry, the back of her throat opening and closing and she wondered if the gamble she'd taken with the cup of tea before they left had been an overly optimistic one. She reached down to get her phone out of her handbag and instantly regretted the movement.

"Brown. Quick. Pull over!"

"Gonna be sick, are you?"

He cursed and slammed on the brakes. She opened the door the moment they stopped, the heavy rain and wind lashing at her, threatening to push her back into the car. She struggled forwards, heading towards the ditch. As the wind slammed the door behind her, she bent over, the violent heaving sweeping through her body, pulling a gush of brown liquid with it. The tea had been a bad idea after all.

She stayed like this for a few seconds, hands resting on her knees until she'd summoned enough strength to pull herself back up into a standing position. She stood for a moment, letting the wind and rain whip at her, trying to decide if she was going to be sick again. The heaving subsided. It was safe to get back in the car.

Brown was shaking his head as she clambered back in, rainwater dripping from the end of her nose.

"Fucking hell, Linton. How much did you drink last night?"

"It was the smell of that pasty."

"Not pregnant, are you?"

She ignored him and sat back in her seat, closing her eyes as he pulled away. She wanted to cry. Her hair was splattered against her face, she could taste the acrid tang of vomit in her mouth and her head was pounding. Brown was driving too fast again and a masochistic part of her hoped he'd crash so she could end this misery.

"Nice love bites by the way. Classy."

She opened her eyes. "What?"

"You've got red marks all over your neck. Bit of an animal, was he?"

Shit. She hadn't noticed. She'd got dressed in a hurry, put her make-up on in a half-light. She rubbed at her neck and tried adjusting the collar on her coat. "Don't be ridiculous. I bought some new washing tablets and it's an allergy from that, I expect."

He grunted. "Are you going to ring Walktall or not?"

Bastard. She grabbed at her phone and pressed the number she'd saved from her earlier attempts. This time she was answered by a cheerful sounding call centre operator called Mandy.

She was new, she explained, when Linton asked whether any of the footwear they sold was Walktall branded. "Hang on. I'll put you through to my supervisor."

She heard clicking followed by the unmistakable voice of Enya singing 'Orinoco Flow'. That's exactly what Linton felt like doing.

No, not sailing away. Too energetic. Maybe crawling away. Into a dark cave.

There was another louder click. "Hello? My colleague said you wanted to know whether we sell Walktall branded footwear."

"That's right."

"To be honest, we mainly sell high street brands. Vans, Converse, Nike, that sort of thing."

"So you don't have your own Walktall brand?"

"No."

"Oh." Linton heard the disappointment in her own voice. She was so sure they'd tracked the shoes down. "Thanks for your time."

The operator interrupted her goodbye. "We did try it as an experiment once though," she said.

Linton felt her heart beat quicken. "What do you mean?" Brown glanced across. She raised her eyebrows and nodded.

"We had a lot of customers asking for desert boots. No one else does them in large sizes so we had a go at making some ourselves."

"Desert boots?" Linton repeated for Brown's benefit. He took his right hand off the steering wheel and stuck his thumb up. "And did they have your logo on them?"

The operator paused. *Come on, come on.* "From what I can remember, it went on the soles. I think it was moulded on."

"And am I correct in saying your logo is your initials, WT?"

"That's right. The boots weren't up to standard though so we knocked it on the head."

"How long ago was this?"

"March, I think."

"And did you sell them online?"

"Hang on. I'll double check."

Enya started singing again, this time about being home. *Only another eight hours*, Linton thought, and hopefully she'd be joining her.

"What did they say?" asked Brown.

"They made some desert boots with their logo stamped on the bottom and . . . yes?"

"Hi." It was the supervisor again. "We didn't put them on the website. Like I said, they weren't up to standard and we didn't get many pairs made. In the end, we sold them off cheap through our shop in Glastonbury."

•••

A couple of minutes later and they arrived at Wick Cottage. They pulled onto a small gravel drive and crunched their way towards the front door. Before they had a chance to knock, it swung open to reveal a tall man in his early forties looking tanned and relaxed. His smile was warm and his hair cut close to his head. He wore an open-necked blue-and-pink checked shirt tucked into a pair of brown cords.

Brown put out his hand. "I'm DI Brown and this is DS Linton. We're looking for Mr Vine."

"Lovely to meet you," said the man, putting out his hand to shake Brown's. "Not what you expected?" He'd obviously caught the split second of confusion that passed across their faces. "We're quite normal, you know, us Druids. We don't spend the whole time in long white dresses chanting and waving staffs around. Come on in."

They followed him into the narrow, oak-floored hallway and through an open door to the right. It led into what Linton assumed was his living room. The walls were painted a deep red and an enormous oak mirror hung on one wall, reflecting a collection of tasteful paintings. Beneath it, in the beautifully tiled antique fireplace, crackled a log fire. Alcoves either side housed shelves crammed with books and CDs. As she moved further into the warm room, she smelt a sweet, sickly perfume.

"Please. Have a seat. Can I get you something to drink?"

"I'm fine, thanks," said Brown, "although Linton might want some water. She mentioned she was feeling dehydrated in the car on the way over."

She forced herself not to glare at him. "I'm fine, thank you."

As they sat at the polished walnut table, she realised it was the large pink lilies responsible for the cloying perfume she could taste. She hoped it wouldn't take long. The heavy scent was making her feel sick again.

"Thank you for agreeing to help us with our investigation," said Brown.

"I work from home, so it's nice to have some company."

"Do you write books full-time?" Linton asked Vine, watching him twist an ornate ring round his left index finger. The red gemstone caught the light from the fire.

"Not enough money in it, I'm afraid. I'm a freelance copywriter."

"You're a Druid in your spare time then, are you?"

Vine laughed. "You make it sound like a hobby. If you're a Druid, you're a Druid all the time. It's the same as if you were Catholic or Jewish or a Buddhist. It's a belief, a way of life. But you're right in a way. I only dress up as a Druid on certain occasions."

"And how did you, um, decide to become one?"

"I studied anthropology at university so I've always had an interest in ancient religion. Then, while I was researching for my book, I got friendly with the Head of the Glastonbury Order. I got more and more involved in it. It's a lot of fun."

Brown nodded slowly and then said, "As I explained on the phone, due to the location and manner of Angel Kingsley's death, there's a possibility it's some sort of sacrificial murder. What would you say to that?"

Vine pushed himself up from his seat and moved over to the fireplace. He picked up a small log from the wicker basket and flicked it expertly into the centre of the blaze, causing the flames to momentarily crackle and spit. The smell of damp, mossy wood filled the room.

"Look," he said, turning back round to face them, an amused smile tugging at the corner of his lips. "You obviously haven't read my book, and I wouldn't expect you to have, but human sacrifice is only a tiny part of what I write about. I'm more interested in how our ancestors viewed their world. In *all* their customs and their beliefs."

"But it *is* something you know about."

"Well, yes. But you're barking up the wrong tree if you think us Druids did it," he said.

"We don't necessarily think that," Brown replied. He paused, as though looking for the right words, and then said, "But I am right in thinking Druids celebrate festivals at Glastonbury and Avebury."

"And?"

"As I'm sure you're aware, two women died at Avebury Stones." Vine nodded as he sat back down at the table. "We're almost certain the same individual is responsible for their deaths and there's a possibility he or she may be part of a group or cult which practises human sacrifice. That's where we think you may be able to help."

"Look," Vine said, twisting at his ring again. "All these lurid stories of Druids and religious ceremonies involving sacrificial killings, they invariably came from hostile sources. The Greeks and Romans trying to turn people against them. Simple propaganda. There's no proof that any of that went on. And, even if it did, that's certainly not what modern day Druidism is about. We don't endorse human or even animal sacrifice for that matter. It's about promoting peace and the harmony of nature."

Brown pushed a piece of paper across the table.

"Can you have a look at these dates? Do you think any of them might be significant?"

Vine pulled the sheet towards him and studied it. "Significant in what way?"

"Do they relate to any ancient ceremonies? That sort of thing."

"Why? Are they the dates the women were killed on?" he asked, as he handed it back to Brown, who nodded. "They're certainly not the dates of any Druid celebrations."

"What about any other religious groups or cults? Would the dates mean anything to them?"

"They don't have any significance to any ancient festivals I know of. But, apart from the Muti in Africa and a small cult in India, I'm not aware of any groups practising human sacrifice nowadays anyway."

"What about satanic rituals?"

"Not my area of expertise, I'm afraid. I know there was a lot in the media back in the eighties, but they were all pretty gruesome. Dismemberment, that sort of thing. From what the media's reported there wasn't anything like that unless of course you're keeping it quiet." He paused but neither detective said anything. "Perhaps if you can tell me more about the murders, I may be able to help. Other than the fact that they were on spiritual places, what else makes you think it might be a sacrifice? Was something else found at the scene?"

"I'm afraid we're unable to reveal anything more."

"Then I don't think I'm going to be able to help much." Vine smiled. It was a very different smile to the one he'd welcomed them with on his doorstep. Linton wondered how her dad would describe it in his novel. Reptilian? Snake-like?

"I suppose we can ask questions around what we saw without giving too much away," Brown relented.

"Be my guest," said Vine and all of a sudden Linton saw him as he really was. An intelligent and gentle man, co-operating with the police. It was just the distortions of sleep deprivation and a hangover.

"What would be the significance of laying something out in a circle?" Brown asked.

"That's a biggy. How long have you got?"

"OK. I'll ask it another way. If something were laid out in a circle near the murder, would you see it as being significant?"

"Possibly. The circle of life maybe?"

"What about the number twelve?"

Vine shook his head slowly. "Not really."

"Can you think of any other groups that consider the Tor and Avebury as having a particular significance?"

"It's hard to know where to start. It holds a multitude of meanings to a multitude of people. There are so many myths and legends connected to the Tor. You should know that, living here."

"Such as?"

"Some think it was the location of King Arthur's stronghold. Others that it's the home of the Fairy King. Then there's the Celtic legend that says the hill is hollow and the top guards the entrance to the Underworld. And, of course, you've got the whole ley lines thing." He paused.

"Go on."

"There's a common belief that Glastonbury lies in a triangle with the stone circles Stonehenge and Avebury, and that they form a world energy point. Some people think aliens built the stones at Avebury because they're identical to ones on Mars called Cydonia, and they're arranged in the same format. And that UFOs travel along ley lines in the same way that cars use roads and motorways."

"UFOs," snorted Brown, shaking his head in disbelief.

"A couple of months ago the MOD released a secret file on UFO sightings," said Vine coldly. "They've got images of mysterious shapes and lights over Glastonbury."

There was an uncomfortable pause then Linton asked, "Did you know Angel Kingsley?"

"Not personally. I ran an evening class at Avalon College about a year ago and Liz, her mum, enrolled on it. She mentioned her daughter a couple of times. Angel's an unusual name and it stuck in my head. Look," he said, shaking his head, "before you get carried away thinking I had something to do with Angel's death because I'm a Druid and I know her mum, I've got an alibi for the night she was murdered. I was in London that weekend giving a lecture at UCL. I stayed at the Comfort Inn, if you want to double-check. It's round the corner from Paddington station."

"I'll do that, Sir," Linton said.

"Thanks for your time," said Brown, handing him his card. "We appreciate it. If you can think of anything else, please get in touch." As they moved into the hall, he turned and said, as though it was an afterthought, "You're a tall bloke. Like me. What size shoes do you take?"

Vine glanced anxiously at his feet. "An eleven," he said quickly. "Why do you ask?"

"Just curious," said Brown.

They said their goodbyes. Linton shook Vine's proffered hand, glancing at the ring on his finger as she did. "It's an amazing colour," she said.

"It's a garnet. The Head Druid gave it to me. In ancient times, gemstones were used as a way of telling the future."

Brown snorted. "Must come in handy when you're doing the lottery."

"Yes, quite," replied Vine, his tone betraying exactly what he thought of the comment.

Back in the car neither of them spoke. Brown seemed distracted and Linton was still feeling sick. Her fingers had turned numb and she fumbled with the harness of her seatbelt, wincing at the crunching noise of the gravel beneath the wheels as Brown reversed out of the driveway. With the belt finally in place, she lay back in her seat and closed her eyes. The images behind the lids were red and fiery. She could see the flames dancing in Mr Vine's fireplace, the ring glinting on his finger as he twisted it around. She opened her eyes again. "What was all that about? Asking him for his shoe size? You don't think . . ."

"No harm in asking. You know The Toad's mantra: leave no stone unturned." Linton had a sudden image of the Chief Inspector pulling up a rock, his long tongue darting out to gobble up a couple of juicy grubs. She shuddered.

"Shame about Vine being away," she said, anxious to dispel the image of Hargreaves. "That would be perfect. A mad anthropologist tries his hand at human sacrifice."

"As if it were that easy." Brown paused. "I know what you mean though," he conceded. "And there's definitely something about him. He's too smooth for my liking. A bit *too* charming."

"Three words," Linton said. "Pot, kettle, black."

"And I've got three for you. I'm your superior." Despite his bad mood, she knew he wasn't being serious. For all his faults, he never pulled rank.

"Do you still think there's something in this sacrifice thing?" she asked.

"What do you think?"

She shrugged. "Perhaps it's a breakaway Druid who wants to have a go at the human sacrifice thing and he's not told any of the others. Or it might be some nut-job who thinks by killing young women he's going to live forever."

"Or maybe the King of the Fairies has had enough of people trampling over his hideout."

"All right, sarky."

He was quiet for a moment, and then said, "After speaking to him I've got my doubts. It doesn't feel right. You'd expect something more. The body laid out in a particular way. Or religious paraphernalia left at the scene . . ."

"We've got the candles . . ."

" . . . and like he said, it's not gruesome enough to be satanic. There was nothing in the killing or the way he left the bodies to suggest it was."

"Unless the killer's too squeamish. Perhaps he doesn't like the thought of chopping them up or eating them or whatever else you do when you've sacrificed someone."

Neither of them spoke for a while; Brown was concentrating on his driving, Linton was concentrating on the horizon. She was the first to break the silence with a loud groan.

"What's up?" asked Brown. "What are you thinking?"

"That you'd better pull over. I'm gonna throw up again."

TEN

ONCE UPON A TIME

"I'd like you all to give our new friend a huge welcome tonight. We're so pleased to have him here."

He looked around the large, draughty hall at the clapping, smiling faces and felt something he hadn't in a long time – a sense of belonging. Acceptance – for who he was, for *what* he was.

"We're so glad you found us and we hope that what you hear tonight will be of help. That you'll realise you don't have to live in fear or shame anymore. That you're not different, or bad, but you're *special*."

•••

As soon as they got back to the station, Linton hurried to the ladies toilets, anxious to see the red marks on her neck. She was shocked at her exhausted reflection staring, glassy-eyed, back at her from the soap-splattered mirror. Tentatively pulling down her collar, she examined the red, mottled marks. *Were they love bites?* She wasn't so sure.

She studied her face more closely in the mirror. Her skin looked red and blotchy, the gentle lines on her forehead horribly pronounced under the unflattering light. She felt tears prickling at the back of her eyes.

She wanted her mum. Not her real one, but the fantasy mum she'd created as a child. The one who wore make-up, of the non-glittery kind, and had a tidy blonde bob. She dressed in jeans and Gap sweatshirts and had a proper handbag, not some horrible raggle-taggle patchwork affair that looked like it was stitched together by a bunch of elves on acid. She attended parents' evenings and school concerts and joined the PTA and all the other parents said, "Look, that's Kate Linton's mum. Isn't she normal?"

She sighed. Rummaging around in her handbag she found a stick of concealer and rubbed it on the marks.

•••

Brown was looking annoyingly fresh when Linton hurried back into the incident room.

"It makes you wonder how the fuck investigations ever get completed," he said, as she slumped down at her desk.

"What d'you mean?"

"I know it's all about the detail, but we know most of it's a waste of time. Look at this." He waved his hand dismissively over a piece of paper. "It's the list of Sam's friends and family. We're going to have to interview every single one of them. How long's that going to take? And what's the point when it's just as likely it's a random killer?"

"Who's first?"

"Danny Hicks. The ex-boyfriend. I rang him just now."

"What did he say?"

"Not a lot. He reckoned he hadn't been in contact with Sam for ages."

"Do you think he's lying?"

He shrugged. "Even if he is, I doubt it's important. Unless we discover he's linked to the Avebury women. But we need to eliminate him from our enquiries. One we can tick off from our list of hundreds." He sighed. "Besides, things like this niggle at me."

"What do you mean?"

"Turley said the sister got all shifty when she talked about him." He paused. "That Turley. She's quite, what's the word, intuitive. Got a good nose for that sort of thing."

"I doubt it's her nose you're interested in."

"Funny. Anyway, I've arranged to see him first. He's a graphic designer." The way Brown pronounced the profession, he may as well have said 'wanker'. She shook her head and winced.

"How's the hangover?" he asked.

"Pretty bad," she admitted.

"What you need is a can of coke and a packet of salt and vinegar crisps. All that stuff about pints of water and peppermint tea is a load of bollocks. You want salt and sugar."

No, she thought, what she wanted was a time machine so she could go back to seven o'clock the previous evening. To the conversation she'd had with her brother on the phone just before she went into the pub. If only she'd gone to see him instead.

She ought to ring him. He'd sounded excited even though when she'd spoken to him the day before he'd sounded low. He periodically jumped between mania and depression, but normally not so quickly.

She promised herself she'd ring him later.

•••

An hour later, Brown pulled off the M5, at junction 17. Linton opened her window slightly. The spittle of cold rain that managed to creep in through the small rectangular slit felt welcoming against her cheek. She wished she could get out of the car and stand in the downpour, let it completely douse her. Even though she'd had a shower that morning, at a skin-peeling temperature, she still felt stale and dirty. Her armpits were sticky and her face itched, as though hundreds of tiny insects were crawling beneath its greasy surface.

Brown turned up the radio when the news came on. They listened to the newsreader discussing Angel's murder, going back over the case again from the beginning, starting with the discovery of the first body at Avebury.

Brown grunted as they ended the report and turned the radio back down.

"I wonder how that American couple are," she said. "The ones who found Angel. Do you think they ever finished their tour of England?"

"I doubt it. It's not something you ever get over, is it?"

He was right. People underestimated how much it affected you, the shock of finding a body. It was always said so glibly when they announced it on the news. *The body was found by a member of the public early this morning.* A jogger or a rambler or some poor sod out walking the dog. It was always uttered so casually. But Linton knew from experience it wasn't like that.

She thought of the bloke who'd discovered Sadie Carter's body, the woman who'd died of hypothermia. She remembered what the vicar had said. About how upset he was, running around like a headless chicken.

"God, this weather's doing my head in," said Brown, interrupting her thoughts. "It's going to be wet for the next few days."

A song came on and Brown turned up the radio again. It was the one that started off with the line about her working as a waitress in a cocktail bar. It reminded Linton of college discos, which made her think of Simon Talbot. *Talbotski.*

It was ironic after what he said, when he'd imitated a profiler. Saying it was probably a bloke who couldn't get it up because he felt inferior to women.

Is that what last night had been about? Surely not. He had two children didn't he? He was drunk, that was all. A classic case of brewer's droop. *Or maybe not*, she thought cringing. Perhaps he didn't fancy her. That would explain the disastrous evening with him all those years ago.

Was she that unattractive? Come to think of it, it was ages since anyone had flirted with her. And look at what Ben had done . . .

She mentally shook herself. *Stop!* It was the 'demons' again.

That's what she nicknamed the thoughts that haunted her the morning after a big night out. The mental equivalent of self-flagellation. Post-session depression, Ben called it.

When Brown finally pulled to a halt in the multi-storey car park, it took every ounce of energy for her to lean over, open the door and drag herself out.

The graphic design office was only a five-minute walk from the car park, but the rain was unprecedented. It was as if the clouds were emptying out by the bucket-load, so, even with coats and umbrellas, they arrived at Danny's workplace wet and bedraggled. In contrast, the third-floor office was smart and sleek. When Hicks greeted them in, she couldn't help glancing at his feet. They looked tiny, only about a size eight, the same size as Ben's.

"Never trust a man with small feet," her granny had said. As usual, she'd been right.

They introduced themselves and chatted about Danny's job, with Linton doing a much better job of feigning interest than Brown, despite the hangover. Then it was down to business.

"Do you think it's odd that Claire Jenkins didn't report her sister as missing until Saturday night?" Brown asked.

Danny shrugged. "Sam's very self-centred. She wouldn't think to ring people to say she'd changed her plans. Especially if something better came up."

"It seems to me that Claire reporting her sister as missing hinged on you."

He paused, then said, "What do you mean?"

Linton detected a hint of anxiety in his tone. "You sent Claire a text just before she rang the police. Is that correct?"

He nodded quickly. "She'd been trying to get hold of me all day. Asking if I'd spoken to Sam."

"Claire didn't mention that," said Brown. "She made it sound like she'd contacted you as an afterthought."

Danny looked uncomfortable.

"Why didn't you answer her earlier?"

"I was busy."

"What did your text say? The one she got *just* before she phoned the police."

"Umm, I can't remember exactly," he said, his eyes darting around nervously. "Probably that I haven't seen Sam for ages."

"If you and Sam weren't in contact then why was Claire trying so hard to get hold of you?" asked Brown.

Danny reached for his cigarette pack, pulling it towards him. He let his hand play absentmindedly with the cellophane wrapper. "Look. I told you on the phone I haven't spoken to Sam for weeks. She sent me a couple of emails recently, but I didn't reply."

"Was it you who ended the relationship?" Linton asked.

He nodded.

"Why?"

He looked longingly at his cigarettes. "Is this relevant?"

"It could be."

"I saw her for what she was and I realised she's not my type."

"What do you mean?"

"She's a good-looking girl, but I reckon she's messed up in the head. She comes across as laid-back and a good laugh, but when you get to know her, she's not like that at all. She's clingy and demanding and self-centred."

"You were relieved when you split up with her?"

"I s'pose."

"Why do you think Claire was so sure you'd have spoken to her?"

He shrugged. "I can't be the only person she contacted."

"And, presumably, you've got no idea where she is," Linton said.

He looked at her as though she was stupid. "She's been abducted by the ley line strangler."

"Nobody knows that for definite, Mr Hicks."

He shrugged again. "Where else would she be?"

•••

"What a tosser," Linton said, as they stood waiting for the lift, just beyond the entrance to the office. "All that stuff about Sam being self-centred. He might as well have been talking about himself. I'll get his alibis checked out, but unless he was wearing someone else's shoes, then he didn't do it."

"It doesn't look like it."

"Do you reckon he's hiding something though? He seemed on edge."

"Don't take it personally, Linton. We're the pigs, the filth. That's the effect we have on people. You should be used to it by now."

Maybe he was right, but she couldn't help feeling there was more to it. The trouble was she felt too knackered to think what it might be.

The lift arrived with a jolly ping that felt like an insult to her mood. As they stepped in, Brown pushed the button to take them to the ground floor. Linton avoided looking in the large mirror, knowing her reflection in the harsh, unflattering light would only depress her. Brown meanwhile, couldn't resist looking at himself.

"You know she's got a record, don't you?" he said, adjusting the collar on his coat.

"Who?"

"Claire Jenkins."

"So? It's hardly relevant though, is it?"

"It's funny," he said thoughtfully. "You wouldn't expect that sort of behaviour from someone like her. She's obviously nothing like . . ." he paused ". . . like you'd expect a teacher to be."

"You were going to say like her sister, weren't you?" said Linton.

He didn't reply, but let out a long, weary-sounding sigh.

"So you're saying you know Sam well, then."

The lift shuddered to a stop and the doors juddered slowly open. Brown was the first out.

"One of these days, Linton . . ." he mumbled.

"One of these days what?"

He didn't answer, just stomped ahead of her, clenching and unclenching his fists.

•••

They didn't speak again until they reached the car park. Linton was the first to break the silence.

"He didn't seem bothered about Sam, did he?" she said, trying to keep up with Brown as he strode across the diesel-stained tarmac. "He was completely uninvolved. As though he was talking about a stranger."

"He's not going out with her anymore, so what does he care?" He pointed his keys at his car, making a click and a long, loud beep that echoed round.

"Yeah. What does he care his ex-girlfriend's been kidnapped by a strangling psychopath? It's amazing how quickly blokes can get someone out of their life and just carry on."

"Is that a dig at me?" he asked, pulling open the driver's door. "Or are we back to the all-men-are-bastards crap? Wanker!" he shouted suddenly at the top of his voice, as a car screeched past, making Linton jump and saving her from having to answer.

Actually she'd been thinking about Ben when she said it. Ben, who'd begged and pleaded and said he'd made the biggest mistake of his life, that if she left him, he wouldn't be able to live without her. Ben, who instead of chucking a bottle of pills down his neck like he promised, had been seen out and about, very much alive and chucking eight pints of lager down his neck instead.

"Fucking arsehole," said Brown, as they listened to the screech of tyres as the speeding car continued its descent towards the exit. *Yep*, she thought, that just about summed her ex-boyfriend up.

•••

Sally Jenkins had been awake for hours. No matter how firmly she ordered her legs and arms to move, she couldn't summon up the momentum she needed to get herself out of bed. She kept telling herself *five more minutes*, but despite her full bladder and dry mouth, she remained hunched in her protective ball, praying the phone would ring. Praying it wouldn't.

For the fifth time that morning, she listened to the bells of St John's clock, counting off the loud chimes in her head, this time to ten, and once again she wondered if Sam could hear them too.

Five more minutes, she promised herself again, and then she would get up. She shifted her position trying to ease the pressure on her bladder, and heard a familiar noise. It was the sound of a key turning in the front door.

Claire must be home. She listened for the customary slam, but instead there was a faint click. Her daughter must think she was asleep; she was obviously trying to be quiet so she didn't wake her. She'd only been gone for an hour, but Sally wasn't surprised to hear her home. She must've got her boss to come in and cover for her. She'd told her she was silly going in. Listening to the slow, drawn-out creaking of the stairs, she thought how considerate Claire was being. Normally an impatient person, always in a rush, prone to thumping up the stairs, two at a time. Slowly tiptoeing just wasn't in her nature.

"Claire?" she croaked, then cleared her throat and shouted more loudly, "Claire? Are you OK?" The creaking stopped. No reply. Why wasn't she answering? It *was* Claire, wasn't it? It must be. No one else had a key apart from . . .

"Oh my God. Sam! Is that you?"

She was out of bed, grabbing at her dressing gown, throwing it on, as she raced through her bedroom door, simultaneously listening to footsteps banging down the stairs followed by the slam of the front door, the letterbox left banging in its wake.

She raced along the hallway almost tripping over the suitcase she still hadn't packed away and hurtled down the stairs. As she reached the bottom, she yanked the door open and a sudden rush of cold damp air slapped her in the face. It was raining; the street was deserted. She looked up and down. No one. *The entrance to the alleyway.* Perhaps whoever it was had turned down there? She considered following, but looked down at her gown and pulled her front door shut, collapsing onto the bottom stair in defeat.

•••

According to Brown's TomTom, the graphic design office and About Face – the TV company Sam worked for – were five minutes apart. But thanks to heavy traffic it took closer to fifteen, giving Linton plenty of time to torment herself with thoughts of Ben.

For the last month, she'd banned herself from thinking about him, knowing it wasn't doing her any good. But now she'd started, she couldn't stop. It was like self-harming. A little cut here, a little nick there.

What pissed her off the most about the whole thing was as soon as she'd offered Ben what he wanted, he didn't seem to want it any more.

For three years, he'd pestered her about having children. "I'm not ready," she kept saying. "I like my job too much."

"You can still be a mum and have a career. Other people do it," he'd argue back.

"I'm not other people."

She'd promised herself from a young age that once she had children, she'd stop working. She wanted them to have a different childhood to hers. Not that it was a bad one, not compared to some she'd come across in her job. She wasn't abused. Her parents weren't cruel. They simply weren't around much.

Her mum painted when inspiration struck, regardless of whether it was day or night, and everything else took second place. Linton got used to meals served at midnight, having no clean uniform to wear to school and rarely arriving before the classroom register was called.

One autumn morning though, Linton's feelings changed.

Less than an hour before, she and Ben had been having *the conversation* in bed. It went along in its usual way with Ben trying to persuade her and Linton simply disagreeing with everything he said.

But as she pulled up at work something happened. Maybe it was the song playing on the radio or the colour of the sky at that precise moment or the September scent of change in the air that did it. It was as if she was at the centre of it all, looking out on everything going on around her. And in that moment she knew exactly what it all meant and precisely what she was meant to do. The feeling passed, a click of the fingers and it was gone, but the decision remained with her.

She'd got out of the car and pulled her phone out of her handbag.

"OK then," she had texted.

Five second later and there was a "beep-beep." She read the reply.

"OK what?"

"OK, let's have kids," she had typed.

Five seconds later and another "beep-beep."

"Get home early then and we can get on with it!"

He had come home that evening with a bottle of champagne, a bunch of flowers and a hard-on. The following morning he had got a taxi to Bristol Airport and then a plane to Amsterdam. And by the time Linton saw him again, everything had changed.

•••

Sitting in the managing director's office of About Face, Linton felt disappointed. Where were all the glamorous, trendy media-types rushing around being arty and creative? She'd expected it to be exciting, dynamic, but it didn't feel that different to anywhere else she'd worked, including the station back in Glastonbury.

"What we're trying to do, Mr Banks," said Brown, "is establish what happened during the hours leading up to Sam's disappearance. Perhaps you can run through what she did at work on Friday?"

"We're doing a programme about complementary medicine, so we were filming at the Healing Show. It was at the Assembly Rooms on Whiteladies Road."

"The Healing Show?" said Brown. "I've never heard of it."

"It's an annual exhibition. Different practitioners can come and demonstrate what they do to the general public."

"What kind of practitioners?"

He smiled. "Hands-on healers, crystal healers, tarot readers. No doubt you're familiar with all that, coming from Glastonbury."

"You mean people who are into ley lines?" Brown prompted. "That sort of thing."

Banks frowned. "I guess so."

"What does Sam's job involve?" Linton asked.

"She's a researcher. Basically she wanders around and chats to people, to see who might be worth interviewing. You could say it's her job to find the story."

"Is she good at what she does?"

"She's great. She makes people feel at ease. It means they're less likely to clam up in front of the camera."

"Did you notice anything unusual in her behaviour on Friday?"

He shook his head. "If anything, I'd say she was in her element. She knew a few of the people on the stands from Glastonbury. She'd been at school with a couple of them. She was showing off; the whole 'I-work-in-TV-aren't-I-cool' type thing."

"Do you remember her talking to anyone in particular?"

"No one springs to mind. Like I said, she talked to loads of people, it's part of her job. I can remember a lot of them were talking about Glastonbury carnival. I know Sam was excited about going back and meeting up with all her mates. She says it's one of the biggest piss-ups of the year."

"Was there anybody there from Avebury?" Brown asked.

He shook his head again. "You'd have to ask the organisers. As far as I know, it was more this area; Bristol, Bath, Glastonbury."

"Did you see anyone taking particular notice of Sam?"

"Why? Do you think he was there?"

"We're trying to get a picture of what happened on Friday."

"I can see why you'd think that," said Banks thoughtfully. "If the murders at Avebury and Glastonbury were some sort of sacrifice, like the papers are saying, then it's possible the killer would be at an event like that. The thing is . . ." He paused.

"Go on," said Brown.

"Look. I'm not saying I'm an expert but I've spent the last few weeks looking into alternative therapies, and all I'd say is there's a danger in lumping stuff together. Just because you're into crystal healing doesn't mean you're into sacrificing people on ley lines."

"Going back to the question," said Brown impatiently, "was there anyone at the exhibition who appeared particularly interested in Sam?"

He shook his head. "She's a pretty girl, so she generates a lot of attention but there's no one I can think of that stands out."

"Were you filming there all day?"

"Pretty much. We went back to the office some time after four to start looking at what we'd got on tape. Sam helps with the editing. She had some experience of that in her last job."

"Where was that?" Linton asked.

"London. She moved down here about a year ago. To be honest I don't think she liked being a small fish in a big pond. She was working for FTN. They're a huge company compared to us. I don't know if you've heard of them?"

Brown nodded. "They make a lot of the reality shows."

"Sam worked on *School Exchange* and *Working Girl*," said Banks.

"The one with Becki Harvey," said Brown.

"Did you watch it?"

"Didn't everybody?"

"It certainly got good ratings, even though the critics hated it. Anyway, she had a good reference."

"After you got back here did anything happen? Did anyone come in to see her? Did she get any phone calls?"

"Not that I know of. You could ask some of the others when we've finished. She generally works alongside Karen and Pete. But she wasn't in the office long. She left early so she could catch the bus to Glastonbury. She doesn't drive."

"Isn't it a problem with a job like this?" Linton asked.

"If I'd known, I wouldn't have been so keen to take her on. Part of her job involves tracking down props and it does make it awkward. The thing is she didn't lie on her application form. She's got a clean driving licence and the issue didn't come up at interview. It's not that she can't drive, she won't. I heard from a colleague that she was in a bad accident a few years ago. Her dad was with her and he was killed outright."

They spent another hour at About Face questioning Sam's colleagues, but none of them had anything further to add.

•••

"We'll need to get a list of everyone who was at the spiritual healing fair," said Brown, as they queued for caffeine in the café underneath the TV studios. "Let's find out who was exhibiting and concentrate on anyone from Glastonbury or Avebury. There's every chance he was there. It may be how he knew she was going to be in Glastonbury that night. Banks said she spoke to a lot of people."

"You're back to the spiritual connection now, are you? I can't keep up. I thought you'd gone off the idea."

"It's called having an open mind. You should try it sometime."

"What's that supposed to mean?"

He didn't answer. Linton could hear two women behind them in the queue discussing their diet, comparing how many pounds they'd lost in the last week.

"I think Banks made a good point though, don't you?" she said. "About the danger of lumping everything spiritual together. Just because someone's into ley lines doesn't make them a sacrificial murderer . . ." She stopped talking, uncomfortably aware Brown was glaring at her. "What?"

He didn't answer, just carried on staring, his lips stretched into a thin line. The two women were now debating whether or not they should buy the last piece of carrot cake to share.

"What?" she asked again.

"Are you taking a course?" he said, the anger in his voice apparent, despite the fact he was whispering.

"What d'you mean?" she asked, confused.

"In how to be an argumentative bitch?"

"What's that supposed to mean?"

"I'm sick of it," he hissed. "Everything I say you disagree with."

"No, I don't."

"You see? You're doing it again."

"I'm not."

"Ever since you split up with Ben, you've been like this. What is it? Are you punishing every bloke for what he did?"

"You're a psychologist now, are you?"

"Why you being like this?"

"Why are *you* being like this? You've been in a foul mood ever since Sam Jenkins was reported missing."

"Can I help you?" asked the harassed-looking man behind the counter.

"Two teas to take away please." As Brown asked, Linton heard the women behind come to a decision; they'd buy the carrot cake and share it. After all, they'd been so good with their diet this week, they deserved it.

"Why were you looking at her on Facebook the other day?" Linton asked, as the man moved away to pass their order to the young girl making the drinks. "Scared you might see something about yourself on there?"

"You know what, Linton," Brown said loudly, "why don't you fuck off?" The two women behind them sniggered. Linton tapped Brown on the arm.

He spun round. "What?"

"Would you mind getting me that last piece of carrot cake?" she said. "It looks delicious."

•••

Back in the car, Linton realised the cake had done some good. Her stomach was feeling settled and for the first time that day she could see a glimmer of light at the end of the murky tunnel of her hangover. It was a shame the atmosphere in the car was so uncomfortable.

She was about to speak, try and call some kind of truce with Brown, when his hands-free rang.

"Yep . . . yep. Still in Bristol . . . What time was this . . .? I presume we're getting SOCO round? Okay . . . well, keep me informed."

"What's happened?" Linton asked, when he hung up.

"That was Hooper. Smarmy fucker. Always the first to know."

"About what?"

"Sam Jenkins' mum just rang the station."

"And?"

"She reckoned someone let themselves into her flat this morning when she was still in bed. It wasn't Claire. And the only other person with a key is Sam."

"Shit. Did she see who it was?"

He shook his head. "She ran down the stairs, but whoever it was had already gone. It's still raining, so maybe we'll get some footprints."

"Do you think it was *him*?"

"I don't know. He's got access to Sam's key."

"But why would he go to her mum's? It's so risky. He could've got caught."

"He must've had a good reason."

"But what?"

They both contemplated her question in silence and then Brown thumped the steering wheel with his right hand. "Of course! Her diabetic kit. The spare one she keeps at her mum's. Maybe he went round to get it for her."

"Which means he wants to keep her alive."

"It looks that way."

"But why?"

ELEVEN

Andrew Chubb glanced furtively at his wife. She sat staring ahead, body stiff, her tapping fingers the only give-away that she was impatient for the journey to end, so she could bring forth the insults forming and growing in the pregnant silence.

As usual, it was her who'd started the argument as they waited for the taxi outside the party, making sure, of course, that they were out of earshot. Andrew breathed a sigh of relief when the cab finally pulled up. Crawling into the car was like entering the sanctuary of a church. He knew Rachel wouldn't say a word until they got out at the other end. She didn't like to lose face in front of anyone and that included taxi drivers.

It was the same old thing. She'd accused him of flirting. He insisted he was only being friendly. "I can't help it if people are interested in what I do."

The stupid slut started it. She'd come up to *him*. Someone must have told her who he was and what he did for a living. He could hardly be rude and tell her to go away.

"I hear you're a ghostwriter. How fascinating," she'd said. "Whose autobiography are you working on at the moment?"

"Becki Harvey's."

"The winner of *Working Girl?*"

"I know. Z-list, I admit, but the money's good. I've done a few A-listers in my time," he said, proceeding to name the three celebrities he thought would impress her the most: a glamour model, a footballer and a singer who'd recently come out of the closet.

"Doesn't it bother you that they don't get your name on the front cover?"

"With one like mine?" he said laughing. "If I ever write my own novel, I'll give myself a pen-name, I think. Something sexier."

She moved closer and arched one eyebrow suggestively. "I wonder what name I could use?"

"I can think of a few appropriate ones," he replied.

"You're not so bad yourself," she said, slowly tracing the rim of her glass with her index finger. And as if she was rubbing a magic lamp, Rachel had suddenly appeared beside them. It was obvious she'd heard every word.

"You wanker," she hissed at him once they were out of the taxi.

"And there I was thinking I was the one who was good with words," he said, following her up the four stone steps that led to the red front door of their Bath town house. He fumbled in his trouser pocket for his keys. Rachel was rummaging around in her handbag, trying to find her own set first. Anything to get one over on him, he thought.

"You're an idiot," she said, turning round to spit the words at him. He looked at her flawless skin, at the glossy black ringlets framing her face, at her sneering, perfectly made-up lips, and in that split second, as he felt the anger coursing through his limbs, he would've liked to put his hands around her neck and squeeze.

Angie was switching off the television as they walked into their brightly-lit sitting room.

"A load of old rubbish on at this time of night," she said. "Nice evening?"

"Lovely, thanks," they both lied.

Rachel quickly set about dimming the lights in order to create a more ambient atmosphere. She was obsessed with lighting, fiddling with it whenever she entered a room, figuring out the most flattering place to stand.

"Did the kids go to bed nicely?" asked Andrew, pulling off his coat and scarf.

"Good as gold they were," said Angie. "The phone rang a couple of times, but I left it to go on to answerphone like you asked me to."

Whoever it was had probably tried his iPhone first. He'd left it upstairs on his bedside table. Rachel banned him from taking it to parties.

"Thanks, Angie. If you don't mind, I'll quickly check the messages and then I'll walk you home."

The hallway felt cold. The heating was on a timer and would've switched itself off an hour ago. He picked up the phone and dialled 1571. There were two messages and one caller. He pressed one and tapped his foot impatiently waiting to hear who'd left a message at nineteen minutes past ten. It was Will. *Money*, thought Andrew, the minute he heard his voice. That's probably what he was ringing for. Another sob story about how his student loan hadn't come through yet. But he was wrong.

"Mum? Dad? It's me. Will. You know, I said I had a couple of days off and was going to come and see you, well, I can't. Sorry. They've sprung a couple of seminars on us that I don't want to miss, so it'll have to be another time. I'll ring you."

That was a turn up for the books. His son wasn't on the scrounge and, not only that, he appeared to be taking his studies seriously for once.

The next message was from Becki.

"Andrew. It's me. Sorry to ring your home so late." *No, she wasn't*, he thought. "I tried your mobile, but didn't get an answer. Just to let you know, I'm sorry, but I'm going to have to cancel our meeting tomorrow. I hope you don't mind. It's just I'm all over the place at the moment. I need to go away and get my head together. I'm going to Glastonbury for a couple of days. It's meant to be a spiritual place and I think it might be what I need."

Andrew laughed. Could that girl be any more see-through? Of course it was what she needed. Half the country's press was in Glastonbury at the moment sniffing around. A murder, a girl going missing and a possible serial killer on the loose? No wonder she was going. Hoping to be photographed. She was unbelievable. Only Becki would use someone else's tragedy to get herself into the papers.

He didn't get it. What was it about Becki that the public loved so much? And not only the public, his own son was infatuated with her. He'd been practically drooling when he'd met her at a party they'd thrown, inviting her before Andrew had got to know her properly. Will had spent the whole evening following her around like a dog, plying her with drinks, laughing like a lunatic at everything she said. At one point, they'd disappeared and, if Andrew hadn't been so busy being the host with the most, he'd have hunted them out to keep his son away from her.

"Perhaps she'll get abducted herself," he muttered. "And then at least I'll have something interesting to write about."

•••

By the time Linton got to bed, her hangover had finally slunk away only to leave her with a raging sore throat. Great, she thought. Now she had tonsillitis. That was all she bloody needed.

The illness had plagued her all her life. The doctors had wanted to remove her tonsils when she was five, but her mum had refused. Unlike everyone else who saw them as useless bits of dangling flesh, she insisted they were the gatekeepers to the body, guarding against invasion from germs and infections.

Her throat wasn't the only thing keeping her awake. She kept going over what had happened on her way home from work, when she'd dragged herself into the supermarket to buy milk and bread for the morning.

Morrisons was the last place she'd expected to find them. Maybe in one of the shops in Glastonbury high street nestled between a green goddess statue and an Indian drum set, but not under the harsh lights of the local supermarket, next to the foil and cling film.

Yet there they were, packed in cellophane and reduced to half-price as they weren't the kind of thing people bought at this time of year. They were a mix of colours. Red, yellow, orange and green. And there were twelve of them in each pack.

"Brown," she said, seconds later into her mobile. They were speaking again. Just. Still, he didn't sound too pleased to hear from her.

"What?"

"I'm in Morrisons."

"Thanks for the update."

"It's important. They sell garden flares. And they come in packs of twelve in the same colours as the wax we found at the crime scene. We've been trying to give some meaning to the number of flares, but I don't think there is any. I think it's how they happen to be packaged."

"I presume you're going to buy some."

"Of course."

There was a pause, then he said, "I wonder if there's a Morrisons near Avebury?"

Five minutes later, as she reached for a six-pack of pickled onion Monster Munch, he rang back to say there was.

"I spoke to the store manager and they sell garden flares in packs of twelve."

"Bingo."

"By the way, SOCO have finished at the Jenkins' house."

"And?"

"A footprint on the carpet. Size fourteen boots."

"Was there a Walktall logo?"

"Too faint to be certain," he said, "but the size is enough. He was definitely there."

"Did he take Sam's insulin?"

"No. He didn't even make it up the stairs."

At the checkout, Linton held out the pack of flares to the teenage cashier who was twiddling with her nose ring. "Do you sell many of these?"

"A few," she said, shrugging.

As she shovelled food into a carrier bag, crushing crisps and bread, more anxious about holding up the queue than getting her shopping home in one piece, she heard a laugh. A laugh that caused her stomach to clench, then flip itself over. She looked round and there he was. Simon Talbot, queuing at the cigarette kiosk with a slim, high-heeled woman in her mid-twenties. Linton thought she recognised her, but she couldn't place her.

"Please enter your PIN number."

She turned back to the cashier and punched in the four numbers. Her hands were shaking. By the time she looked again, Simon had finished paying and was unwrapping a packet of chewing gum. Linton watched him stroll towards the exit, his hand in the small of the woman's back, as if he was guiding her. Perhaps she was a work colleague? Maybe he was giving her a lift home from work and they'd stopped at Morrisons on the way. But as they reached the automatic doors, Simon's hand slid down the woman's back and pinched her bum.

What had last night been about then? Had he used Linton to get information? But what information? She hadn't told him anything anyway. Had she? What *had* they talked about when they'd got back to her house? She couldn't remember a thing . . .

Now, lying in the bed she'd shared with Simon less than twenty-four hours ago, she wondered how she could've been so stupid.

She glanced across at her bedside clock. It was coming up to midnight. She needed something to help her sleep. And then she remembered. Her dad's book! That would help her nod off. The next instalment had arrived today.

In less than a minute she was back in bed with it, her head resting on the pillow she'd propped up behind her.

It was no good. She couldn't concentrate so she leant back on the pillow and closed her eyes. If she were a detective in a crime novel, she thought, she'd find a clue to the case in her dad's narrative. It would point her towards something she'd previously overlooked and she'd solve the case single-handedly.

She closed her eyes and wished her throat didn't hurt so much. Putting her hands around her neck, she felt her swollen glands, like two small eggs. She pulled her hands tighter, remembering what she'd learnt about manual strangulation; about how it was impossible to do it to yourself because once you lost consciousness you couldn't keep up the pressure.

A professor called Fox had run a session on strangulation a while back. He was one of the experts they wheeled in from time to time so they could be seen to be giving on-going training.

"Did you know ten per cent of violent deaths in the UK every year are due to strangulation?" he'd said by way of introduction, before going on to explain how strangulation was often about anger and power. "When perpetrators use strangulation to silence their victims," he said, "it's a form of control."

Was that what these murders were about? Was the killer trying to establish control?

She felt herself starting to doze off, but a sudden image of Simon Talbot bearing down on her woke her with a jolt. An hour later, she was still wide awake, wondering whether Sam Jenkins was asleep.

Her abductor had gone to the trouble to try and get her insulin so he could keep her alive. *But why?*

Her thoughts were tripping over each other, trying to pull her attention in different directions until her mind was a tangle of disjointed words and pictures. She felt her eyelids drooping. Last thing she saw was Brown bearing down on her and this time she didn't wake with a jolt.

TWELVE

The following morning, Linton nearly collided with PC Lucy Wilson as she ran head down through the pouring rain across the station car park. They yelled "Hi!" at one another and legged it to the shelter of the entranceway for a quick chat.

It had been a while since their paths had crossed and, once again, Linton was struck by how attractive Wilson was. It was no wonder she was nicknamed Juicy Lucy. Linton had always suspected Brown of having a thing for her and it wasn't long before his name came up.

"How's your lovely DI?" Wilson asked with a grin.

"Annoying as ever."

"You're only saying it to hide the fact you like him."

Linton laughed. "He's not my type."

"Type doesn't come into it. He's bloody gorgeous and that's all there is to it."

"He's the biggest womaniser I've ever met."

"Perhaps he hasn't found the right one yet." Wilson wiggled her perfectly plucked eyebrows suggestively. "Or maybe he has but he hasn't got the nerve to tell her."

"That's because he knows you'd tell him to fuck off."

"I'm not on about me."

"Who then?"

"You."

Linton laughed again, aware of how forced it sounded. "Hardly. I don't think Brown even thinks of me as female."

"Somehow I doubt it," said Lucy, looking her up and down. "With a figure like yours and those gorgeous green eyes. Anyway, according to Hooper . . ."

"Hey, Wilson!" It was PC Bridges splashing across the car park, another one of Lucy's many admirers. No doubt with some mundane information that would give him the excuse to walk into the building with her, so for those few seconds he could fantasise they were a couple.

"I'll see you later. Say hello to Brown for me," said Wilson, winking.

According to Hooper *what?* Linton thought as she followed them into the building.

She was still pondering this when she reached the incident room a few moments later. Brown was already at his desk looking fed up. She knew Lucy's message would cheer him up, but as she approached his desk and opened her mouth to tell him the PC said hello, something stopped her. She didn't want to see the smile of pleasure he'd get from hearing her name.

"All right?" he asked, looking up. "I've just got off the phone from your boyfriend."

"Ben?" she asked, confused.

"You're not back together, are you?'

She shook her head. "Of course not. Who are you on about then?"

"The charming Simon Talbot. Wanting to know if there've been any developments he should know about."

"He's not my boyfriend."

"I'm glad to hear it."

"Why?" She felt her face growing hot. "Do you think I'm going to tell him about the case? I bet that's the only reason you think he was talking to me in the pub. So he could get an exclusive."

"Fucking hell, Linton. Calm down." He shook his head. "You've read too many Lynda La Plantes. He's a small-town journalist with no ambition. If he had any, he wouldn't still be writing for the local rag at his age, would he? I meant I'm glad because he's a tosser and you could do a lot better. I know what he's like and how he treats women. A mate of mine used to play rugby with him. They went on tour and, the minute he got on the bus, he was taking his wedding ring off."

"You can talk."

"I'm not married. Look, I'm getting pissed off with everyone giving me a hard time. If I found the right woman and settled down, I'd be faithful."

"Yeah, right," she said. "And anyway, for your information, he's split up from his wife so in theory he's single."

"Tell that to his girlfriend."

"What girlfriend?"

"Apparently he's going out with a pharmacist and it's serious."

Linton remembered the pretty woman he was with in Morrisons. She knew she'd looked familiar. So that's where she'd seen her. Behind the counter in Boots.

"My advice is to stay away from him, Linton."

She shrugged. "Whatever." God. The stroppy teenager was back again. Brown didn't seem to notice. Instead, he picked up a handful of typewritten sheets and handed them to her.

"It's some of the statements from the exhibitors at that healing thing in Bristol, where Sam's company were filming the day she went missing."

Linton glanced at the top page, which listed the exhibitors. The ones from Glastonbury were grouped separately. She ran her eye down it.

Organisation	Representative	Stand No
Alchemy	Miss M Gates	6
	Mr Philips	
All that Glitters	Mr and Mrs Littleton	27
	Mr S Child	
Divining for Health	Mrs J Whitehead	18
Hands on Healing	Miss S Lovington	2
	Mr A Matthews	
The Glastonbury Experience	Mr J West	7
Zodiac Dreams	Miss J Budd	28

"Did any of the exhibitors come from Avebury?"

Brown shook his head. "The whole thing's probably another bloody waste of time."

"Nothing from any of the Glastonbury lot?"

"Hooper got a bit overexcited when he interviewed Littleton and his nephew."

"Why?" She glanced back at the list: All that Glitters, Stand 27.

"Child, the nephew, was interviewed earlier in the week, by one of our house-to-house team. He's got a place on the high street."

"But?"

"He didn't leave Bristol until after 6 p.m., so he couldn't have met Sam off the bus. He's got his uncle as an alibi and a timed receipt from a café to prove it."

"I know Littleton," she said. "He's one of my mum's friends. Bit of a pothead, but a nice enough bloke."

She flicked through the pages and pulled out their statements, so she could read them for herself.

Statement: Mr Tony Littleton, owner of All That Glitters
I was exhibiting at the Healing Show in Bristol on Friday, 20th November 2009. My wife and my nephew assisted me on the stand. We arrived at 8.15 a.m.

Apart from one coffee break and one toilet break, I spent the day on the stand with my wife and nephew. I would have remembered if I'd spoken to anyone filming a documentary, but I do not. I certainly do not recall speaking to a woman called Samantha Jenkins. Nor do I recall ever having met her although the name is familiar because I've heard it on the news.

The event finished at 4 p.m. My wife wanted to visit her sister at St Michael's Hospital. She's had a lump removed from her throat. Visiting hours don't start until 6.30 p.m. so she agreed she would get a bus home in the evening, which she did, arriving back in Glastonbury just after 9.15 p.m. Meanwhile, my nephew and I packed up the stand and loaded it into the van. It took us approximately one hour. At 5.15 p.m. my nephew and I went to a café near the Assembly Rooms, where we bought cakes and a pot of tea and we read the papers until 6 p.m.

(Note: Mr Tony Littleton produced a receipt for the Madhatters Café, dated 20th November. A pot of tea, a doughnut and Danish were purchased at 5.11 p.m.)

At just after 6 p.m. my nephew and I left the café and walked to the car park, got into the van and drove home.

(Note – Mr Tony Littleton produced a receipt for the car park which showed his exit time as 6.15 p.m.)

We arrived back in Glastonbury just after 7.15 p.m.

Quarter past seven in the evening. That was an hour after Sam's bus arrived in Glastonbury, thought Linton. His wife and nephew's statements were next in the pile. She read them both and they corresponded with what he said.

"Oi, Brown!" Linton looked up to see Keen pulling off his dripping coat. "I just saw Hooper taking care of your, um, young lady from the other night."

"What?"

"She was down in reception asking for you. Hooper told her you were working on a case, so you'd be tied up for a while. She didn't look too pleased. Nice, umm, eyes," he said, obviously changing the noun for Linton's benefit.

Brown pushed himself out of his chair and hurried over to one of the windows overlooking the car park. He yanked the handle back pulling with it a rush of cold, damp air. Putting his fingers to his mouth, he whistled.

"Hey! Kim! Hang on a sec," he shouted, leaning out of the window. He turned back to Linton, his face wet with rain. "I'll be back in a sec."

"That's a first," said Keen, as Brown rushed out of the room.

"Perhaps he likes her."

They both moved to the window. Keen smelt damp and fetid, like the water at the bottom of a vase when the flowers have gone over. It amazed Linton he had kids, that someone had had sex with him; perhaps his wife had no sense of smell.

"There he is."

They watched Brown run out from the front entrance of the station, jumping over and around puddles until he reached the woman. Her face was hidden from view by a large navy umbrella, but Linton saw from the hair poking out beneath that she was blonde. She was tapping a high-heeled foot and Linton wondered whether it was from nerves or impatience. After less than a minute, she swung around and marched away.

"What was all that about?" Keen asked a few minutes later, as an out of breath Brown sat back down at his desk.

"Not that it's any of your business, I told her she was a nice girl, but I couldn't get into a relationship at the moment. I said I was too busy with work."

Linton tried to catch Keen's eye, but he was staring open-mouthed at Brown.

"What?"

"Have you had some kind of personality bypass?"

"What d'you mean?" asked Brown.

"Where's all your 'treat 'em mean, keep 'em keen' talk?"

"Maybe I've changed." Linton realised he was looking at her as he said it. She held his gaze for a few moments, trying to decipher the expression on his face, but in the end she looked away, hoping he wasn't able to read hers.

•••

ONCE UPON A TIME

The locum seemed genuinely nice, despite his accent.

She normally hated Americans, which was understandable. Her husband had run off to California with one. Perhaps if he hadn't, things might have turned out differently. Or their son might have done.

The doctor nodded sympathetically as she explained. "He obviously needs help," he said, when she'd reached the end of her tearful monologue.

"And he gets these obsessions," she continued. "First it was dinosaurs, now it's outer space. And these people he hangs round with don't help. Filling his head with rubbish."

"What sort of rubbish?"

"Stupid stuff," she said, suddenly too drained to go into it. She sighed and said, "He keeps going on about his *real* family. How he needs to get back to them."

"Can you persuade him to come and see me?"

"I'll try but he's so *changeable*." She thought of his violent mood swings; how easily he switched from angelic to aggressive. Unstable was the word she really wanted to use.

It's his father's bloody fault, she thought as she traipsed up the hill afterwards. Buggering off like that. Thinking that the odd chirpy phone call and present in the post would make up for it. Sending him comics and clothes and shoes. Things he couldn't get over here. Not understanding that what he couldn't get, what he really needed, was his dad to come home.

•••

The day dragged. Brown drove to the Willoughby Estate to interview the staff at Walktall, but came back even more down in the mouth, having drawn a blank. Nobody remembered anyone coming in to buy the desert boots, nor did they keep a database of shop customers, only those who ordered by post or online.

Linton spent the afternoon going over statements from the drivers of the cars captured on CCTV around the time Sam disappeared after walking away from the Town Hall bus stop.

There was only one that caught her attention. It was an ex-teacher from St Dunstan's school.

"Now you've jogged my memory, I think I do remember seeing her. She was with a man; they were stood near the entrance to the alleyway that runs down the side of St John's church. I couldn't see his face, but I knew it was a man by his build and stance. Thinking back, I've got a feeling he was familiar, but I wonder now whether I'm only thinking that in retrospect. I've got a vague impression he was wearing a long coat, but I'm not entirely sure. She was standing under a streetlamp and I remember now, I said to my wife, 'That was Samantha Jenkins. I taught her in Year Seven.'"

"Listen to this, Brown," she said, reading the statement aloud to him.

"So?" he said, when she reached the end. "He couldn't see the bloke's face."

"It's not that, it's what he said about the alleyway."

"What about it?"

"It leads to St John's car park. Maybe that's where they went after the teacher saw them. Perhaps the abductor had his car there. Maybe he's not keeping her in Glastonbury. He might have picked her up and driven her somewhere else."

Brown sighed. "Even if he did, there are no sodding CCTV cameras in the car park."

"God, Brown, you want to be careful," she said, shaking her head. "You're starting to sound like The Toad."

•••

It was only a couple of weeks until the shortest day of the year, but today had felt like one of the longest.

It had been hard to concentrate at work, not to think about Sam, about the exciting future that lay ahead for them. He'd flicked through some of the tabloids, laughing at what one of them had called him. *The ley line strangler*. He'd read article after badly written article, full of false conjectures and mistakes. He'd have done a much better job if he'd had the chance.

It had rained again all day. And it was set to be another wet night. Hopefully it would clear by Friday. At least that's what they'd said on TV this morning, before they went on to talk about Sam again.

THIRTEEN

Andrew Chubb was not in a good mood. He'd spent the day rewriting the beginning of Becki's autobiography. Her childhood and adolescence hadn't been an interesting one. There was no drug-taking, no child abuse. The only noteworthy event had been some underage sex with a fifteen-year-old boy, but that was the extent of it.

"It's flabby," the editor had said, but what did she expect? He didn't have a lot to work with.

God, he thought, *she is a silly cow, running off to Glastonbury*. How was he meant to get the damn thing finished? And why was she being so bloody coy about the famous bloke she'd slept with? He'd like to throttle her.

Rachel had yoga tonight, so at least he could watch *Top Gear* repeats on Dave without her moaning in the background. He was putting a glass of red wine to his lips when his mobile rang.

He looked at the number displayed. Talk of the devil. It was her – Becki. She'd better be ringing to tell him the name of her mystery man or he was hanging up.

"Becki," he said, reaching for the remote and pressing mute. "How's your chi or whatever it is you're working on in Glastonbury?" he said, ladling his voice with sarcasm.

"Andrew? Thank God you're there."

"I hope you've come to your senses and you're ringing to tell me the identity of you-know-who?"

"It's not that. I . . ."

"Sorry, Becki, someone on the other line. I'll call you back."

He hung up. *Silly cow.*

A second later his phone rang. It was her again. He let it go to answerphone.

It was bedtime before he got round to listening to the message, and what a load of rubbish it was. Did she really expect him to believe any of it? She was such a bloody drama queen.

•••

"The important thing is that you didn't do it," said Adam.

"But I wanted to."

They were in Claire's bedroom. She was sitting on her bed with her back against the wooden headboard; he was on the floor, leaning on the radiator and chewing gum. She'd felt uncomfortable at first. There was something intimate about sitting in a room with a bed. She wouldn't normally bring Adam in here, but her mum's friend was round trying to console her.

It had taken him a while to work out what she was trying to say when she'd rung his mobile twenty minutes earlier.

"Don't be silly," he'd said, once she managed to get her sobbing under control. "Of course I'll come round. We're in this together."

"I opened the bottle and poured it into a glass," she now said. "I felt like I was watching somebody else. I saw this person swishing the liquid around and then put it to her lips. She almost took a sip and then I thought, what the fuck is she doing, what the fuck am *I* doing? And then I was me again and I knew I had to stop myself. I took it into the bathroom and tipped it down the sink. Then I came back in here and got the whole bottle and tipped it down as well. I knew I couldn't put it in the kitchen bin in case mum found it. I didn't even want it in our dustbin. I didn't want it anywhere near me. I know this sounds mad, but I walked up the road and put it in the bin on the corner."

"Claire," he said gently. "You don't have to explain it to me. Don't forget I've been there too."

"At least I'll have something to say at our next AA meeting," she laughed humourlessly. "A whole year of sobriety," she said, thinking guiltily of the flowers and cards and congratulatory email from her mum. "And I nearly messed it up."

"It's not surprising you were tempted. With all this stuff with Sam going on."

She sighed and leant over to her bedside table, reaching for her cigarettes. She pulled one out and lit it. "Pass me that mug, will you?" she said, pointing at one she'd left on her windowsill earlier. Balancing it precariously on the mattress next to her, she felt like a student again, enjoying the loud sizzle as the hot ash hit the tepid remains of her tea. She threw her head back and exhaled loudly, watching the smoke drift towards the Christmas cake icing finish of the Artex ceiling.

"What do you think's happened to her?" she asked finally.

"The same as you, I suppose," he said, looking away.

"If she dies, it'll be my fault. I should've reported her as missing straight away."

"But you thought she'd stood you up and couldn't be bothered to tell you."

She took another deep drag. "Only at first."

"What d'you mean?" Adam's tone was wary.

Claire looked across at him and sighed. "Do you remember that night I went out in Bristol for Ali's birthday?" He nodded. "I wanted to prove I could do the whole pub thing without drinking. We ended up in Danny's local, in Clifton Village. He was in there with a group of mates."

She stopped and took a deep breath.

"Go on," said Adam.

"I went over to him. He was drunk. He started talking about Sam and why he ended it. He was horrible but instead of sticking up for her I agreed with him. I said she wasn't good enough for him. He invited me back to his flat for a coffee and one thing led to another."

"You slept with him?" said Adam quietly. She nodded.

There was a pause. Adam cleared his throat then said, "So what? It's not as if they were together anymore. They'd split up."

"But Sam still likes him," said Claire. "She told me. Just before I got off with him."

"It doesn't make you responsible for what's happened to her."

"Yes, it does," she insisted. "I thought she'd found out about Danny and was avoiding me. Because she was upset. If I'd have gone to the police earlier they might have found her."

"It wouldn't have made any difference," said Adam. "Trust me."

"How do you know? Aren't the first twenty-four hours of an investigation the most important?"

"But why didn't you want the police to find out?" he said, ignoring her question. "About you and Danny?"

"It was bad enough being done for ABH. I didn't want them thinking I was a slapper on top of everything else. I even told Danny not to say anything; that if he did, I'd tell them about his coke habit."

"But it was the alcohol. You'd never have hit that woman if you weren't drunk. And she should've spoken to the school if she had a problem with your teaching. It's not professional, is it, going up to someone in the pub like that?"

"And smacking the mum of one of your six-year-old pupils in the face is?"

"But, if you hadn't done that, then maybe you wouldn't have stopped drinking. Perhaps you needed something to shake you up. To make you want to get sober."

She shrugged. "I don't think bumping into Simon Talbot today helped. That prat from the paper. It just brought everything back. He wanted to interview me. Invited me into The Pendragon for a drink. I told him to get stuffed."

"Didn't Sam get off with him once?"

She sniffed. "Only because she was pissed."

They were quiet for a minute. Claire dropped her cigarette end into the mug, leant over and placed it on her bedside table. She saw Adam glance nervously at the alarm clock on her bedside table.

"Look, I've got to go," he said, standing up abruptly and pulling on his gloves and hat. "I'm knackered and I'm on an early shift tomorrow. We've got a massive delivery of shoes tomorrow that'll need unpacking."

"You're not fed up with it already, are you?" Adam's job in the Walktall warehouse was his third in as many months, and it wouldn't surprise Claire if he was already thinking about leaving.

"Nah. It's great." He pointed to his feet. "Look. I got a third off. There are some advantages in working for a company that sells big shoes. It's funny. All those years I've been buying stuff from them. I never thought I'd end up working there."

"Well, thanks for coming over. I appreciate it."

"Don't mention it. Oh, by the way," he said, zipping up his coat, "did you know Becki Harvey's in Glastonbury at the moment?"

"How do you know?"

"I saw her in the high street this afternoon; coming out of The Pendragon. She must be staying there."

"Are you sure it was *her*?"

"Positive."

"She looks different in real life from when she was on telly."

"I know. Don't you remember? I met her at that party Sam threw?"

"Oh, yeah, so you did." She'd been drunk that night, but had a vague recollection of Adam making an unsuccessful pass at the reality star. She wouldn't embarrass him by bringing it up. "Did you speak to her?"

"I said hello, but she looked right through me." He sounded hurt.

"I expect she couldn't place you," she said. "She must have met hundreds of people since the show."

"Even so," he replied angrily, his face clouding over. "She didn't have to be so rude. I can't stick women like that."

•••

"Can you hear me?"

Sam opened her eyes and tried to focus, but it hurt too much, so she shut them.

"Are you OK?"

"Mmmm," she grunted. He sounded calmer now. He'd been cross after her mum had nearly caught him. She'd explained over and over that she'd got confused about when she was coming back from her holiday. It must have been the drugs he'd given her.

"Sometimes, I can't tell if you're asleep or pretending. I wanted to tell you I walked to the spot earlier, but I'm afraid we're going to have to wait until the weather changes."

Not that again. She wished he'd stop going on about it.

"They've got it all wrong you know," he said, leaning over, smelling faintly of cigarette smoke. "They think I'm a psycho who gets off on strangling women. I just don't like being laughed at, that's all. That's what Hannah did. She said she'd made it all up; that she hadn't seen them after all. Then Angel said she'd only dreamt it. As for Sadie," he said, pausing to shake his head, "they came and took her and didn't even wait for me."

Shut up you nutcase, she wanted to shout. *Just get me some insulin.* Didn't he realise she was going to die if he didn't?

He stopped talking and for a moment she thought he was going to rip off the duct tape. But instead he pushed himself off the bed and said, "I saw your sister again today. Poor Claire. She's so worried about you." He was quiet for a moment and then said thoughtfully, "Maybe I should put her out of her misery."

PART TWO

THE
DISAPPEARANCE

FOURTEEN

Linton shunted her high-backed blue swivel chair a couple of inches along the floor to get a better view of Hargreaves and the Superintendent. They were out in the corridor, deep in conversation. Both of them had their back to her, but something about Milne's stiff stance told her it wasn't a light-hearted one. She glanced at Brown to see if he'd noticed them, but he was looking intently at his screen, apparently deep in thought.

The Toad suddenly turned and caught her eye. She looked away, struck by a horrible thought. Were they talking about *her?* Was she in trouble? Maybe she *had* said something about the case to Simon Talbot the other night and they'd found out.

Now, out of the corner of her eye, she saw Hargreaves and Milne staring at her. Milne was looking serious, her hair even more unruly than usual, as though she'd run her hands frantically through it. Linton quickly fixed her eyes on her computer screen, her neck and cheeks turning hot as they continued to look in her direction. A few seconds later, The Toad strode across the room towards her. *Shit.*

"Brown. Linton. I want you in my office now. Chop-chop." *Shit. Shit. Shit. He's going to give me a bollocking and he wants a witness.* She looked at Brown as they got up, hoping he might have an inkling of what this was about, but he simply pulled a face and shrugged.

"Sit down," said Hargreaves as they followed him into his office. Linton sat on the chair nearest the door, swallowing in an attempt to push what little saliva she had past the throbbing lumps of pain that were once her tonsils.

"Have either of you heard of Becki Harvey?"

"Who?" she asked. Even though she had, she was momentarily thrown.

"The one from *Working Girl*," said Brown. "That TV programme Sam Jenkins worked on."

"She's disappeared," said Hargreaves gruffly, "from Glastonbury."

"I thought she lived in Bath," Linton said, recovering herself, her body flooding with relief, now she knew this wasn't about Talbot.

"She does, but she's staying at The Pendragon. Some sort of mini-break by all accounts. She went out for dinner last night, but didn't come back to the hotel. No one's seen her since. Obviously, in view of recent events, we're treating this extremely seriously. Particularly as she and Sam Jenkins worked together."

"Who reported her as missing?" asked Brown.

"The hotel manager. He insisted on speaking to me. Went on and on. Didn't think I'd ever get him off the sodding phone."

"Maybe she met up with someone," Linton said.

"Hopefully that's all it is. But we need to follow it up."

"What about family? Friends?" she asked. "Have they heard from her?"

"Not so far. I've got Hooper working on it."

"Was she here on her own?"

The Toad nodded. "Oddly enough. We've had a murder and an abduction in the last week. It's hardly the place you'd want to come for a sodding holiday."

"Did she tell anyone at the hotel why she chose to come here?" asked Brown.

"That's what you need to find out. I've told the hotel manager to expect a visit from you in the next half hour. So go on. Chop chop."

•••

The Pendragon was a popular destination for tourists partly because of the fifteenth century architecture, but mainly because of its ghost.

According to legend, the building was once the home of a vicar who got his young servant girl pregnant. She'd come to him asking for help and in a fit of temper, he strangled her with his bare hands. Over the years, scores of people claimed to have seen the apparition of a pale-faced woman wearing a long dress and apron, gently stroking her protruding stomach.

Mr Cartwright, the gangly hotel manager, welcomed Linton and Brown like royalty, seating them on a red velour two-seater sofa in the reception area, next to a roaring log fire.

When Brown asked if they could go somewhere more private, Cartwright apologised profusely, explaining they wouldn't fit into his tiny cubbyhole of an office, before proceeding to give the exact dimensions of the room.

"I can't take you into the dining room either," he continued. "It's full of guests taking their morning coffee and given the nature of your visit it wouldn't be appropriate."

"Mr Cartwright, why you don't find a chair and sit down?" Linton said, interrupting him.

He nodded enthusiastically and scuttled off in the direction of the reception desk.

"For fuck's sake," said Brown. "I've heard of verbal diarrhoea, but this is more like dysentery."

Cartwright returned a moment later with a stool dangling from his skinny wrist. Linton watched, fascinated, as he scurried back over, tripping on the edge of a rug. It was as if he'd borrowed someone else's feet and was trying to get used to them. He placed the stool opposite them and sat down awkwardly, rubbing his bony hands together and clearing his throat as though something was stuck in it that he couldn't cough up.

"I can't tell you how pleased we were Becki Harvey chose to stay here. Of course, she's not our first famous person. We've had the novelist Gilly Murphy and the comedian Bill Diamond and Kate Moss *almost* stayed here during the festival. Who else? Let me think . . ."

"Did Becki tell you why she was in Glastonbury?" Linton asked, hastily.

"I got the impression she was here for a quiet break and to do some sightseeing."

"Didn't you think it's odd considering we've had a murder and a woman go missing in the last few days?"

"It's not my place to comment. I never question my guests. I believe one should maintain a professional distance."

"Is that the receptionist who was on duty last night?" asked Brown. They turned to look at the young woman standing behind the long polished counter who was glancing uneasily over at them. Her face was heavily made-up, and under the camouflage it was difficult to tell what her features were like. She was wearing a low-cut top that showed plenty of cleavage, and chewing on her scarlet painted lips. Linton smiled at her reassuringly, but the girl turned away and started rearranging some paperwork in a way that suggested the activity was unnecessary.

"No. That's Gail Chapman." The name was familiar, and Linton wondered if she'd come across her through her job. "She hasn't been employed for long. It was Jenny who was on duty last night. Jenny Heller. She's been with us for years. Let me see. She would have been on the desk until nine in the evening and then, after that, we have a night porter. It was Mr Cooper's shift last night. He's ready for you to question him whenever you are."

"We'll need to speak to Mrs Heller," said Brown.

"Don't worry, it's all in hand. She isn't due in until three o'clock but she's fully aware of the situation and I've told her you'll want to talk to her. I can ring her and instruct her to come in if that's what you wish. She lives relatively close by, so it shouldn't take her long to get here . . ."

"Thank you," Linton said, interrupting him before he started telling them Jenny's route. "We may as well see her and Mr Cooper together."

"And if you need to question Gail, I'm happy to cover for her."

"That won't be necessary at the moment," said Brown quickly. "Whilst we're waiting for Mrs Heller to arrive, perhaps we can take a look at Becki's room?"

"Of course. There are only six rooms in The Pendragon and Becki's booked into Room 2. It's the biggest one we have."

Brown pulled himself up from the sofa. "Shall we then?" Linton could hear the impatience in his tone.

•••

ONCE UPON A TIME

"How dare you? You have no right to say that."

The phone was in the hallway, two flights down, but he could still hear every word she was saying. Her anger made her forget about keeping her voice down.

His fists were clenched, his nails nearly drawing blood. He wanted to run down and yank the phone away, smash it against the side of her head and knock some sense into her. But it wouldn't make any difference. To what she thought, to who he was, to the truth. She was too stupid to ever understand.

"If anyone's ruining him, it's you," she was screaming. "You're a bunch of charlatans. Filling his head with rubbish. Telling him he's special. You're not the one who has to put up with him every day."

He'd heard enough. He'd heard it all before. Uncurling himself, he crept back into his bedroom, climbed onto his desk and pulled himself out of the skylight onto the roof.

He liked it up here. He liked to think it brought him closer to his *real* family. It made him feel less homesick. He stared up at the night sky, whispering the words of a child even though it was a long time since he'd been one. Not that she seemed to have noticed. She still wanted to control him with the bottle of pills she claimed was their salvation. Over and over again, he murmured the rhyme, willing tonight to be the night that they finally answered his plea.

"Star light, star bright, first star I see tonight.

I wish I may, I wish I might, have the wish I wish tonight."

"Please," he begged, "just take me home."

•••

"It has the best views of any of the rooms in the establishment," Mr Cartwright explained proudly, as they mounted the ornate staircase, the smell of disinfectant and furniture polish heavy in the air. "You can see into the Abbey Grounds and it boasts a four-poster bed and an en suite bathroom."

Linton felt she needed to say something in response to his enthusiasm. "It sounds lovely."

"Here we go," he said, bending to unlock the second panelled door they came to. "No one's touched her room since she checked in. I specifically asked the chambermaid not to go in there this morning and to wait until after you'd been."

"Very commendable," said Brown. "We'll see you downstairs in a bit." Cartwright looked disappointed, but backed awkwardly out of their way. Linton followed Brown through the open door.

They spent a few seconds looking around, taking in the scene as they pulled on their gloves. The room was tidier and far less cluttered than Linton had expected. She'd imagined celebrities to be messy, used to people picking things up for them.

They explored the room methodically. There were red lipstick marks on the rims of both the white china cups and the remains of a milky liquid in the bottom of them. Two empty sachets of UHT milk had attached themselves, through static, to the sides of the thin white bin-bag that lined the otherwise empty wicker basket. On the floor near the open bathroom door lay a couple of damp-looking towels. A pair of jeans and a pink T-shirt were neatly folded on one of the armchairs. Some tourist leaflets were spread across a coffee table; the top one promoting Glastonbury's famous Chalice Well.

Linton checked the four-poster bed, noting an indent in one of the pillows. The quilt was crooked as though someone had been lying on top of it. It was obvious, from the tightly tucked-in sheets, that no one had slept in it.

They went into the en suite bathroom and Linton pulled back the white shower curtain revealing the expected plastic bottles of complimentary washing stuff; one was a body wash, the other an all-in-one shampoo and conditioner. On the sink were a toothbrush and a new tube of toothpaste.

They stepped back into the bedroom and Brown checked the chest of drawers. He held up a tiny black thong and a see-through, black lace bra. Linton waited for the lascivious grin, but it didn't appear. Instead he walked over to the wardrobe. She followed and, as he pulled open the door, they peered into its fusty interior to see what it held. A couple of tops hung limply from the hangers. Linton looked at the labels.

"Miss Selfridge and Topshop. I thought she'd be into designer labels."

At the bottom of the wardrobe, on top of the requisite spare blankets that made her feel itchy just looking at them, was a holdall. It looked brand new and similar to the one Ben bought for his weekend away in Amsterdam. Definitely *not* designer.

The route to the window was blocked by a table but just as Mr Cartwright had boasted, Linton could still see the Abbey ruins opposite. She thought about the last time she was there, only a few weeks ago, on a warm August evening. Van Morrison had played an open-air concert. She thought of all the trouble Ben had gone to that night: the picnic he'd packed; the punnet of strawberries and the bottle of chilled champagne; the blanket he'd taken in case she got cold. How he'd looked across at her and beamed when Van Morrison started to sing *Moon Dance*. Then she remembered his confession two weeks later and felt the anger rising up inside her again.

"Let's go down and see if Jenny Heller's arrived yet."

"OK," she replied, relived to have her thoughts interrupted. She followed Brown onto the dimly lit landing but, before closing the heavy door behind her, she took one last look around the room. There was something odd, something that didn't quite add up, but she couldn't put her finger on it.

•••

Jenny Heller was waiting in the dining room. The guests had finished their coffee so it was safe to let the police in. Mr Cartwright introduced them and excused himself, explaining he had some important hotel business to attend to. *Thank God.*

Jenny was a jolly woman in her late fifties, attractive, with dark frizzy hair and a gravity-defying bust that Linton found it hard to take her eyes off. She was the type of woman who filled a room with her presence and, like the one they were seated in, she had something of a faded grandeur about her. She was obviously having a great time, enjoying being at the centre of whatever this might turn out to be. Mr Cooper, sitting quietly at her side, was about the same age, but that was all they had in common – where she was large and loud, he was small and subdued.

"Do you think the ley line strangler's got her?" she asked, her eyes glinting.

"We're not sure, Mrs Heller," Linton said. "At the moment, we're trying to establish Becki's movements after she arrived at the hotel."

"But you have to admit. It's a bit of a coincidence. Her going missing, I mean, what with Sam Jenkins. And that Angel whatshername being murdered."

"Perhaps you can start with telling us when you first saw Becki."

"Let me see, lovey. I don't normally start until three p.m., but I did a longer shift than usual yesterday on account of Gail feeling poorly." She raised her eyebrows meaningfully. "Morning sickness," she said in a whisper that was remarkably louder than her normal speaking voice. "At least that what *she* reckons. I wouldn't believe anything that comes out of her mouth. She's one of those who has to be the centre of attention. There's always some drama in her life. One minute, her boyfriend's pushing her down the stairs, the next minute she's been mugged. Always in trouble at school she was. Don't know why Mr Cartwright ever employed her. She's trouble, she is. I told him, but he wouldn't listen."

Linton remembered now why Gail's name was familiar. It was back when she was a PC. She'd arrested her for shoplifting. She must've been thirteen or fourteen. Linton had felt sorry for her when she found out about her family background and was softer on her than perhaps she should've been.

"She was kicking herself when she found out she'd missed Becki. She loves her. Reckons she's her idol," Jenny continued.

"Were you working when Becki checked in yesterday?" Brown asked.

"Like I said, I was covering for Gail. It must've been about midday."

"How did she strike you?"

"Very pretty. Lovely figure."

"What about her mood?" Linton asked.

Mrs Heller paused. "Jumpy."

"You mean frightened?'

"I wouldn't say that. More like anxious, impatient maybe."

"Did she say much to you?'

"She was chatty. I asked her about the show and she didn't seem to mind. She said she was here for a bit of a break and that it felt weird because she wasn't used to going places on her own."

"Did she say *why* she was on her own?"

"I didn't like to ask, lovey. I thought perhaps she wanted a bit of time to herself. I know I could do with some." She laughed and nudged Cooper again who responded with a grunt.

"Do you think that's why she was on edge?" asked Brown. "Because she was on her own?"

"Maybe. She asked if she could have a sandwich sent up to her room. She said she didn't fancy eating in the dining room alone."

"Did she have much luggage with her?"

"Only a small bag. I was surprised because I thought she'd have more stuff." She paused. "Ooh. I've remembered something. There was one thing she asked me which I thought was odd."

"Which was?" asked Brown, leaning forward.

"She wanted to know where the nearest public car park was. I told her she could park behind the hotel, but she said she didn't have a car because a friend dropped her off. Don't you think it's odd? Her asking about the car park, I mean."

"Did you tell her?"

"What?"

"Where the nearest car park was."

"I told her about the one behind the church." *The one that Sam and her abductor may have walked towards*, Linton thought, remembering what the teacher who'd driven past had written in his statement. How he'd seen Sam and a man at the bottom of the alleyway that led to St John's car park.

"When did you next see her?" asked Brown.

"She came down from her room an hour later and handed in her key. She said she was going out to have a look round the shops. She came back at five-thirty and then I didn't see her again until she handed her key in again at seven."

"Did Becki say where she was going?" Linton asked.

"Gigi's for a pizza. She never made it though because Mr Cartwright rang this morning and checked."

"You didn't see her again after that?"

She shook her head. "I finished at nine and she hadn't come back by then. You were on your own after that, weren't you, Mr Cooper?"

"And did you see her at all?" asked Brown, addressing the impassive-faced man.

"Nope. I knew she was staying here. Mr Cartwright said so. When I came on duty, I seen her keys hanging up so I knew she was out, but she never come back and asked for 'em."

"Did you think that was odd?"

"I didn't really think about it." Linton could believe it. He didn't look the type to take an interest in what celebrities got up to. "Anyway it's none of my business. As long as they behave themselves in here. I s'pose I thought she'd met a man and decided not to come back for the night."

"Did anybody come into the hotel asking for Becki at any time?"

"No," said Jenny, as both she and Cooper shook their heads.

"Did she, at any point, come into the hotel with anybody else?"

"Not that I know of," said Jenny. "Anyway, every time she went out, she left her key behind, so we'd have known if she'd taken someone up to her room."

"And did either of you see anyone hanging around outside? Anyone you might describe as suspicious looking?"

"Only half of Glastonbury," she said, cackling as once again she elbowed an unflinching Cooper in the ribs.

•••

Within minutes of returning from The Pendragon, The Toad summoned them to his office, demanding an update before giving one of his own.

"I've just spoken to Andrew Chubb," he said. "He heard about Becki's disappearance on the lunchtime news." The name was familiar but Linton couldn't place it. "The ghostwriter who's writing Becki Harvey's autobiography," he explained, rolling his bulging eyes to show his contempt.

Of course, thought Linton. She'd read about her proposed book; the press had already been scathing.

"Becki left a message on his mobile yesterday at around five-thirty p.m.," Hargreaves continued. "He forwarded it to Keen's phone. I've got a copy of the transcript here."

He picked up a sheet of paper, cleared his throat and read aloud.

"Andrew. It's me again. I'm scared. I think I'm being followed. I just looked out my hotel window and there's someone on the pavement below staring up at me. What if it's the ley line strangler? What if he's after me too?"

With no hint in his tone or expression that he'd reached the end, Hargreaves stopped reading and placed the piece of paper back on his desk.

"Why the hell would Becki Harvey think the ley line strangler was after her?" said Brown.

"Someone was following her," said Hargreaves. "She obviously jumped to conclusions."

"And why the hell didn't she tell someone in the hotel if she was scared? Why ring Chubb? Is he her boyfriend?"

"I asked that but he laughed. I get the impression he doesn't like her much. Can't say I blame him." The Toad wrinkled up his bulbous nose and shuddered. "I saw her on a chat show once. Dreadful woman."

"Why does *he* think she phoned him?" Linton asked.

"He says she's so self-obsessed that if someone was following her, she'd want him to know so he could put it in her autobiography. In fact, he thinks that's why she came to Glastonbury. Because the media are here and she was hoping she'd get in the papers."

"She had an affair with a famous man, but she won't reveal his identity. She's scared he might hurt her. Do you think it might've been *him* at her window?"

"Why would he follow her to Glastonbury?" said Hargreaves, with obvious disdain. "If he wanted to threaten her, he could do it in Bath."

"There could be another reason for her being here," said Brown thoughtfully. "She asked for a sandwich in her room because she doesn't like eating alone in public, but told Heller and Chubb she was going out for dinner . . ."

"Because she was meeting someone," said Linton, cottoning on. "But who?"

"Our perpetrator," said Brown.

"But why?" Linton asked, frustrated that they'd raised yet another question they couldn't answer.

And there was something else. Another thing bothering her about Becki's hotel room. But what the hell was it?

FIFTEEN

Claire hoped she wouldn't see anyone she knew during her forced excursion to Fags 'n' Mags for a packet of Silk Cut. She didn't want to talk to anybody, to have to venture out of the surreal world she'd found herself inhabiting.

Inside the newsagents, she couldn't help glancing at the local paper. Sam was front-page news of course. Simon Talbot, that wanker of a journalist, had written the story. She hoped he was racked with guilt now after taking advantage of her sister that time.

She thought she'd managed to get away without bumping into anyone she knew, but as she almost reached the counter, she spotted Dave, one of Adam's workmates, coming towards her from the other direction. She saw the panic in his eyes as he realised he was going to have to speak to her.

"All right?" he asked. Claire could see he regretted the question as soon as it left his lips. But how else did you greet someone whose sister was missing, possibly murdered? She could almost see his fingers desperately riffling through his mind's filing cabinet, searching for something to say.

"How's the car?" she asked, saving him.

"The . . . car?" he replied, the momentary relief turning to confusion.

"Adam said you've got a new car. He said you took him for a spin on Friday." She left *the night my sister went missing* off the end of the sentence.

He frowned and shook his head. "I haven't got it yet. I'm not picking it up 'til tomorrow."

"Oh." It was Claire's turn to frown. "I must've got confused."

How weird, she thought as the shop assistant asked if he could help her. Why had Adam told her that then? Why had he lied about not walking home that night? She couldn't be sure anymore. Was she simply losing her mind and imagining things?

•••

The phone call came as Linton was dragging herself out of her car into the unrelenting rain. For once she'd managed to find a parking space outside her house and it struck her as desperate that this piece of good fortune was the highlight of her day. She was giddy with tiredness. Her throat was still raw with tonsillitis and her head was pounding. She'd been fantasising about the bath she was going to run, imagining herself soaking in the hot, steamy water thickly scented with lavender and geranium oil.

The voice on the other end was frantic, trying to explain what had happened.

"How?" Linton asked. "When?" She barely took it in. "Oh God. I'll come over now."

That short conversation was the equivalent of a double espresso. Now it was hard to imagine she'd ever felt tired. She felt the adrenalin kicking in as she jumped back into her car. She turned off the radio unable to bear the soothing tones of the evening DJ she normally enjoyed and arrived five minutes later, parking on a double yellow line, every space on the road taken up. She didn't bother locking the car, just legged it along the pavement, up the steps to number 47.

Once inside the house, she was ushered into the large living room. The scene before her stopped her in her tracks, filling her with a mild horror. She didn't know where to look first. Her eyes tried to follow the haphazard trail of books, CDs and cushions strewn across the floor. The coffee table was hidden under pieces of paper. If there was any order to them, there was no suggestion of it now. Some of the paper was ripped, others cut. There were crimson handprints all over the table. A pair of scissors lay on the laminate floor next to a pool of dark red liquid.

On the far side of the room, next to a radiator, lay a body: large, black and familiar.

"Bloody hell," she said, turning to look at her sister.

"I know," replied Jasmine. "I've only just got Harry to bed. I haven't had a chance to tidy up yet."

"What's up with Rufus?" Linton asked, nodding towards the dog, relieved he was asleep, so she didn't have to endure his slobbering.

"He's knackered. We took him up on the hill after school. Before I spoke to Angela."

Her sister's eyes looked puffy and bloodshot from crying. It's funny how different they were, Linton thought. How Jasmine cried at anything whereas she rarely shed a tear and only in private. Mum always said Jasmine was the sensitive one, whereas Linton was the 'tough nut' of the family; 'cold and unfeeling' if she was being particularly derogative.

"What exactly happened?"

"Angela found him. Luckily, she'd left a file at home and went back to get it."

"How bad was it?"

"She said the cuts were vertical as opposed to horizontal although I don't know what that means."

"It means Michael wanted to kill himself. It wasn't a cry for help. Across for attention, down for death. Sorry," she said, as Jasmine winced. "But they're sure he's going to be OK?"

"I think so. Physically at least." Linton heard the catch in her breath.

"Have you told mum?"

"She's going to try and fly over tomorrow. Alone." Jasmine raised her eyebrows as she uttered the last word.

"She's going to try, is she?" said Linton, sniffing her disdain, and ignoring Jasmine's insinuation. "How thoughtful of her."

"Why can't you forgive her? I have. And don't you feel a bit sorry for her. After what happened with . . ."

"Stop," interrupted Linton sharply, putting her hands up to cover her ears. "Don't say it."

"I rang dad," said Jasmine, exhaling slowly through her nose.

"And?"

"He didn't answer his mobile. He's probably out *partying* and couldn't hear it." Linton shuddered as she imagined their dad, red-faced from too much sun, sweating profusely despite the air-conditioning. A middle-aged, balding ex-pat sporting dribbles of Malaysian beer and curry down the front of his open-necked shirts, his arm casually slung round the shoulder of a woman at least a third of his age. Oblivious to the ringing in his pocket as his daughter tried to tell him his son had slashed his wrists.

"I should've known something was up," said Linton. "He sounded so upbeat on the phone the other night. That's one of the warning signs isn't it? Excessive cheerfulness. Knowing it's all going to be over soon." She stopped, seeing the pained look on her sister's face. "When can we see him?"

"They're sending someone in to assess him, to see if they think he needs to be sectioned again." Jasmine started crying again. *Why couldn't I cry like that?* Linton wondered. It's not that she didn't feel things, of course she did. Perhaps her friend Gemma was right. Maybe growing up in a house where everything seemed so chaotic and out of control meant her emotions were the only thing she could keep in check.

"Did he leave a note?"

"It said he was sorry," said Jasmine said, choking on a sob. "But he didn't want to be here anymore."

"Auntie Kate! Auntie Kate! Auntie Kate!" It was Harry.

"You're meant to be asleep," Jasmine shouted up the stairs.

"Ohhhh!" he replied, expertly turning the word into a three-second octave. "I want Auntie Kate to give me a kiss and a cuddle."

"Do you mind? I'm not in the mood to argue with him tonight."

"I'd love to." Linton meant it. She couldn't resist basking in the glow of the unconditional love and admiration radiating from her nephew. She knew it wouldn't last – the drawings, the love letters, the complete unwavering belief she was the most cleverest, most beautifulest girl in the whole world.

"Hello, sweetheart," she said, stepping into his bedroom. He looked so safe and snug, all wrapped up in his Power Rangers duvet.

"Have you caught any baddies?" he asked.

She shook her head. "Everyone was very good today."

"Are policemen ever naughty?"

Linton thought of Brown and suppressed a smile. "It's impossible to be good all the time, sweetheart."

"But you are," he said stubbornly.

"Not always."

He looked cross. "You have to be because you're a police lady."

"It's not that simple. Sometimes goodies do bad things and sometimes baddies do good things."

She realised she'd lost him. Things were black and white in his world, not the messy shade of grey you came to expect as a grown-up. She tried to think of something meaningful to say. Something he'd take with him into adulthood, so he'd look back at his bedside chat with Auntie Kate and realise what a wise and wonderful woman she was.

"Do you want to hear a joke?" she said.

"OK."

"Why did the banana go to the doctors?"

"I don't know, why did the banana go the doctors?"

"Because he wasn't peeling well."

He laughed so much that in the end Jasmine came up to see what was going on. Linton was pleased to report that not only was she the cleverest, most beautifulest woman in the whole world but now, apparently, she was the funniest too.

•••

Claire found the slim white envelope on the floor when she came back from buying her cigarettes. Her name was handwritten across the front of it. Her boss must've pushed it through the door on her way home from A Helping Hand. She'd rung earlier and said a letter had been hand-delivered for Claire at the shop. *No*, she said, she didn't know by whom. She'd found it waiting on the doormat when she'd unlocked the shop. It was probably an invoice, thought Claire, although for what she couldn't think.

She ripped open the envelope, pulled out a piece of lined notepaper and unfolded it. It most definitely wasn't an invoice.

SIXTEEN

"I didn't know you'd moved to Special Branch," said Brown, tossing his briefcase onto his desk.

Linton stopped typing and glanced up, confused.

He nodded at the three boxes of tablets lined up on her desk: paracetamol, aspirin and ibuprofen. "It looks like you've been on a drugs bust."

"It's this bloody tonsillitis," she said. "I'm juggling them for maximum pain relief."

"Isn't that bad for your liver?"

"I don't care. If I end up in hospital, at least I'll get some rest." She thought of Michael and winced. She'd rung first thing. He was under observation they said but wouldn't go into detail.

"For fuck's sake. Just go and get some antibiotics."

"I will when I get a chance."

She carried on typing. She was part way through her report of their visit to The Pendragon. There was still something bothering her about it. What was it about Becki's hotel room that felt wrong?

She closed her eyes and imagined herself back in the room, looking out across to the abbey . . .

"Brown!" she exclaimed, her eyes pinging open.

"What?" He was tipping the remains of his tea into the large plant pot next to their desk. The leaves of the once luscious fern were now brown and drooping and it smelt of rotting vegetables. Linton had given up telling him to stop.

"Remember what Becki said about seeing someone on the pavement below staring up? She couldn't have done."

"Why not?" he said, banging his mug back down on his desk.

"She couldn't have got near the window. There was a table in front of it. And besides, it would've been dark. She couldn't have seen anyone unless she had the curtains open and the lights off."

"What are you saying? That she made it up?"

"I don't know," she said, lamely. "But I'm not convinced our killer's got her. Why would he abduct another woman? Unless Sam's already dead . . ."

"We'd have found her body by now if she was," he snapped.

"But . . ."

"Let's get on with some work shall we," he said, crossly picking up a pile of papers and waving them at her.

"What's that?"

"A list of the all the people involved in *Working Girl*. And someone's going to have to speak to every bloody one of them."

A few minutes later he said thoughtfully, "I wonder why the 'I'?"

"Whose eye?" asked Linton looking up.

Brown pointed to the list of names. "The letter 'I'. Why is she Becki with an 'I'? Her real name's Rebecca, so why not Becky with a 'y'?"

"It's different I suppose."

"Do you think you grow into your name? Like Angel. She looked like one with her pale skin and long hair. Do you think she'd have turned out the same if she was called Sharon?"

"That's rather deep for you, isn't it?"

"My point exactly. That's because I'm called Rob. If I was called Tao or Shaman, you'd expect me to talk about that sort of stuff."

"All I can say is thank God I was born first. My mum's favourite auntie died when she was young. She was called Kate. Mum always said she'd name her first-born daughter after her."

"That's a bit morbid."

"But better than the names she gave my brother and sister: Saturn and Venus."

"You're joking!"

She shook her head. "I think she was planning on working her way through the solar system except she had to have a hysterectomy."

"Lucky she didn't get as far as Uranus."

"If I had a penny for every time I heard that one."

"Anyway, I thought you said your brother was called Michael?"

"That's what he calls himself now. My granny talked her into giving them normal middle names. Funnily enough it's what they both go by now."

"What about you? Doesn't anybody ever call you Katie?"

She shook her head. "It's not me. Katies are pretty and feminine. I'm definitely more of a Kate."

Brown looked over and frowned. "You look like a Katie to me."

She felt herself redden.

"You know there's still something else about Becki's hotel room that's bothering me," she said hurriedly, letting the comment pass in the hope of lessening her flush.

"How d'you mean?" he asked, nonplussed by her sudden subject change.

"I don't know," she said, as Brown's phone rang. "But I'm sure it'll come to me eventually."

•••

They were called into a briefing at midday.

"I'll keep this short," said Hargreaves. "Sam Jenkins' sister has received a note. She brought it in this morning. It was hand-delivered to the bookshop where she worked. The original's gone off to the FSS, but I have a copy of it here." He stuck the magnified narrative on the whiteboard behind him:

> Please don't worry. It won't be like the others. I promise I'll get it right this time. Sam will be home soon.

"Note the graphic on the bottom-right hand."

Linton already had. Her eye was drawn to it before she even read the note. Someone had drawn a small circle of candles.

"I think he drew it so we know it's not a hoax," continued Hargreaves. "He knows that no one outside the investigation is aware of the flares. The media would've mentioned them otherwise." He paused to let the information sink in then said, "Any thoughts or questions?"

There was a flurry of hands. Hargreaves' face was a mask of indifference as he listened and responded to the various queries and comments.

After a while, Linton switched off and looked out of the window. She was finding it hard to concentrate thanks to the razor blades lodged in her throat. She couldn't believe it was still raining. They hadn't had a dry day since last weekend. The weekend Angel Kingsley was murdered . . . She put up her hand.

"Linton?"

"Sir. It's about the flares." He looked at her expectantly. "I was thinking. They won't work as well if they're wet. Maybe he's just waiting 'til it stops raining." There was a murmur of agreement from the rest of the team.

"It's meant to change at the weekend, Sir," said Wells.

"Well, whatever he's planning to do to Becki and Sam," said Hargreaves grimly, "it doesn't leave us much time. Besides, we'll be lucky if Sam survives 'til then without any insulin."

•••

He didn't look like a police officer, Claire thought. It wasn't simply the absence of a uniform. It was just he was so handsome. He'd have looked more at home on the glossy pages of *Hello!* magazine than on her mum's floral settee.

He introduced himself as DI Brown and then said, "Call me Rob." The name didn't do him justice, she thought. He looked more like a Brad or maybe a George . . .

"We're looking at the possibility our perpetrator knew both women before he abducted them," the officer said. "There's a good chance he met them whilst they were making *Working Girl*."

None of this matters now, Claire thought. *His note said Sam was coming home.*

There was silence. He was looking at her expectantly. He must have asked her a question.

"Can you say that again, please?"

"Did Sam and Becki know each other before they met on the programme?"

She shook her head. "But they were good friends by the end of it. They kept in touch for a while. Until Becki got *really* famous."

"Did you ever meet her?"

Claire nodded. "Once. At one of Sam's parties."

"What about other family and friends? Did any of them meet Becki?"

"Loads of them came to the party." She watched his face fall, no doubt aware the list of people who knew both women was growing longer by the hour.

When was he going to let Sam go? she wondered. *Did he mean she was coming home dead?* No. He promised it wasn't going to be like it was with the others. He'd said so in his letter.

"We're interviewing everyone they worked with on the programme," the officer continued. "Is there anyone you can think of she might've fallen out with?"

She shook her head. She couldn't think of anything except that her sister was alive and coming home.

"What about men? Did she get involved with anyone working on *Working Girl?* Someone Becki might've known as well?"

"There was someone," she said hesitantly, remembering her earlier conversation with Adam. "But he didn't work with them."

"Go on," he said, encouragingly.

"Simon Talbot. He's a local journalist."

The officer licked his lips. "Simon Talbot," he said, repeating the name slowly. She noticed he didn't write in his notebook.

She nodded. "Sam called him Slimon because he was, well, slimy. It was just after she got the job on *Working Girl.* He interviewed her about it. And then he got her to organise an interview for him with Becki."

"And?"

"After he interviewed Becki, he took Sam out to say thanks for setting it up. She's not much of a drinker. He plied her with alcohol and she ended in his flat."

"What happened?"

"That's the thing. She was so pissed she can't remember. And she was too embarrassed to ask."

"And what about Becki?" he asked, leaning forward, his pen poised above his notebook. "Did he try anything on with her?"

"Probably. Nothing he did would surprise me."

•••

Brown returned from the Jenkins' household looking like he'd won the lottery.

"You'd better see if he's a Walktall customer then," Linton said, after he recounted his conversation with Sam's sister. "Although I can't see why him taking Sam to bed would have anything to do with her going missing."

She felt sick. The nausea worsened when Brown slammed down his phone five minutes later and shouted, "Yes! It's got to be him. Simon fucking Talbot. He's a Walktall customer."

Could it be him? Could she have gone to bed with a murderer? Lost her virginity to a serial killer all those years ago? No. It was ridiculous.

"Does he take a size fourteen?" she asked casually, trying to remember how big his feet were, but realising she hadn't paid much attention to *that* part of his body.

"According to the database he's always bought shoes in a size twelve but . . ."

"Hang on a minute," she interrupted. "He's a size twelve. Not a fourteen."

Brown brushed her doubt away with a flick of his hand. "Perhaps they'd sold out of his size."

"But what about the Timberland footprints found at Avebury? They were a size fourteen as well." She shook her head. "You're bending the facts to suit your case."

"Look," he said, sounding irritated now. "We've got a suspect. The first one. You might not like who it is, but don't knock it. Ring him. Tell him to come into the station."

"Why me?"

"Because it's your job," he said, sounding exasperated. "Anyway, you said yourself nothing happened the other night. So why do you care?"

Reluctantly, Linton picked up her phone and rang the *Daily*. She asked to speak to Talbot, but was told he'd taken the afternoon off.

"In the middle of a big story?" said Brown, in disbelief.

"You said yourself. It's only the local paper."

"Where the fuck's he gone?"

"They don't know."

"Ring his mobile."

"Why would I have his number?"

"Phone the bloody paper back and get it!"

She did. Then rang the number they gave her but it went straight to answerphone. She left a message asking Talbot to ring back as a matter of urgency then continued to ring throughout the afternoon. He didn't pick up.

"He's a journalist," said Brown. "Why would he turn his phone off? It's fucking odd."

"It doesn't make him a serial killer," said Linton.

"But you've got to admit. It's not normal behaviour."

•••

Jasmine rang as Linton was pouring boiling water into a Pot Noodle. "I'm phoning to let you know mum's flying over tomorrow."

"That's nice," Linton said, pulling open the kitchen drawer to retrieve a fork.

"I thought you might want to come for dinner."

She stirred the steaming water round, watching the powder miraculously transform into floating pieces of food. "Sorry," she said, pleasantly, "but I'm busy. I know I shouldn't put other commitments before my family, but I'm sure she'll understand."

"Kate!" The exasperation in her sister's voice was evident. "Don't you think this has gone on for long enough? So she didn't turn up for my wedding. It wasn't exactly a shock. We know what she's like."

"That doesn't make it OK," Linton said, stirring the mixture more quickly. "God, Jasmine, she's spent her whole life letting us down. Don't you remember what she was like when we were at school? How many mornings were we late? How many parents' evenings did she forget? How many parties did we miss because she couldn't be arsed to write them on a calendar? We were lucky if she remembered to send us in with a packed lunch."

"It only happened a couple of times."

Linton put the fork down. "It shouldn't have happened at all. Can you imagine being like that with Harry?"

"But I'm not mum, am I?"

"That's the whole point. I'm fed up with forgiving her because that's the way she is."

"You can't change people. You have to accept that's the way they are. Once you stop having expectations, then they can't disappoint you."

"God, do you realise how depressing that sounds? Well, this is the way I am. An unforgiving judgemental bitch."

"I know you're angry. But you obviously care about her because you didn't tell her what happened with . . ."

"Jasmine! I didn't tell her because I don't want to talk about it!"

"But I thought what with Michael and everything . . ."

She interrupted again, "This isn't some Hollywood movie where my brother nearly dies so I realise the importance of family and then mum and me have this gushy reunion. He's probably like he is because of her."

They always blame the mum. It isn't fair, Linton remembered Angel's mum saying.

"Michael's like he is because he's Michael. He's got a chemical imbalance. It's nothing to do with mum. You and I are OK, aren't we?"

Just great, she thought, watching the steam rising out of the plastic pot.

"I can hear Harry shouting down the stairs. He wants to speak to you. Do you mind?"

Poor Jasmine, Linton thought as she waited for her nephew to come to the phone. She was always piggy-in-the-middle of any argument, jumping up to try and catch the insults before they reached the person on the other side.

"Hi, Auntie Kate." He sounded much younger on the phone. "Did you catch any baddies today?"

"Not today, sweetheart. I've got a good joke though. It's a bit rude so don't tell your mum."

"I won't."

"Doctor, doctor. I've got a piece of lettuce poking out of my bum." She paused before letting him have the punch line. "Well, I'm afraid that's just the tip of the iceberg."

Harry laughed, then said, "Auntie Kate, I don't get it."

"Don't worry. I don't get stuff most of the time either."

When he passed the phone back to Jasmine she heard him say, "Mum, Auntie Kate said bum." Men. You just couldn't trust them.

Ben. Simon. *Any of them.*

She thought of Brown and the look he'd given her when they were talking about names. *You look like a Katie to me.* For the rest of the day, she'd scrutinised his comment, turning it over and over, like a kid with a special pebble in her pocket.

SEVENTEEN

Linton was in bed, half-asleep, when her mobile rang. She thrust out her hand, groping for it on her bedside table, almost knocking over a glass of water. It was Brown. He didn't even give her the chance to say hello.

"We got hold of Talbot. He rang the station last night."

"Did he say where he'd been?" she said, pulling herself up into a sitting position.

"He was very vague. Anyway, we'll find out soon enough when we interview him."

Linton felt her mouth turn dry. This was her opportunity to admit what had happened the other night. "You know, I had that drink with him in the pub."

"So?"

"Well . . ." she stopped.

"Did something happen?" Brown's tone was sharp.

Come on, Kate. Tell him how you got so drunk you took him home and went to bed with him. "He saw me pissed. That's all. It's not very professional."

"For fuck's sake, Linton. You need to lighten up."

•••

"The interview room is serious looking with only a desk and three chairs; two for the detectives and one for the suspect. There's nothing on the walls which I assume is done to create a sense of exposure and isolation."

"You what?" said Brown. Talbot laughed. "I did a piece for the paper about the station when it first opened. I can remember it word-for-word."

Brown ignored him, leant over the desk and switched on the video recorder, then slowly spoke the date, time and their names. "Mr Talbot . . ." he began.

"At least call me Simon," he interrupted. "It's not as if we don't know each other. Kate and I go way back." Linton looked down at the table, swallowing hard, wincing at the pain from her enlarged tonsils.

"*Mr Talbot*," he repeated, "before we start, I want to emphasise that this interview is purely routine. Your name's come up as part of our investigation into the disappearance of Samantha Jenkins and Rebecca Harvey. It's important we follow every lead and it's as much about eliminating you from our enquiries as anything else."

"So how exactly has my name come up?" he asked, pleasantly. "The officer I spoke to last night wouldn't say."

Brown ignored him. "Perhaps you can start by telling us exactly where you were yesterday afternoon."

He looked wary. "Is that relevant?"

"It might be."

"At a place a friend recommended."

"What sort of place?"

Talbot paused and licked his lips. "A healing centre."

"You mean a hospital?" Linton could tell Brown was enjoying himself.

"A spiritual healing centre."

"And what exactly were you having *healed*?" Brown put as much stress as he could on the word.

"They run a meditation course. I'm not into that sort of thing normally. I've been stressed recently. I thought it might help."

"And did it?" asked Brown.

He flashed a smile but it didn't reach his eyes. "It had until I switched my phone back on. Look, are you going to tell me what this is all about?"

"What was the name of the place?"

"The Sacred Angel Healing Centre." Talbot leant forward and pulled his wallet out of his back pocket. They watched him flick through a pile of receipts until he came to a business card. "Here," he said, passing it to Brown.

Brown took the small, white card, turning it over so he could read the details. Linton glimpsed an illustration of an angel with gold-trimmed wings. *Angel.* She thought of her blue, swollen face on the Tor a few days ago and felt the hairs on her arm rise up.

"Perhaps you can tell me the last time you saw Sam Jenkins?"

"Let me see," said Talbot licking his lips a couple of times. "I interviewed her back in, um . . ."

Linton looked up from her notepad. "May 2007."

"That sounds about right."

"I've got a copy of the interview here."

"Excellent police work." His tone was mocking.

"How about Becki Harvey?" asked Brown.

"Around the same time." Talbot leant back in his chair and put his hands behind his head in an effort to look casual. Linton noted the small circles of sweat forming under his arms. "I'm sure Kate can tell you *exactly* when."

She looked down at her notes. "June. Just after you interviewed Sam. Have you been in contact with either woman since?" she asked. "Telephone? Email? Facebook?"

"I interviewed them. I didn't make friends."

"Apparently you were more than friends with Sam," said Brown evenly.

Simon licked his lips again. "Who told you that?" His mouth sounded dry and sticky when he spoke. Brown simply shrugged.

"Listen," he said, sounding irritated. "I had a one-night stand with her, but that's all it was."

"You mean you had sex," Brown said.

"Does it matter?" He was obviously taken aback by the bluntness of the statement.

"I'm trying to establish your relationship," said Brown.

"We didn't. Have sex I mean."

"Blimey. Two consenting adults and you didn't have sex. How did you manage that?" Brown sounded genuinely intrigued. It was no doubt a concept that was alien to him.

"We were drunk."

"And?" prompted Brown.

"We fell asleep." He laughed, but it sounded unnatural.

"And what about Becki? Did anything happen with her? Or not happen."

"No," said Talbot, emphatically and Linton wondered if he could hear how forced his answer sounded.

"Where were you three nights ago?" she asked. "The night Becki Harvey went missing."

"I went to Saffron's for a curry with a load of us from work."

"What time was that?"

"About eight. We finished work at six and went for a couple of drinks in the Star and Garter first."

According to Jenny Heller, Becki had left The Pendragon at seven to go out for dinner. If Simon was in the pub at the time and then went straight to Saffron's, thought Linton, he couldn't have met up with her. Unless . . .

"Did Becki join you for a drink and a curry?" she asked.

"Why would she do that? I hardly know her."

"And after the curry?"

"I went home. Well, back to the flat I'm staying in. I'm looking after it for a mate while he's away. I was telling Kate all about it the other night." He smiled smugly at her.

"Can you remember what time that was?" she replied.

"About half ten, eleven."

"And were you alone?"

This time he paused before answering. "Yes. I said goodbye to everyone outside Saffron's and went straight home."

"What about Friday the 20th of November?" asked Brown. "The night Sam Jenkins disappeared."

"I went to the cinema straight after work. In Taunton. It was the five p.m. showing."

"Blimey," said Brown, looking impressed. "Again, no hesitation at all. You've got a good memory."

"*The Men who Stare at Goats* was on. I'm a big Kevin Spacey fan."

"Who did you go with?"

"I wanted to see it on my own. You know, no distractions."

"How did you pay? Debit card, credit card? Would you have any financial record to show you went?"

"Cash. We had a poker game the night before and I had loads of it on me."

"What about a cinema ticket stub?" Linton asked.

He shook his head. "I doubt it."

"A petrol receipt? Perhaps you stopped at a garage in Taunton?"

He shook his head. "You could ring the cinema. They might remember me."

"I'm sure one of your neighbours would have seen you when you got home. Which would have been . . .?"

"About half seven, I think. Look, you don't seriously think I've got anything to do with their disappearance. It's the ley line strangler you should be after."

"What about Angel Kingsley?" Linton asked. "Did you know her?"

"Not personally."

"So you've never met her. Maybe interviewed her for the paper?"

"Not to my knowledge." He was sounding rattled now. "Look, what's going on?"

"Were you in Glastonbury on the night of Thursday, the 19th of November?'

"Probably. I'll have to check."

"How about Hannah James and Sadie Carter?" asked Brown. "Did you know either of them?"

"The girls who were murdered in Avebury?" he said crossly. "Why the hell would I know them?"

"Doesn't your mum live nearby?"

"Hang on a minute . . ."

"Is it true," said Brown, interrupting him, "that your mum lives near Avebury?"

"She moved there a couple of years ago."

"Perhaps you met Hannah and Sadie there when you went to visit her."

"This is ridiculous," he said, pushing himself up from the table. He was bright red.

"Sit down!" Brown demanded.

Talbot obeyed reluctantly then said in a calmer voice, "I've never met them."

"So, just for the record," said Brown. "*To your knowledge* you've never met Angel Kingsley, Hannah James or Sadie Carter and the last time you saw Becki and Sam was in the summer of 2007."

He nodded. "I was meant to do a follow up interview with Sam . . ." he stopped.

"Go on," Brown prompted.

Talbot swallowed hard before replying. "I was going to interview her after she'd finished working on the programme, but I wasn't able to. For personal reasons."

"And what were they?" Brown's face was impassive, but she knew his brain was firing away. Hoping for some small nugget of information he could hang the case on.

"I was ill," Talbot said eventually.

"With what?"

He sighed. "I suffer from manic depression. The correct term is bipolar. I'm on medication but every now and then I have a wobble. That's why I went on the meditation course. I thought it might help."

They were silent for a few seconds. When Linton spoke her tone was gentler. "I think that's all my questions for now," she said.

"By the way," said Brown as they got up from the table. "I couldn't help noticing your feet."

"What about them?" Talbot asked. Linton thought she detected a hint of anxiety in his voice.

"You're like me," continued Brown. "Big feet. What do you take? A size thirteen, a fourteen?"

"A twelve."

"I'm a size eleven and I have enough trouble getting shoes sometimes."

Talbot nodded. "Some shops go up to twelve. But since Walktall opened, I tend to order online."

"Isn't it easier to go into their shop?"

He shrugged. "I know my size, so I get them delivered to work."

"Have you ever bought a pair of desert boots?"

"No," he said, "I haven't."

"One more thing," said Brown, casually. "We'll need you to provide us with a sample of your DNA. Don't look so worried. It's painless. They take a saliva sample from the inside of your cheek with a cotton bud."

"Doesn't it end up on the DNA database?"

"And?" said Brown.

"What if the data's lost or stolen? I might be accused of something in the future because my DNA's found at a crime scene. You hear of mistakes being made all the time."

"I think that's a bit of an exaggeration."

"What if I say no?"

Brown shrugged. "We'll arrest you so we can take it without your consent."

"I haven't got a lot of choice then." Talbot looked at Linton. Had he sensed her softening towards him? She shrugged. "Fine," he said tersely.

•••

After interviewing Talbot, they went to the canteen.

Linton asked for a pot of tea and slipped a pack of Scottish shortbread onto her tray as she reached the till to pay. Brown bought a Coke, self-served in a large cardboard cup. He jammed a yellow straw into the plastic lid and slurped on it noisily as they made their way to the corner of the room, nodding at people they knew as they passed them.

"My money's on Talbot," Brown said, when they finally sat down. "He's into all that spiritual stuff."

"He was on a meditation course. It doesn't mean a thing."

"He knows Becki and Sam," he said, reaching over to pick up Linton's biscuits.

"I don't think it's him."

"Why not?"

Because I don't want to have slept with a serial killer. Because he's bipolar like my brother and despite everything I feel sorry for him. "Because it's a stupid theory," she said, as logic took over from emotion. "His feet are too small. And he's got alibis . . ."

"Which we haven't checked out," Brown interrupted.

"You can't get away from the fact he's only got size twelve feet. The killer's are two sizes bigger."

"The killer wore *shoes* that were two sizes bigger. There's a difference."

"But what's his motive?"

"He doesn't need one. He's not your average bloke, is he?"

"Meaning?" she asked. She felt herself growing hot. She knew where the conversation was heading.

"He's mental. He said himself he hasn't been well lately. Perhaps he flipped."

She slammed her cup back down in its saucer. "I expect it was the voices in his head," she said angrily.

"What's up with you?" asked Brown, bemused. She knew she was bright red now, but she didn't care.

"He's bipolar, for God's sake, it doesn't mean he's a maniac. He's more likely to kill *himself* than anyone else." Brown stared at her as though she'd gone mad. "God, you're an arsehole," she snapped. "I'm going to the loo."

Inside the cramped room the air was thick with pine air freshener. She felt the hot, red, itchy rash of anger creeping up her face towards her forehead. She leant back against the wall and closed her eyes. She thought about her brother, how he'd once described what it was like to be bipolar.

"The worst time is when you come out of the manic bit," he'd explained. "You're in the middle of this adventure, having the time of your life and then suddenly you're thrown into a dark room. It's like a vault. It's suffocating and you can't sleep or eat or think properly. A closed world with no way in or out."

It had helped her understand, but sometimes she wished he hadn't said anything. She hated imagining him in that room, alone and frightened.

She sighed. She was certain Brown was wrong about Talbot but more than that she *wanted* him to be. Not just because she'd slept with him but because it would only reinforce people's prejudices about mental illness. It was true, she didn't always know what her brother was going to do next, but one thing was for certain, she knew he'd never try to hurt anybody.

•••

When Linton walked into the incident room ten minutes later, Brown appeared to have forgotten about her earlier outburst. He didn't mention it, just pointed at a large stack of A4 paper on his desk.

"Becki Harvey's autobiography," he said. "That ghostwriter, Chubb, emailed it over. Turley's gone through it. She's made a list of names that appear in the text along with the relevant page numbers. Talbot's is on pages 178 and 179." Linton sat down, feeling her stomach lurch as Brown flicked through the sheets until he found the sheet he was looking for.

He cleared his throat and read aloud: "'I know this sounds big-headed, but the minute Simon saw me, I knew he fancied me. Sam, one of the researchers, arranged for him to interview me for his local paper. The thing is, I can't stand it when older blokes think they can have you. I suppose he was good-looking, but he was at least ten years older than me, the dirty bastard! I'd rather have a toy boy than a sugar daddy any day. I like my men with a lot more muscle, which is why I couldn't resist Gavin Shanks. But more of that later . . . Anyway back to Simon. Or Slimon, as he was known behind his back! And no wonder! I later found out from Sam that he'd got her drunk and taken advantage of her.'"

Brown paused and shook his head. "God, this is utter crap. Do people really want to read about this?"

"Go on," she urged.

"'I thought it would be fun to wind him up, so I kept smiling at him, wiggling my eyebrows at him suggestively. When the interview finished, he went to kiss me, but instead of my cheek, he went straight for my mouth. I couldn't believe it! I gave him a slap across the face and asked him what he thought he was doing, the pervert. He was so shocked, he didn't say a thing! I flicked my hair back and stormed out. I wasn't really angry, but I thought I'd make him sweat. Make him wonder if I was going to report him to the producer. I didn't, of course, but I'll tell you what – me and the other girls had a right laugh about it that night.'"

Brown got up then sat down again. "It's him. I'm sure of it," he said, tapping his fingers impatiently on his desk.

"Because Becki slapped him round the face two years ago," Linton said. "It's hardly grounds for abducting and murdering her, is it?"

"Surveillance," said Brown, as though she hadn't spoken. "We need to speak to Hargreaves and get him to authorise a team. The interview today may have spooked him. It might push him into doing something."

Brown's phone started ringing. He picked it up and mouthed *Keen*, wafting his hand in front of his nose.

"What time?" Brown asked, as Linton leant forward and switched on her computer. "No *fucking* way!" She could tell by his emphasis on the swear word it was good news. "You're not going to believe this," he said, after slamming the phone down. "Keen spoke to one of Talbot's workmates from the paper. He didn't go home alone after the curry."

"Who was he with?"

"Some work experience girl. His mate saw them both go into the flat he's staying in. That proves he's a liar."

"But he's got an alibi. For the rest of evening."

"He hasn't."

She felt her blood run cold. "What do you mean?"

"He was at the pub like he said, but he popped out for some cigarettes. The vending machine had sold out of the ones he smoked."

"What time?"

"About seven. The same time Becki was seen leaving The Pendragon. He was gone for twenty minutes. Plenty of time to persuade her to go somewhere with him."

"But where? Not his flat. He took the work experience girl back there."

"Maybe she saw something suspicious. Perhaps that's why he didn't mention taking her back because he didn't want us questioning her, which, before you ask, Keen's about to do."

Linton thought for a moment and then said, "Isn't work experience something you do at school? Maybe she was under age."

"Who cares if she was?" said Brown crossly.

"If he slept with someone under age, then he's broken the law in case you'd forgotten."

Brown's furious indrawn breath was audible. "For fuck's sake, Linton, you're going off at a tangent now."

"Why are you getting so angry?"

"Look," he said more calmly. "I think we should talk to The Toad about organising surveillance."

"That's just over the top. Let's get him back in again."

"He'll make something up. And if he's got those girls, he's not going to tell us where they are, is he? The only way we're going to find them is if we follow him." He paused then said, excitedly, "I've just thought. He was one of the first people on the Tor that morning."

"That's because his sister-in-law works in the call centre."

"Or because he hung around after he killed Angel."

Linton tutted, "And I suppose you've got a theory for the Avebury murders have you?"

"He's got connections to the area."

"You mean his mum lives nearby. Look. Don't you think we need to do more first? Check out his other alibi. The one he gave us for the night Sam went missing."

"Which reminds me, don't you think it was slick the way he instantly remembered he was at the cinema? I'd have a job to remember what I was doing a couple of nights ago."

"I think you mean *who* you were doing, don't you?"

•••

He pulled back the duct tape and popped the tablets in her mouth. It took four attempts before she swallowed them.

He shook his head sadly. "You don't look well, Sam."

"Please," she croaked, "let me go. You said yourself you don't want me to die."

"That's because I need you. You're my only hope now. Without you I might not get home again."

"You need to get me some insulin or I'm going to die."

"And how do you propose I do that?" he said coldly, pushing the remaining tablets back into the packet. "Go back to your mum's flat again and get caught? I haven't forgiven you for that."

"Take my repeat prescription. I'll sign it and you can take it in for me and pick it up."

"I know how repeat prescriptions work, Sam. I've become an expert recently. What do you think will happen to me when I hand a prescription over with your name on?"

"But I'm going to die."

"You can't. They won't let you. You're special."

I am not special, she thought. She was all the things Danny had said. He was right. She was self-centred, big-headed. And she was a liar. She was worse than a liar.

"I need to speak to Claire," she croaked.

"That's not going to happen."

"But I need to tell her what happened." She stopped, coughing, gagging, the acrid taste of bile in her mouth. "The night dad died."

"I don't think that's going to happen, Sam."

"Yes it is," she said desperately. "The police will find me. They probably know where I am already."

She saw a hint of panic in his eyes. "Then maybe I'll move you," he said, his tone tense. "Take you somewhere they'll never find you."

•••

Brown put forward his case, quickly and succinctly, listing the things that, in his opinion, made Simon Talbot their, or rather *his*, prime suspect.

Hargreaves' initial reaction was the same as Linton's. Doubt.

"We don't have enough evidence to justify sending out a surveillance team. Do you know how much it would cost?"

"Sir, I can see what you're saying but you've got to admit he's the only real lead we've got."

The Toad's eyes narrowed to slits, "I don't have to admit anything."

"What I meant, Sir . . ."

"And I can see what *you're* saying, but all you've got is that he had a thing for Sam and Becki. So what?"

"But there's more to it than that. I reckon he tried to shag Sam but he couldn't get it up. He must have felt humiliated. And then Becki Harvey slapped him." He stopped to pause for breath, then said, "We know he's got mental health problems. What if the anger turned into something nastier? What if the humiliation pushed him over the edge?"

Linton thought about the other night with Talbot. *Did that mean she was in danger?* She rubbed at her neck instinctively, feeling the oily coating of cover-up coming off on her fingers. No. It was ridiculous.

"Just because he's bipolar . . ." Linton started to say but The Toad interrupted.

"Brown," he said, his eyes so narrow, she wondered if he could see out of them, "it was two years ago. And you've got no evidence linking him to the Avebury victims."

"Sir, we need to dig deeper and I think we'll find there is. Maybe he tried it on with them when he was visiting his mum. Maybe they turned him down and that's why he killed them."

The Toad sighed loudly. "This is all circumstantial," he said, but Linton saw he was buckling under the weight of Brown's argument.

"Look. He's the only suspect we've got. What's the harm in following him whilst we make some further enquiries into his past? A lot more harm could be done if we don't."

Hargreaves was silent for a few seconds. "It'll need authorisation," he said gruffly.

"Thank you, Sir," said Brown, visibly relaxing. "You won't regret this."

As they stood up to leave, there was a brisk knock at the door.

"Come in," barked The Toad. "Chop-chop."

The door flung open to reveal Hooper looking flushed and excited. Brown looked over at Linton and rolled his eyes. "Sir, we've got a man down in custody. He's turned himself in. He says he's the killer and he's holding Sam and Becki."

"Is he for real?" The Toad was already hauling himself up on to his feet, using his desk as leverage.

"He knows a lot about the cases."

"Maybe he can read," said Brown. "There's been quite a bit about it in the papers."

"There's something about him," said Hooper. "He seems genuine."

"Well, Brown," said The Toad, bright red and wheezing, "it looks like we won't need your surveillance team after all."

EIGHTEEN

It was coming up to five a.m. Linton was in bed, her eyes closed, half-asleep as Brown chattered excitedly in her left ear.

"Did I wake you?" he asked when she initially picked up her phone.

"It's the middle of the night," she mumbled. "Why would I be asleep?"

"I was right," he said triumphantly.

"About what?"

"I've just got off the phone from Hooper. Stupid twat. What the hell was Hargreaves doing listening to him?"

"What are you on about?"

"It was a false confession. The bloke that came in last night. He was just some nutter with nothing better to do."

"Hang on. You never said it was a false confession."

"I mean I was right about Talbot."

"Oh, for God's sake," she said, pulling herself up so she was leaning against the headboard. "Just because it was a false confession doesn't mean Talbot's guilty."

"We need to carry out that surveillance."

"Speak to Hargreaves in the morning. When it's *proper* morning."

"I mean you and me."

"Very funny. Can I go back to sleep now please?"

"I'm not joking. Even if Hargreaves says yes, it'll take time to get a surveillance team authorised and briefed. What if it's too late by then? What if we spooked Talbot? We don't know what he might do. We need to follow him and see where he goes."

"We can't do that. We don't know anything about surveillance. We're not trained."

"It's common sense. Anyway, I've got a book on it."

She laughed. "We'll be fine then."

"Hasn't anybody ever told you sarcasm is the lowest form of wit?"

"And this is coming from someone who thinks *Carry on Camping* is one of the funniest films of all time?"

"I said it was underrated."

"It's a ridiculous idea. For a start, he knows what we look like. What if he sees us?"

"He won't if we're careful. And even if he does, he won't know it's us. I'll drive my own car and we can disguise ourselves."

She snorted. "I'll get my fake moustache out and give it a dust-off. Do you want me to cut a hole in a newspaper?"

"Fuck off, Linton. I mean wear a hat and some glasses. Or what about the wig you wore to Wells' fancy dress party?"

"I went as Marge Simpson."

He paused. "Maybe a hat then."

"Hargreaves'll expect us in first thing. What are you going to tell him?"

"That we're following up another lead."

"What lead?"

"Someone from the crew who worked with Becki and Sam."

Linton groaned. "It's Saturday. He might not even be going anywhere."

"So? We'll sit in the car outside his flat. Bring a book with you."

"It's not his flat, he's . . ."

"I know," he said, interrupting her. "He's looking after his mate's place. I also know there's only one exit out the back of the building. He parks his car in the residents' parking area, so he can't go anywhere without us seeing him."

"How do you know he's not keeping the women at his flat?"

"He isn't."

"And you know that, how?"

"Keen spoke to the work experience girl. She didn't see anything suspicious."

"So? She may not have gone into every room."

"True," there was a short pause. "That's why I checked it out late last night."

"What?"

"I took a bottle of whisky round to apologise for coming across a bit tough when we interviewed him. Before I left I went to the loo. I stuck my head round both bedroom doors. There was no one there."

"Do you realise how unprofessional that is?" *And not telling your superior you went to bed with the prime suspect the other night isn't?* "Not to mention that, if we follow Talbot without authorisation, it'll mess up the court case. If it ever gets that far."

"Isn't it more important that we save Sam and Becki? Think about what we saw on the Tor. Think about Angel Kingsley's mum and what she's going through. We can stop that happening again."

It was emotional blackmail. They both knew it, but it didn't make it any less effective.

"OK," she sighed, "I'll come."

"Great. I'll pick you up in ten minutes."

"Why? He won't be going anywhere yet . . ."

She didn't bother finishing the sentence because Brown wouldn't have heard. He'd already put the phone down.

"For fuck's sake," she said out loud.

•••

Fifteen minutes later she opened her front door and laughed. Brown was dressed in a suit and wearing a cap and sunglasses. She hummed the soundtrack to Miami Vice.

"Fuck off," he said.

"It's November. It's pouring with rain. Don't you think the sunglasses are a bit much?"

"At least I've made the effort."

"You haven't seen my hat and wig yet."

He followed her through the hall and into the kitchen. "Bloody hell, Linton," he said. "How d'you keep it so clean? It's like a show home."

"Thanks," she said, even though she knew he was being critical. As if living in filth was what everyone should aspire to.

She picked up the blonde bob and brown beret she'd left on the table and put them on. "What do you think?"

It was Brown's turn to laugh. She realised it was the first time she'd heard the sound in days.

•••

"God, this wig is so itchy. It's driving me mad."

"Don't you ever stop moaning?" asked Brown.

That was unfair, Linton thought. She'd been a relative saint in terms of keeping her complaints to herself. And she had lots of them. Like the fact she had two tennis balls lodged in her throat, so she could barely swallow, and that, thanks to Brown, she'd had less than five hours sleep the night before, and that there was so much litter in the passenger footwell it was like sitting with her feet in a bin.

She glanced at her watch again. Eight thirty-five a.m. They'd been parked opposite the block of flats where Talbot was staying for three hours.

"It's not exactly edge-of-your-seat stuff, is it?" Linton said, as a lady in a duffel coat shuffled past, pushing her tartan shopping trolley.

"If we were doing it properly," said Brown indignantly, "we'd have at least three cars involved so we could mix it up. Change tail cars to stop him getting suspicious or use parallel routes."

"This bloody wig," she said, in response, pulling it off and scratching her head vigorously.

"Quick," hissed Brown. "Put it back on. It's him. He's going to pass us any second."

Linton shoved the wig back on her head.

"Pretend to talk to me," he said.

"What do mean?" she said, turning to look at him. "How do you pretend to talk? You're either talking or you're not talking."

"That was great! He didn't even see us." He started up the engine and she was suddenly hit by the ridiculousness of what they were doing. It was farcical. Two adults – highly trained police officers – looking like the arse-end of a fancy dress party, following a man whose only crimes involved impotence and large feet.

"Let's go." She swore she could hear the testosterone rattling in his voice.

"It's like an episode of *Law and Order*," she said. Brown didn't answer.

•••

Trailing Talbot wasn't as difficult as Brown had made out it would be. He followed behind, careful not to get too close. It helped that it was still raining heavily so visibility was poor.

At the Street roundabout, he took the M5 Bridgwater turning.

"That doesn't give much of a clue," said Linton. "If he's heading for the motorway he could be going anywhere."

They drove in silence, the atmosphere thick with concentration, as though every particle of air was compacted. After fifteen minutes, they reached the turning to the M5. Talbot took the route signposted, THE MIDLANDS, LONDON, BRISTOL.

"Bloody hell, Brown. We could be stuck in this car all day."

But after five minutes, as they approached Junction 22, Talbot started signalling.

"Weston-super-Mare," she said. "Maybe he just fancies a walk on the beach." Brown grunted.

As they reached the outskirts of the town, Talbot slowed down and signalled, pulling up outside a chemist. Brown parked on the other side of the road, and they watched him enter the shop.

"So what did you and Talbot talk about last night?" Linton asked, as casually as she could.

"You."

She felt her face heat up and her stomach constrict. "What?"

"I'm joking. We talked about rugby. I was only there for five minutes. Look. He's coming back out."

Talbot was carrying a large plastic bag containing a bulky packet. "It looks like nappies," Linton said.

Straining to see through the cheap plastic carrier, she could make out a word – *Confidence*. "Not nappies. Incontinence pads."

"If he's got them drugged and tied up, they're going to need something to go in."

They followed Talbot's car for another minute or so before he turned into a side road. Laburnum Avenue. Halfway along he slowed down, indicated left and came to a stop at the bottom of a steep driveway that led up to a pink bungalow. Brown had no choice but to carry on driving up the road, stopping when they had almost reached the end of the cul-de-sac.

"Can you see him?"

Linton took off her seatbelt and clambered round, looking over the top of her seat.

"He's got out of his car and he's walking up the driveway. There's an empty space just along from where he's parked."

"I'll give it a sec then I'll turn round."

A minute later, they were sitting just down from the bungalow Talbot had disappeared into. It was a tatty building in need of a coat of paint. Yellowing net curtains hung from the grubby windows. Brown rang the station and gave the address of the house so they could find out who was registered as living there. Whoever he spoke to said they'd call him back.

"What now?" Linton asked.

"I'm going round the back."

"He'll see you."

"I'll go into next door's garden and look over the wall. Those fir trees should hide me."

"What if there's someone in?"

"There's no car on the driveway. I'll risk it." Brown swung his long legs out of the car. "I'll be back in a minute. Get ready in case we need to make a quick getaway."

Linton watched him walk confidently up to the house next to the one Talbot had gone into and disappear up the side passageway. She pulled herself into the driver's seat and checked for the keys in the ignition. She had a sudden childish urge to drive off and abandon Brown there; make him get the bus home. It would serve him right for putting her through this.

She looked around. The road was deserted. After a couple of minutes, a plumber's van drove past followed by a portly woman with bright red cheeks cycling slowly by on a sit-up-and-beg style bike. "Cheeks like a cabbage-cutter," her Granny would've said.

Then she heard the sound of a car behind slowing down. She turned and watched with disbelief as it indicated and pulled into the driveway of the house Brown had disappeared alongside of.

"Shit," she muttered, under her breath.

Linton watched the driver get out. She was a starched headmistress of a woman with a steely expression and a perm to match. Clutching her shopping bags like she was lifting weights, she marched purposefully towards her front door.

Surely Brown must've heard the car. Linton watched the passageway anxiously, waiting for him to appear. A minute passed. *Where was he?*

She was considering ringing his mobile when she heard shouting followed by Brown careering down the driveway. He yanked open the passenger door and pulled himself in.

"Quick. She's coming."

As Linton started the engine, the front door opened and the woman she'd seen earlier came storming out.

"I've got a good mind to call the police, you pervert," she shrieked. "I've heard about your sort on the radio. You're one of those gerontophiles."

"Quick. Go! She saw me from her kitchen window," he panted. "Shit. I hope she didn't get the registration."

"She's probably the local Neighbourhood Watch Coordinator. So were Sam and Becki there?"

"Not that I could see. Unless one of them's aged sixty years in the last three days."

"What d'you mean?'

"There was an old woman in the kitchen sat at the table. I'd say she was in her eighties. His granny probably."

A few seconds later and a message from the station confirmed his suspicion. The house was under the name of Talbot. Mrs Veronica Talbot.

"Anyway, what's a gerontophile?" Linton asked, as they passed the chemist Talbot had stopped at earlier.

"The opposite of a paedophile. Someone who's into sex with old people."

She laughed, "She thought you were a Peeping Tom. Spying on her neighbour. That's hilarious."

"They could still be in there, you know," he said, stubbornly. "The old lady might not realise. Not if she's old and bedridden."

"But she was sat at the kitchen table, so she's obviously mobile. Anyway, don't you think Lady Thatcher's doppelganger might have noticed? "

"Not if he brought them here in the middle of the night."

"You're clutching at straws, Brown."

"Talking of clutches, pull over. I don't like other people driving my car."

They stopped next to the predictable row of housing estate shops, with a newsagent, a florist and a hairdressing salon. As Linton walked around the back of the car, her phone rang. It was Jasmine. Linton didn't say much as she listened. She could barely get the word "bye" out.

Hanging up, she looked at the sign above the hairdressers. Whoever owned it obviously had a sense of humour. Or pretty poor taste when you considered what it was next to. It was called Curl Up and Dye, which wasn't far off what she felt like doing. She shoved her mobile back into her handbag. As she got back into the car she could feel a fiery lump building in her chest.

"Are you all right?" asked Brown.

Later, when she looked back, she wasn't sure how it happened. Perhaps, it was the way he asked, or the fact he even bothered, but the next thing she knew she felt tears running down her face.

"What's happened?" he asked. He sounded genuinely concerned.

"It's my brother. It's a long story."

It took fifteen minutes. She started with Michael's diagnosis over ten years ago and ended with the phone call she'd just had telling her he'd been sectioned.

"They're going to put him on suicide watch. I hate the thought that he wants to die."

"The ultimate escape," said Brown quietly.

"I s'pose we all want to escape sometimes," she replied.

"Speak for yourself."

"What about all those women you sleep with? Isn't that just a way of escaping reality?"

"I like shagging, that's all. What's yours then? Cleaning?"

"Fuck off. I don't know. Reading."

"Crime novels? Hardly getting away from real life, is it?" He paused. "Look. I am sorry. About your brother. And for being such an arsehole. No wonder you got in a piss with me when I called Talbot a nut-job."

"We'd better get back," she said. "And, thanks. For listening, I mean."

Brown looked over and smiled as he started up the engine. "You don't seriously think I'm taking you back to work, do you?"

"What d'you mean?"

"Have you seen the state of you? I'll drop you off at home."

Neither of them spoke during the twenty minutes it took to reach her house. But it was a companionable, comfortable silence. A silence that nuzzled into Linton's weary body, leaving her feeling drowsy and warm.

She unclipped her seatbelt the second they stopped outside her front gate. "Thanks again," she said, quickly pulling open the door, anxious to get her blotchy, mascara-streaked face out of the car and inside before any neighbours spotted her. As she scurried towards her gate, Brown called after her.

"Hey, Linton. Wait."

She turned round.

"Don't forget this," he grinned, climbing out of his car and walking towards her. He stopped when he reached her and handed her the wig. "I know how much you enjoyed wearing it. And look. What I said before about Ben being a twat. I don't just mean for telling you. He was a twat for doing it to you in the first place."

For a second neither of them moved. Linton was certain something was about to happen – something that would alter everything. Brown tilted his head to one side, narrowing his eyes as though he was studying her. She felt dizzy suddenly. She stepped sideways to balance herself and as she did, she felt something beneath her right foot. Her brain registered something soft and squidgy beneath her shoe just before the stench hit her nostrils.

"For fuck's sake, Linton," said Brown, his expression instantly changing to disgust. "That's dog shit you've trodden in. Sorry. I'm going before I throw up."

With the slam of a door, he was back in his car and driving off.

•••

Was he mad?

That's what they were saying on *Crimewatch*. Not exactly saying it, but that's what the criminal psychologist was insinuating.

But surely if you were mad, you heard voices, like those people who claimed God or the Devil was talking to them, instructing them to do things.

The only voice he heard was his own and it sounded sane to him. When he killed Hannah and Angel it wasn't an act of madness. It was just something that happened.

A mistake, an accident. He was angry and frustrated and disappointed and, if he was honest, humiliated.

Afterwards, when he realised Hannah and Angel were dead, he

hadn't felt crazed. If anything, he was calm, sanely thinking things through. How he'd better get away quickly in case someone saw what he'd done.

And anyway, as he kept telling himself, it was *their* fault. They should've delivered what they'd promised.

"What do you think happened the night Sam Jenkins went missing?" Kirsty Young was now asking an amphibian-looking police officer, his eyes bulging as he sweated under the glaring lights of the *Crimewatch* studio. As she asked the question, the camera zoomed in on her face so it felt like she was asking *him*. He was the right person to ask after all. He was the one that knew.

He closed his eyes and thought back to that evening. It was like watching the events on his own little screen inside his head. He saw himself looking at his watch, illuminated by the streetlight he was waiting under. It was just after six. *Not long to go now*, he remembered thinking five minutes before the bus was due. It would pass him on its way down to the bus stop at the town hall and then Sam Jenkins would get off and walk back up towards the pub, and towards him. He knew it would all work out this time. It was meant to be. That's why everything was falling into place so easily.

He'd already planned how he'd entice her back to the flat. He would appeal to her vanity, her obvious need to talk about herself. He'd tell her his girlfriend was interested in a career in TV and ask if she'd mind popping in to talk to her for five minutes. Perhaps give her some pointers.

He was certain it would work. He'd had no trouble persuading Hannah or Sadie or Angel to go with him when he asked. Politeness tended to prevail. You were taught that being rude could get you into trouble, but in fact most of the time it was good manners that did. The fear of offending someone by saying no.

PART THREE

NOT LONG
TO GO NOW

NINETEEN

It was still raining. Claire could see Adam in the distance, slightly stooped, his hands in his pockets as he strode ahead. A man on a mission. She quickened her pace, finally breaking into a slow jog. As he reached the church, he took a sudden left turn into the alleyway that led to St John's car park.

Claire was running now. "Adam," she shouted. She turned the corner into the unlit passage, gasping with surprise as she smacked into him.

"Claire?"

She was breathing heavily, unused to exercise. "I saw you walking past the flat," she panted, her hands on her knees. "Where are you off to?"

"Nowhere. I mean, home," he added quickly.

"That's a funny route to take."

"I fancied a walk."

Claire pulled herself back into an upright position, still panting. "Why did you tell me Dave gave you a lift home from work the night Sam went missing?"

He paused. "Did I?"

Despite the gloom, Claire could see he looked wary, his eyes darting from left to right. "I bumped into Dave," she said. "He reckons he didn't."

"It must've been another night." He was fiddling with his gloves now, pulling at a loose thread he'd found on one of the fingers.

"But he hasn't even got his car yet." She paused, waiting for a response, but none came. "Why did you lie, Adam?" He didn't answer, just continued to pick at the dark, grey wool. The only sound in the alleyway was the rhythmical dripping from the bottom of a nearby drainpipe. "Adam? Are you going to tell me what's going on?"

He looked up, holding her gaze momentarily before taking a step towards her. She instinctively stepped back. "I'm sorry," he said.

•••

After the incident with the dog shit, Linton wanted to crawl into bed, pull the duvet over her head and stay there for the rest of the night. But she couldn't. It was their weekly girls' night out and she'd promised Gemma and Lisa she'd definitely make it tonight.

Once in the pub, it wasn't long before she was wishing she'd stayed home. While she was standing at the bar waiting to buy their second round, Simon Talbot sidled up to her. He waved, a flutter of fingers, the mocking action mirroring his sardonic expression.

It was that deed alone that banished all feelings of sympathy. She couldn't care less what was wrong with him. There was no excuse for the way he'd behaved.

"This is a coincidence," he said, his breath warm and beery against her face. "I was just thinking about you." She could tell from his slurred greeting his second round had been and gone some time ago.

She turned away hoping he'd take the hint and pretended to read a poster behind the bar about a cider promotion. For a split second she thought, *I must tell Ben*, then remembered the only thing she should be telling him was to fuck off.

"I didn't know if you'd be allowed to speak to me seeing as I'm a suspect in a murder enquiry."

Was he? She was so confused. Now he was here in the flesh, Brown's allegations seemed ridiculous. She didn't know *what* to think any more.

"It's because I'm bipolar, isn't it?"

"Don't be ridiculous," she said, trying to catch the barman's eye. "It's got nothing to do with that. And anyway, we've only interviewed you once. To eliminate you from our enquiries."

"So why were you following me today?"

"What are you on about?" She felt her stomach seize up.

"You and Brown."

"I was at the station all day. Writing up reports."

His eyes narrowed. "It looked like you. With a wig on."

She forced out a laugh. "A wig! What do you think this is? *Scooby Doo*?"

"I was beginning to think you might have it in for me," he said, visibly relaxing, "because I didn't ring you after the other night."

"I couldn't care less. It was a stupid, drunken mistake." She raised her hand, but the barman moved towards a burly bloke waving a twenty-pound note.

"Good. I'm glad you see it that way too." Talbot was smiling, obviously pleased to be off the hook. Linton looked at his smug, bland face and wondered how she'd found him attractive. Suddenly she didn't feel like letting him get away with it so easily.

"Do you think your girlfriend would mind?"

His smile vanished. "What?"

"She's a pharmacist, isn't she?"

"And?"

"I wonder if I should I mention our night together next time I'm in Boots."

"You go for it," he said, his eyes darkening. "And the next time your DI pops round with a bottle of whisky for a matey chat, I'll tell him what happened the other night."

She laughed. "That you couldn't get it up? Yeah, that'll impress him."

His face hardened. He raised his hand and for a split second Linton thought he was going to hit her, but he simply flicked his fringe out of his eyes. She waited for him to reciprocate with an insult, but instead he said coldly, "What I mean is, I doubt he'd like to know we spent the night together."

"Why?"

"You know what I'm getting at. You and Brown. You're an item, aren't you?"

She laughed and this time it was genuine. "You must be joking."

"Why did you call me by his name then?"

She swallowed. "When?"

"The other night. When I was up on top of you. You kept moaning his name in my ear."

•••

Adam was leaning forward, his forehead resting on his clasped hands. He'd been sitting like that for a while. Had anyone passed him, they might have thought he was praying.

"I've started drinking again," he finally said.

Claire expelled a long plume of cigarette smoke into the frigid air. "I thought as much. After I found out you'd lied about getting a lift with Dave."

They'd moved out of the alleyway and were sitting on the wooden bench in the shelter outside the church. By day it was home to dreadlocked men drinking cans of cheap lager and smoking skinny rollups.

"If you knew, then why did you ask?"

"I wanted to hear you say it."

Adam laughed, but it was a noise devoid of humour. "Come on, Claire. You of all people know what it's like."

She ignored the dig. "So that's why you didn't walk home through town the night Sam went missing. You went straight to the pub."

He nodded.

"That's where you're going now, isn't it? Why couldn't you tell me? I'm meant to be your buddy. We're supposed to help each other."

"You've got enough stuff going on. And I was worried about what you'd think of me."

"Why?"

"Can't you guess?" he said, moving towards her.

"Please, Adam. Not with Sam and everything. I can't think straight. Just go home. Promise me you won't go to the pub. I'll ring you tomorrow to make sure you're OK. And we've got a meeting in a couple of days. I wasn't going to go but I'll make sure I do." She stopped talking and took a deep breath. "Sorry. I'm babbling."

They were silent for a few moments, both of them looking at the ground.

"Is it because you still like Danny?" Adam asked finally.

"What? No!" she said, shaking her head adamantly. "I don't know what I saw in him."

"I do." He paused. "If only I fancied your sister."

It was a verbal slap, but she felt it physically.

"You wanker," she spat, pushing herself up from the bench.

Adam grabbed her arm, pulling her back down again. "You don't understand. I've been thinking about this. If I fancied Sam, then you'd like me."

"What are you talking about?"

"It would be like it was with Danny. It'd be a challenge. To get me to like you instead of her. So you can stop feeling inferior all the time."

"Fuck off, Adam."

"What I'm trying to say," he said, looking her in the eyes, "is that I'm not interested in her. It's you I want. She doesn't even come close. Doesn't that count for something?"

•••

A couple of hours later, Linton was lying fully clothed on top of her duvet replaying the earlier conversation she'd had in the pub. Not the one with Simon. She didn't want to think about that. But the one afterwards, when she told Gemma and Lisa about breaking down in front of Brown earlier in the day.

"We know you fancy him," Gemma had said, looking at Lisa for confirmation.

"I do not!" Linton didn't like the way Gemma said 'we'. It made her think that conversations had gone on which she wasn't privy to. "How many times do I have to tell you he's not my type? He thinks monogamy means shagging one woman at a time. I could never trust him and, anyway, apart from the job, we've got nothing in common."

"Kate," said Gemma, "you're ranting. And anyway do you really want to be of those pukey couples who wear matching coats and go mountain-bike riding together?"

"It's pointless even discussing it. I don't like him and he doesn't like me."

"Why were you testing him then?" said Emma, looking smugly all-knowing as though the Bacardi Breezers she was guzzling were some sort of divining potion.

"What do you mean?"

"Why did you tell him about Michael? You never tell anybody anything personal, except us, of course, but we don't count, and even then we have to drag it out of you." She paused, as though she was about to deliver a punchline. "I think you wanted to see how he'd react."

Was she testing him? Linton didn't think so. Though she did wonder what had possessed her to unburden herself like that. Maybe it was the wig, making her feel like she was someone else.

She picked up her book then threw it down again, knowing she didn't have the patience for it. There was nothing on TV. She'd watched every episode of *CSI*, some of them twice, and didn't fancy *100 Best TV Car*

Crashes or a documentary about a woman enduring extreme plastic surgery. She'd have a shower, she decided. A long, blistering hot one.

•••

Earlier there were carol singers, children; their voices thin and reedy and out of tune. She recognised *O little town of Bethlehem*, then heard his voice, saying good-naturedly, "It's a bit early for carols, isn't it?"

The children laughed and carried on. Behind the duct tape, she tried to make her own sounds.

He'd gone out, then come back later smelling of beer.

"It won't be long now," he said. "And when you get home you'll remember and then you'll understand."

He started to sing.

"Yet in thy dark streets shineth
The everlasting light
The hopes and fears of all my years
Are met in thee tonight."

Then there was silence. A door slammed. He was gone.

•••

It was as Linton was reaching for the shampoo that it struck her. The thing that had been bothering her ever since she and Brown had searched Becki's hotel room.

She quickly squeezed a dollop into her hand, rubbing it vigorously into her hair, then tipped her head back to rinse it. She wanted to get out and call Brown.

With the last of the suds rinsed away, she opened her eyes to see the handle on the bathroom door wobbling. She put it down to a lorry thundering past the front of the house, causing a vibration. That was the thing with these old houses: they never seemed to be still. Walls cracked, floorboards creaked. She thought for a second how much she'd freak out if the handle started to turn.

And then it did.

A second later, the bathroom door was pushed wide open. She screamed a high-pitched scream as she found herself staring at an all too familiar face.

TWENTY

"How the hell did you get in?" Linton shrieked, over the pounding water. She crossed one arm over her chest and used her other in a feeble attempt to cover her pubic area. He raised his eyebrows and grinned, waving a silver key at her.

Bastard. He must've hung on to a spare.

"Ben!" she spluttered. "You nearly gave me a heart attack. Pass me the towel."

"Oh, come on," he said, his words coming out thick and slurred. "It's not like I haven't seen it all before."

He pulled the towel off the rail and handed it to her. She snatched at it, wrapping the warm fabric around her as quickly as she could and then hurriedly turned off the water. The pounding was replaced with the sound of large droplets hitting the enamel followed by a gentle gurgle as the remaining water escaped down the plughole. The subsequent silence made her feel as self-conscious as her nakedness had seconds before. She clambered out of the bath.

"You're drunk."

"You're gorgeous."

"Fuck off, Ben. What do you want?"

She moved to push past him and he reached out to touch her shoulder.

"I said, fuck off." She watched him recoil, the playful twinkle in his eyes quickly replaced by tearful hurt.

She marched into their, *her,* bedroom and grabbed the dressing gown from the back of the door, pulling it on and belting it tightly. He was close behind, like a dejected dog kicked in his side but determined to follow his master, ever faithful. *Faithful.* Yeah, right. That was a bloody joke. She sat on the bed and sighed.

"What do you want, Ben?"

"You."

She shook her head. "Why didn't you phone?"

"I did. You didn't answer," he said, collapsing onto the bed next to her. "I've been on the doorstep ringing you for the last ten minutes." He stumbled over his words; made answer sound like 'ansher'. "I knew you were in 'cause the lights were on."

"You scared the shit out of me."

"I couldn't resist. Knowing you were in there with nothing on."

"Is that what happened in Amsterdam?"

He sighed, "Here we go again."

"What did you expect? That I'd forgive and forget?"

"I thought you might've missed me."

"I miss the other Ben. The one I could trust."

"For God's sake, Kate," he shouted suddenly, springing off the bed. "It was a stupid drunken mistake. I know it's a crap excuse, but I was off my head. And at least I was honest with you."

"Aren't I lucky? That, when my boyfriend decides to act like a complete dickhead, at least he has the decency to tell me."

Ben collapsed back on the bed and put his face in his hands. "The thing with you is," he said, sounding choked, "you've got such high expectations of everyone. Why can't you give people a break sometimes?"

"I am giving you a break. A permanent one."

She realised tears were running down his face. He looked so needy, so vulnerable. Seeing him on their bed reminded her of why she'd fallen for him. She thought of those first few weeks together, going to work after being up all night. Everyone telling her how well she looked despite only grabbing snatches of sleep in between grabbing Ben. She was about to reach out and touch him when an image of Brown flashed in her head. She needed to ring him, to tell him about the revelation she'd had in the shower. It was important.

"I've got to make a phone call," she said gruffly.

"What, now?" He looked up. His eyes were red-raw and lopsided. She realised just how drunk he was.

"It's work. I'll go downstairs, it's confidential."

He opened his mouth as if to argue, but must've seen from her face that there wasn't any point.

"Fine," he said tersely. "I'll wait."

Linton went into the kitchen to make the call. Brown picked up straightaway.

"What's up?" he asked.

"Why's it so noisy?"

"My flatmate's got his mates round. Hang on a sec. I'll go into my bedroom." The sound of raucous laughter gradually faded away until all she could hear was Brown's breathing. "That's better."

"It's about Becki. I've thought of something."

She told him as quickly as she could, conscious of Ben upstairs on her bed.

"What do you think?" she asked, when she'd finished.

"We'll go to The Toad with it in the morning."

"OK." She paused. "By the way," she said reluctantly, "I saw Talbot in the pub tonight."

"And?"

"He reckons he saw us following him."

"Shit."

"I told him he'd got it wrong. I think he believed me."

He was silent for a moment, then said quietly, "You were right."

"About what?"

"Talbot. We've got no evidence. Nothing. I've been clutching at straws. Why would he abduct two women because they pissed him off a couple of years ago."

"Back to the drawing board then."

He cleared his throat. "Kate?"

"Yeah?"

There was a long pause. "I'll see you tomorrow." It was only after he put the phone down she realised it was the first time he'd ever called her by her Christian name.

•••

Linton could recall the evening perfectly.

Ben's flight got into Bristol at four p.m. He'd phoned her from Amsterdam to say not to bother picking him up, he could get a lift with one of the other stags. He was on his way to her mum's flat when he rang. Jasmine had let slip that Ben would be in the city for the weekend and their mum had a birthday present for Harry. Would Ben mind collecting it from her?

Linton decided she'd drive to the airport anyway and surprise him. He was travelling with seven other blokes so she hadn't expected him to rush over and whisk her off her feet. Even so, she thought, as he shuffled through arrivals looking pale and hung-over, he could've acted more pleased to see her.

"So you saw her then?" she asked, as they walked to the car.

"Who?" he replied, sounding oddly panicked.

She turned and looked at him quizzically. "Mum."

He nodded. "Her flat's just around the corner from the hotel."

"And what about Eva?" she asked scornfully. "Was she there?" He nodded again and she shuddered at the thought of her mum's girlfriend. 'The lipstick lesbian', as Ben called her. Young, blonde, big-breasted. It was embarrassing.

She'd met Linton's mum while she was staying with an artist friend in Glastonbury. Apparently they'd just clicked. Linton had had to endure a toe-curling monologue from her mum about how Eva had awakened her sexuality, that, until they met and fell in love, she'd been living a lie. Within the month, her mum had put her house up for rent and moved to Amsterdam.

"I can't get my head round it," she'd said to Ben. "What does Eva see in her?"

"Your mum's a good-looking woman. And perhaps she liked the challenge of an older, straight woman. Mind you," he'd conceded. "I can't see it lasting. Eva doesn't strike me as the monogamous type. I give it three months."

So far it had been six and there was no sign of it ending.

As soon as they got home, Ben went upstairs to have a shower. Linton undressed to her underwear and lay on the bed waiting for him. When he finally emerged from the bathroom with a towel wrapped round his waist, instead of flinging it to the floor like he normally would, he stood staring at her, his expression a mix of anguish and terror. She could see tears forming in the corner of his eyes.

"What's wrong?" she asked anxiously, pulling herself up so she was kneeling on the bed.

"I'm so sorry, Kate," he said, looking down at the bedroom carpet. "I've fucked up."

Linton could feel her heart speeding up, her stomach turn to mush. *Was life really that predictable? Amsterdam. A stag do. The remorseful apology.*

"I don't believe it," she said. "You slept with a prostitute, didn't you?" She leant over and grabbed at the t-shirt she'd discarded on the floor.

To her relief, Ben looked genuinely shocked. "What? No. You've got it all wrong." He paused and took in a breath, as though psyching himself up for what he had to say next. "You know I love you, Kate. And that I'd never do anything to intentionally hurt you . . ."

"Just cut the crap, Ben," she said, raising her arms to pull her top on, noticing as she did that her hands were shaking. "Tell me what you've done."

He took another deep breath. "You know I said I saw Eva."

"And?" she prompted.

"She offered to come out with us. Show us the real Amsterdam."

She had a vision of Eva and her mum, their arms draped around one another. She felt nauseous. "So it was that cow that took you to a prostitute."

"Kate," he said grabbing at his hair, clearly frustrated, "will you stop going on about bloody prostitutes?"

"What then? She took you to a sex club. You had a lap dance. Just tell me."

"I had sex with her," he said quickly.

Linton jerked backwards involuntarily, as if she'd been slapped. "Who?" she said, knowing precisely but unable to process it.

"Eva," he replied, flinching as he said her name. "But I was pissed and stoned," he added hastily. "I didn't know what I was doing. I'm so sorry, Kate. Please forgive me."

"You had sex with Eva," she shrieked, over the top of him. "But she's my mum's girlfriend. She's gay." She let out a strangled laugh as the reality hit her. "Oh my God. I bet you're the group hero, aren't you? Persuading a lesbian to shag you."

"I think she's bisexual," said Ben quietly.

"You don't fucking say," she screamed. "So where did you do it? Mum's flat? In her bed? Did she watch as well?"

Ben winced. "The hotel," he paused, chewing on his lip. "In the lift," he said finally. "It sounds worse than it is. It was over within minutes. It meant nothing . . ." he trailed off as Linton let out another abrupt laugh. She realised with an odd sense of satisfaction that she sounded deranged.

"You shagged a lesbian in a lift," she hissed, waving her finger at him demonically. "No hang on. Let's be completely accurate," she paused then said, pronouncing every syllable for effect, "you shagged your girlfriend's mum's lesbian lover in a hotel lift in Amsterdam. For God's sake, Ben! It's like an episode of Jeremy Kyle. You complete arsehole!"

Screaming the last word at him, she picked up the alarm clock from her bedside table and threw it at his head, watching with delight as it ricocheted off his head with a loud crack and landed on the carpet.

Up until then she'd agreed, in public, with the declaration that 'men are all the same'. She didn't really think it, but no one wanted to hear that she, alone, had a bloke who wasn't interested in other women, a bloke who, no matter what, would be faithful. It would be smug. Now she thanked God she'd never uttered the words, 'Ben's not like that', because he obviously bloody was.

By the time Linton came back upstairs, Ben was asleep, face-down on the bed, snoring loudly, his feet dangling over the edge.

She went into the spare room and tried to sleep.

TWENTY-ONE

Linton left the house early without bothering to wake Ben. Her sore throat had come back with a vengeance, so she went on a quick detour to buy some more painkillers. By the time she arrived at work, Brown was already there.

"Did you speak to The Toad?" she asked, popping a couple of the tablets from their foil wrapper into her hand. "About what I thought of last night?"

"He said he'll see us when you get in. He's on the phone at the moment."

"Not any more," she said, as Hargreaves flung his door open.

"Brown. Linton," he shouted. "In here."

Linton shoved the tablets into her mouth, swallowed them dry, which wasn't easy with her tonsils in their current state, and followed Brown into Hargreaves' office.

"Linton. I hear you've got something you want to tell."

She nodded and cleared her throat. "I was in the shower, washing my hair when it struck me." She stopped. Now she was sitting opposite The Toad, his rheumy eyes trained on her, last night's eureka moment seemed ridiculous.

"Come on. Chop-chop."

"There wasn't any shampoo or conditioner in Becki's bathroom. Only the hotel stuff."

"And?" prompted the Toad with frown when she didn't continue.

"Well, don't you think that's odd?" she finished feebly.

"Linton. I hope this is going somewhere because frankly I've got more important things to worry about than what Becki Harvey uses to wash her hair."

"The thing is she loves it. She's always flicking it about or running her hands through it. She's described it as her best feature. There's no way she'd wash it in any old rubbish."

"Linton . . ." he growled.

"Where was her *own* shampoo and conditioner?" she said, hurriedly. "She wouldn't have used the hotel stuff. It's crap. You might as well use washing up liquid. Why wasn't it in the room when she went missing?"

"She probably forgot to bring it with her," Hargreaves said frostily. "Is there anything . . ."

"But it's not just that," she interrupted. "There was no make-up. No cleanser. No moisturiser. No hairspray, gel, deodorant, perfume. Nothing."

"I expect she took it out in her handbag. Now unless . . ."

"But she's not the type of person to have a couple of lipsticks and some mascara," Linton interrupted again. "So where was it all?"

"And her knickers," said Brown, unexpectedly. Linton and Hargreaves turned their heads to stare at him. "I've just thought about it. The only knickers we found were the clean ones in her drawer."

"So?"

"She'd obviously had a shower because there were damp towels on the floor."

"And?" The Toad's tone was growing more impatient.

Brown turned to Linton. "Do you put on clean underwear after you've had a shower?"

"Of course."

"So where was her dirty stuff?"

"Maybe she's not as hygienic as the women you know."

"Or perhaps she didn't want anyone finding them," he said, ignoring her sarcasm. "It's as if she knew someone would be in there looking through her stuff."

"Or that she wouldn't be coming back for her stuff," Linton said, warming to the theory. "She wouldn't mind losing the things we found in her room. That cheap holdall, a couple of tops from high street shops."

"What exactly are you suggesting?" Hargreaves sounded like his patience had finally run out.

"What if Becki isn't really missing?" said Brown.

"Of course she's bloody missing," yelled The Toad. "No one's seen or heard from her." He grabbed at a pile of papers and pulled them towards him, his other hand already reaching for the phone. "Go on. Out. Both of you. Stop wasting my time and come back when you've got something worth sharing."

A couple of minutes later, it looked like they might. Hooper came off his phone looking like he was about to wet himself.

"Here we go," said Brown. "What's wonder boy come up with now?"

"That was the Contact Centre," the skinny trainee called out, hurrying over to their desks. "A young woman saw Becki Harvey getting into a car in St John's car park just after seven o'clock on the night she went missing."

Linton remembered what Jenny, the receptionist, had said, that it was odd how Becki had asked where the nearest car park was. She exchanged a knowing glance with Brown.

"Voluntarily?" he asked.

"According to the witness," said Hooper breathlessly, bouncing from one foot to the other, "Becki got into the passenger seat herself. The driver was in the car and didn't get out. It was dark but she could see he was male and young. Probably in his early twenties. Good looking, apparently. She couldn't be any more certain than that. Anyway, she saw Becki lean over and kiss the man on his lips and then they drove away."

"Any description of the car?" asked Brown. "Did she manage to get a registration number?'

"She said it was small, possibly a Ford Ka or a Volkswagen. It was dark, so she couldn't be sure of the colour, but she thinks it was either blue or green. The only other thing she remembers is a UCL sticker. She noticed it because it's one of the universities she's thinking of applying to."

"And she's certain it was Becki?" Linton asked.

"Definitely. She knew it was her straight away. She heard her laughing when she opened the car door and she said she sounded like she did on the telly."

"Why she didn't report it sooner?"

"She was ringing from Turkey. She's on holiday. The first she heard about Becki's disappearance was when she saw it in one of the English papers."

Brown looked thoughtful. "And she's sure about the date and time?"

"Her flight was that evening. She said she remembered looking at the church clock and thinking she only had a couple of hours to go until she needed to leave for the airport."

"Maybe it was the mystery man she was having an affair with?" Linton suggested. "Perhaps he arranged to pick her up in the car park in the hope no one would see him?"

Brown shook his head impatiently. "The witness said the man was in his early twenties. That doesn't sound like a description of a married man with four children."

"Let's get the details of the car out to the media," said Brown, "and see if it rings a bell with anyone else."

•••

UCL. If anything was ringing a bell, the university's initials were, thought Linton as she watched Hooper loping back to his desk.

Of course.

It was where Vine, the Druid author, had given his talk the weekend Angel was murdered. Apart from Talbot, he was the only person they'd spoken to who was a credible suspect. It was a pity, she thought, that he had a night in a London hotel as an alibi.

Didn't he?

Oh shit, she thought. She'd forgotten to chase it up. It was the morning after the night she spent with Simon and she'd had that massive hangover.

Fingers shaking, she typed Vine's name into the database and searched through the notes from his interview. It took her less than a minute to find the name of the hotel he said he'd stayed in. The Comfort Inn, Paddington.

She rang 118118 and asked to be put straight through.

"GoodmorningComfortHotelTinaEvansspeakinghowcanIhelpyou?" recited the receptionist, only pausing for breath when she reached the end of her singsong salutation.

Linton asked her question and felt like crying when she heard the answer.

She put the phone down and looked over at Brown. He was typing, listening to his iPod, in a world of his own. A world she was going to have to disturb.

"Brown?" There was no answer. "Brown!"

"What?" he shouted, yanking the headphone piece out of his left ear. Linton felt sick. He was going to kill her.

"Do you remember Mr Vine said he was in London the night Angel was killed?"

"Yeah."

"Well, you know I had that hangover?" She stopped.

Brown had pulled the other earpiece out and was staring at her. His expression was neutral, but she knew in a couple of seconds his eyes would narrow and his face harden.

"I didn't check it out with the hotel," she said quickly. "I'm sorry." She winced, curling up in anticipation of the verbal blow she knew was about to hit her.

"Oh, for fuck's sake Linton!" he shouted, slamming his fist down on his desk. "Simple, fucking police procedures. Five minutes. That's all it would've taken you . . ."

"I phoned them just now," she said interrupting him, "but you're not going to believe this." He glared at her. "They've got a new computer system. It's playing up and they can't get into it at the moment, so they don't know if he stayed there or not."

"For fuck's sake."

"But it's unlikely he'd have lied," she said, trying to reassure herself. "Not when he knows we can check it out so easily."

"Unless that's *why* he lied. Because it was so fucking easy, he didn't think we'd bother."

It made Linton cringe to hear her fears aloud. It was bloody obvious. They'd even joked about it. What was it they'd said? A mad anthropologist. He knew Angel, at least he knew her mum. He probably knew Sam as well.

Of course.

The exhibition in Bristol. It was his sort of thing. That's how he'd have known Sam was coming back to Glastonbury that night. And he might've met the Avebury women when he was researching his book.

But hang on.

The man in the car was young. It couldn't have been him. Unless the witness got it wrong. Maybe she didn't see him, but assumed he was younger because of the university sticker.

This was all her fault. She'd have to resign. But that was the least of her worries. What was far worse was if he murdered Sam and Becki she'd have the death of those girls on her conscience.

Perhaps she could ring him and do a deal: "Hi. It's the police officer who came to your house. Brown hair, green eyes, with breath that smelt of vomit. I was wondering if you could release Sam and Becki and take me hostage instead. You'd have to strangle me? That's fine. I'm shit at my job, my ex-boyfriend prefers lesbians and my brother keeps trying to kill himself. And my throat is bloody killing me anyway, so you might as well finish the job off."

She placed her hands around her swollen neck, imagining him strangling her. She didn't wearing a necklace like Angel so he'd have to do it manually.

Angel's necklace.

She pictured the pretty green gemstone. It was the same size as the one in Vine's ring, the one that glowed in the firelight. What was it he'd said? Something about Druids using gemstones to predict the future.

Was there a connection? Had Vine given Angel the pendant? But no, the stone was different. His was red. A garnet. Unless . . .

"Linton?" She looked up. It was Hooper. "Have you got a minute?"

Fuck off. I'm having a nervous breakdown.

"Not really," she snapped. "What is it?"

"There's a woman in reception who wants to talk to you. She reckons some bloke tried to get her to go up the Tor."

"When?"

"About a month ago."

"What's her name?"

"Gail Chapman."

The receptionist who worked in The Pendragon. She remembered what Jenny Heller said about her: "I wouldn't believe anything that comes out of her mouth. She's one of these who has to be the centre of attention." She was just trying to muscle in on the action.

Tell her to fuck off, she wanted to scream.

"Look," she said as calmly as possible, "Can you take a statement from her? I'm right in the middle of something."

Hooper shrugged, "Whatever you say."

Linton rang the hotel back a few minutes later. The computer system still wasn't working and it was going to be a couple of hours before it was up and running. Brown had stuck his headphones back in, but every now and then he looked over at her and shook his head.

Right. That's it, she thought. There was no way she was going to sit there sweating for two hours. She'd go mad.

"I'm going out for a minute," she said, to no one in particular.

•••

Linton pulled out of the station car park without a destination in mind. In the end, she found herself driving up the High Street. She couldn't stop thinking about Vine. Had he lied about modern-day Druids not carrying out sacrificial killings?

Every shop she drove past seemed to exist to torture her, to remind her of Vine. A Helping Hand, with his book displayed in the window; The Witch and Wand with a large, handwritten sign advertising Druid tea; All That Glitters, the gem shop that no doubt sold garnets like the one on his finger. *"Did garnets come in green?* she wondered."

Bugger it. She had nothing better to do for the next hour. She might as well go into All That Glitters and find out.

There was nowhere to stop on the High Street, so she pulled into St John's car park, managing to find sixty pence for the machine after scrabbling through the bottom of her handbag. She ran up the High Street, swearing under her breath at the rain, at the slippery pavement, at anyone who happened to get in her way. She had to resist the urge to shout in people's faces and push them into the road.

By the time she reached the shop, she was panting. Its door was covered with posters, advertising the plethora of events available to Glastonbury residents: Yoga days, Reiki workshops, Buddhist mediation, a UFO conference organised by someone called Star Child. The first thing that hit her as she pushed it open was the heavy scent of patchouli oil. With it came the memory of Angel, her face bluish-grey, her eyes bulging.

The man behind the counter looked over at Linton and smiled. Even in her overwrought state, she could see how good-looking he was, with his long dark hair pulled back into a ponytail and tawny owl eyes.

"Can I help?" he asked softly.

"Please," she gasped, desperately trying to get her breath back. "It's a question actually."

He smiled reassuringly. "Ask away."

"Is there such a thing as a green garnet?"

He came out from behind the counter and walked over to a wooden table covered in small wicker baskets. He put his hand into one and pulled out a jade gemstone.

"A green garnet," he said, holding it out to her. "They come in almost every colour, including green."

She felt sick.

"Have you sold one in the last couple of weeks? In a pendant?"

He shook his head, then tipped it to one side and said, "I don't mean to pry, but are you OK? You don't look very well."

Linton was so taken aback by his gentle enquiry she said, "I feel terrible. I've got tonsillitis."

"I've got something that will help," he said, reaching into one of the other baskets. He picked out a small blue gemstone and held it up to the light. "Lapis lazuli. Carry one in your pocket and your throat will clear up in no time."

"That's very kind," she said, hoping she sounded as though she believed him. "How much do I owe you?"

He smiled warmly and once again she was struck by his good looks. Take away the hippy top and the long hair and he was gorgeous. "Have it for nothing," he said. "It's my pleasure."

•••

Half an hour later and Linton was back at her desk absentmindedly rolling the little piece of smooth blue stone between her thumb and forefinger. Luckily Brown was in a meeting, so she didn't have to suffer any more of his head-shaking and eye-rolling.

The more she thought about it, the more convinced she was it was Vine. All she needed now was the phone call from the Comfort Hotel to confirm her fears.

Eventually GoodmorningComfortHotelTinaEvansspeakinghow-canIhelpyou rang back.

"DS Linton," she said, wincing as she waited for the receptionist to tell her there was no record of Vine staying in the hotel.

"Hiya," Tina trilled. "We're up and running now."

"And?" Linton asked, holding her breath.

"I can confirm that Mr Vine stayed here that night and didn't leave until the following morning. In fact, I've got a copy of his bill and it shows he was in the hotel bar from ten-thirty in the evening until midnight."

Linton's stomach did a little flip. "Are you absolutely sure?"

"Positive. He settled his bill the following morning at eight twenty-five a.m. It's all recorded here."

"And it was definitely him?"

"I've got his car registration and it matches the one you gave me. His car was in the hotel car park all night." Tina was beginning to sound irritated. What with the computer system being down all morning and a mad policewoman hyperventilating down the phone, it wasn't surprising.

"That's great, Tina. Thank you so much."

Linton couldn't help it. As she put the phone down, she let out a loud whoop. How had she got so carried away? That whole thing with the gemstones. What was she thinking?

"Have you won the lottery?" Hooper called out across the room.

"Something like that. By the way," she said, remembering their earlier conversation, "What did Gail Chapman have to say?"

He shrugged. "When I told her you were busy, she got in a right snot and stormed off."

"I don't think she's much of a fan of the police," said Linton.

"If you ask me, she was making it up. She's my sister's mate and by all accounts she's full of shit."

"I'll ring her anyway," said Linton. She didn't want to make any *more* mistakes.

Gail wasn't on duty at The Pendragon. Linton tracked down her home number but there was no answer. She left a message apologising for earlier and asked Gail to ring her as soon as possible.

TWENTY-TWO

Enough was enough, Linton decided when her bedside alarm clock went off the following morning. It didn't wake her because she wasn't asleep. She'd spent the night balanced between consciousness and unconsciousness, half-dreaming, but aware of every noise. Each time she felt the scales tip towards sleep, she made the mistake of swallowing and the razor blades in her throat jolted her awake.

"It's repressed emotion," Gemma had said when she'd phoned the night before. "There's something you need to say to someone and it's literally got stuck in your throat."

Linton had laughed.

"Honestly," insisted Gemma, who balanced her diet of celebrity magazines with self-help books and popular psychology. "I've been reading why people get certain ailments. A sore throat means you're not saying what you think."

"I'll tell you what I think. It's a load of hippy shit. Ooh, hang on a minute, now I've said it, I can feel my sore throat miraculously clearing up."

"Very funny," Gemma had replied huffily.

It was no good. Linton was going to have to make an appointment at the doctor's. She would call into the surgery on her way to work.

•••

The doors to the surgery had only been open for a minute, but there were already seven people waiting in the queue.

Linton joined the end of it, smiling to herself as she heard the man at the front announcing to the unimpressed receptionist that his name was Starchild. *Only in Glastonbury*, she thought. His voice sounded familiar and when she looked more closely at his profile, she realised it was the good-looking man from the gem shop. A name like that was probably a basic requirement to work there.

"Bloody druggies," said the man in front of her. "After his methadone, I expect."

It was ten minutes before Linton made it to the front of the queue. "Sorry," announced the receptionist triumphantly. "All of our appointments have gone for the day."

"But you only opened a few minutes ago," said Linton, in disbelief.

"A percentage of our appointment slots are pre-booked. Plus, we've been taking appointments over the phone since the lines opened at half-past eight."

Linton took a deep breath. "OK then. I'll make one for tomorrow please," she said, already dreading the uncomfortable night ahead.

"Sorry," relied the receptionist, smugly. "You'll have to ring first thing. All of our pre-bookable appointment slots have gone, so we can only make same-day appointments."

Linton remembered what Gemma had said, about the importance of telling people what you thought. She looked at the woman, puffed up and ready for a fight and decided she'd rather suffer a sore throat than give her the pleasure.

•••

Linton had been planning to ring Gail Chapman as soon as she got into work. She hadn't rung back and it was niggling at her. But with The Pendragon only a few doors away from the doctor's surgery, it made sense to go and speak to her in person.

She'd almost reached the entrance when she saw something that made her stop dead in her tracks.

It was Simon Talbot, running up the steps into the building.

He was the last person she wanted to see. She decided she'd ring Gail when she got into work after all.

"She's certainly popular today," said Jenny Heller an hour later when Linton finally got a chance to phone.

"How d'you mean?"

"That bloke from the local paper was in again this morning wanting to talk to her. Simon what's-his-name. But, like I told him, she's got the day off today."

"Did he say why he wanted to see her?"

"I didn't ask. I don't like the bloke. He gives me the creeps, if I'm honest, and I'm normally a good judge of character."

If only I'd been, thought Linton. "Has Gail ever mentioned that a man tried to get her to go up the Tor last month?" she asked.

Jenny laughed. "She's not on with that again, is she? She's a bloody liar. She never mentioned it 'til Becki Harvey went missing."

"You think she's making it up?"

"Of course she is! It's because she worships Becki. It's her way of getting in on the action."

"What did you mean when you said 'again'?" Linton asked, picking up on something Jenny had said a moment ago.

"Sorry, lovey?"

"You said that Simon Talbot was in to see her *again.*"

"He's been hanging around here all week. Like a bad smell. That's what I mean about him giving me the creeps."

Before Jenny rang off, she gave Linton a mobile number for Gail. Linton tried it immediately, but the phone was switched off. She rang her home number a couple of times, but no one picked up.

•••

"What are you going to do when this is all over?" asked Brown. He'd followed Linton into the staff kitchen and was sitting on the Formica table, his legs dangling down, watching her swill their mugs out in the sink.

She looked across at him suspiciously. "What are you on about?"

"You know, have you got any plans to go anywhere to celebrate?"

"Like where?"

"The pub, the club."

"Since when do I go clubbing? Why are you asking?"

She knew why. He was creeping. Feeling bad about shouting at her yesterday when she thought she'd messed up over Vine's alibi.

"It's called making conversation."

"You don't normally care what I get up to," she said, reaching down to get a carton of milk out of the fridge.

"Aren't you going to ask me?" said Brown.

"Ask you what?"

"What I'm going to do when this is all over?"

Linton put the carton of milk down on the worktop and turned to face him. "What is this all about?"

He glanced over his shoulder, checking to see if anyone was standing in the open doorway, then said, "You're meant to ask me what I'm going to do when this is all over," he said, hurriedly. "Then I say I'm not going to the club because there's no point. Then you ask why not, and I say it's because I'm not into chasing women any more."

"Brown," said Linton, "what are you on about?"

He ignored her interruption. "Then you say, 'Why aren't you?' and then I say, 'So I can get this off my chest once and for all. It's been driving me mental.'" He paused. "Sorry. Bad choice of word."

Linton felt her heart thumping in her chest, like an out-of-kilter washing machine and the familiar hot redness creeping up her neck, curling its way onto her jaw line. This wasn't about him trying to make it up to her for losing his temper. This was about something else. Something she'd thought about as an abstract, too frightened to put it into words in case she jinxed it. She swallowed the lump that had lodged itself in her already swollen throat.

"OK then," she said. Her voice quivered as she spoke. "Why aren't you chasing women any more?"

He uncrossed his legs and leant towards her, so the tops of their heads were almost touching. She licked her lips involuntarily.

"It's because of Sam Jenkins."

Linton pulled back, folding her arms simultaneously. "What do you mean?"

"I slept with her."

She felt the words, rather than heard them, each syllable stabbing at her.

"You said you didn't!" Her mouth felt dry and tacky. "Why did you lie?"

"Because I knew you'd all take the piss. I'm getting fed up with all the Casanova jokes."

"I thought you loved it. All the lads jealous of you, a different woman every night."

"This isn't about what everyone else thinks. It's about me. When Sam went missing, it got me thinking about how I've treated women, in the past. I've slept with so many they're turning up in our murder cases. Can you imagine how you'd feel if you'd slept with one of the victims?"

"Firstly, that would make me a lesbian," she said cringing as an image of Eva sprang to mind, "and, secondly, aren't you jumping ahead of yourself? We don't even know if she *is* a victim."

"It's only a matter of time."

"We might still find her."

"And what if we don't? And I treated her like shit. She didn't deserve it." He stopped, then said quietly, "That's why I wanted it to be Talbot. It would've been easy."

"And you're still certain it isn't," she said, remembering what Jenny Heller had said earlier. About how she didn't trust him.

"I had a ridiculous theory and I was twisting the facts to suit it." He looked as though he was about to say something else but stopped.

"There's more, isn't there?" said Linton. It was a statement rather than a question.

He looked down at the floor and licked his lips nervously. The action reminded her of Talbot.

"Sam was under age," he said quietly.

She looked at him with disgust. "Fucking hell, Brown." *No wonder he'd got so agitated when she'd made that comment about Talbot's work experience girl.*

"I didn't know," he said hastily. "She was in the pub and she looked eighteen."

"So what happened? Did she get up in the morning and put her school uniform on?"

"Don't be stupid. A couple of months later I went to St Dunstan's to do a drugs talk to Year Eleven and she was in the audience. I nearly shit myself."

"Year Eleven? She could've been sixteen."

He shook his head. "I remember she told me she was a Leo. I slept with her at Christmas. She was definitely fifteen."

"Was that why you were on Facebook? To see if she'd mentioned you?"

"I knew it was unlikely. It was years ago, but I wanted to check no one else knew. That would be great, wouldn't it? Ending up in the Sex Offender Register."

"Why are you telling *me* this?"

"It's been driving me nuts. I wanted to get it off my chest." He paused. "Do you think I'm a complete tosser?"

"Honestly?" she said, trying to keep her tone light. "Yes."

Brown laughed. "You see, I knew you'd understand. I feel better already."

She turned back to finish making the tea, her hand shaking as she spooned sugar into the *World's Best Golfer* mug that Brown was using. She passed him his drink before sitting down at the table with her own.

"Aren't you coming back through?" he asked.

She shook her head. "I'm going to sit here for a while. My throat's killing me. Besides," she said, reaching for the office copy of the local paper, "I haven't had a chance to read this yet."

Brown stood in the doorway, not moving.

"Was there something else?" she asked, keeping her eyes firmly on the paper.

He paused for a few seconds. "No," he said finally, and walked out taking his steaming mug of tea with him.

•••

ONE WEEK EARLIER

"Don't call me that," he snapped, stepping off the pavement to overtake an old man and his guide dog.

"Sorry," Angel replied. "It's just that . . ."

He interrupted before she could finish her apology. "Do you think it'll happen again tonight?" It was the second time he'd asked since they'd left his flat.

"Don't get your hopes up," she said. "I was off my head last time."

They walked in silence, leaving the blind man and his dog behind. Angel wished she had something to tie her hair back to stop it flapping in her eyes. Swiping it away with her hand, she smelt the musky-sweet scent of the incense oil he'd spilt on her sleeve when they'd gone back to his flat for a smoke. It made her think of her mum and she felt a stab of guilt. She shouldn't have said those horrible things. If only her mum wouldn't get so wound up about it, as though she was about to commit a crime. She just wanted to be on television. What was so wrong with that?

She'd make it up to her tomorrow, she decided. Give her the painting of the Tor she'd finally bought from the gallery at the bottom of town. It could be an early birthday present. It had taken eight months to save up for it, but she knew her mum would be thrilled.

In the distance, she heard St John's church bell ringing out the time. The chimes reached twelve and stopped. The beginning of the witching hour. *How appropriate*, she thought as they passed the Witch and Wand shop. Not that she believed in any of that crap, of course. That was much more up mum's street. Still, she couldn't help glancing at the shop window to see what bizarre display they'd put up *this* week. But all she saw was their reflections. He looked sinister with his dark hood and long coat flapping out behind him. The Grim Reaper came to mind. God, she must be more stoned than she thought.

"Come on, Angel. Not long to go now," he said, as they reached the top of the High Street.

"D'you bring a lighter?" she asked breathlessly, jogging to keep up.

"Of course I did." He sounded tense, no longer the laid-back charmer she'd spent the last hour sharing spliffs and stories with. She felt the skunk wearing off and what made sense at the time now seemed nuts. All that stuff he'd said. All that shit about going home that she'd gone along with, not wanting to offend him. She shivered; a jolt of cold and something else.

"I wish I'd worn some more clothes," she said. "It's gonna be freezing up there."

"The flames'll keep you warm."

She could see the pointed tips of the candles sticking out of his rucksack. The wax looked orangey-brown under the light from the street lamps. His face was serious. She licked her lips. Her mouth felt sticky. Metallic tasting. It wasn't fun anymore. She didn't want to go up there; she wanted to go home. Maybe her mum would be awake and she could tell her she was sorry.

"What if someone sees us? Won't we get into trouble?"

"With who? And anyway, there won't be anyone up the Tor this time of night."

"I s'pose."

He stopped walking and turned to face her, slowly rubbing the tip of his nose with his thumb and forefinger.

"I hope you haven't changed your mind, Angel."

"It's not that," she said, looking down and noticing for the first time the size of his boots. They looked like they belonged to a clown.

"What then?"

"It's just . . ." she paused, searching for the right words, fiddling nervously with her necklace. What she wanted to say was that she thought he was a freak, that he was talking shit.

"Please, Angel," he begged. "You promised you'd help me."

She looked at his earnest expression and in that split second she felt total empathy; she knew what it was like to be desperate for something. It was why she'd bought the green garnet and hung it round her neck; it was meant to bring the wearer luck and success. Of course she didn't believe in any of that new age stuff, but to be honest, she'd do anything if it helped when she auditioned for *Second Chance* in a couple of weeks.

She thought about what her mum said: how you reap what you sow; how if you were good, then good things would happen to you. Maybe if she helped him out, however mad he was, she'd get her place on *Second Chance* and she'd be famous at last, the headline in all the papers. It was all she'd ever wanted.

"OK," she said.

TWENTY-THREE

As it turned out, Linton didn't get much of a chance to read the local paper. She was only halfway down the front page when Hooper stuck his head round the door to say there was a phone call for her. She took the paper with her so she could finish it later, hoping the call was from Gail. It wasn't.

"It's me. Chantelle. From the gallery." It took Linton a second to register. Of course. Annoying-cat-woman. "I, um, spoke to Mikey. He rang to say he's going to be travelling for a bit longer." She stopped. Linton remembered that getting information out of her was like pulling teeth.

"And?"

"What? Oh. Yeah. I asked him about the painting."

"And?" she repeated, not bothering to hide her irritation.

"Yeah, sorry. He can't remember who he sold it to."

"And that's it, is it?"

"Um, yeah."

Great, Linton thought, putting the phone down. Nothing was coming together. They were no closer to working any of it out. The wax flares, the spiritual locations. The connection between three dead women, a missing diabetic and a reality star spotted getting into a car. It was so frustrating.

She picked her phone up and tried Gail again. There was still no answer.

"Brown," she said, after she left yet another message. "You know I told you about Gail Chapman? How she came in to speak to me?'

"Mmm," he murmured absentmindedly.

"Well, I can't get hold of her."

"So?"

"I've been thinking. What if her story's true?"

He looked up and frowned. "What are you trying to say?"

"What if something's happened to her?"

"Like what? No one's reported her as missing, have they?"

"No."

"Well then. It's her day off from the hotel. She's probably gone shopping or something."

"But I've left messages on her mobile."

He shrugged. "You told me yourself she hates the police. And she's obviously pissed off because you didn't have time to see her. That's why she's not picking up."

"You're right." She was jumping to stupid conclusions. The thing with Vine not chasing up his alibi had shaken her, made her paranoid that she was missing things.

•••

It was a frustrating day of loose ends being tied, but without reaching any conclusions. A Tox Report came back to say Angel's blood had contained alcohol and cannabis and nothing stronger, but all it did was reinforce their initial speculation she'd gone up the Tor willingly.

Wells had finally finished chasing up every pharmacy in the surrounding area, his enquires taking him as far as Taunton, Yeovil, Bristol and Bath. So far, nobody had come in with a repeat prescription for insulin in the name of Samantha Jenkins.

"That's worrying in itself, don't you reckon?" he said. "Even if she's alive, she can't have long. Not without her medicine."

Brown merely grunted a response, but when he looked up a second later and caught Linton's eye, she knew what he was thinking. He was still feeling guilty about sleeping with Sam.

Not long after lunch, The Toad came back from a press conference in a foul mood, announcing that no one was to go home until they'd tracked down the car Becki was seen getting into.

Linton spent the next few hours pumping paracetamol into herself while she sifted through transcripts of the numerous calls they'd received relating to sightings of small, bluey-green cars on the night Becki went missing. After ringing half a dozen people, she still hadn't got anywhere. At seven o'clock she had a cup of tea and a muffin and then started on the batch that had come through during the evening. At ten she stopped, deciding it was too late to ring people back, besides which she needed a break. Her throat was on fire and her eyes felt like they'd been soaked in washing up liquid.

She opened the window behind her desk and stuck her head out, hoping some fresh air might wake her up. She could hardly believe it. For the first time in days, it had stopped raining. The dark, velvet sky looked clear and fresh, as though the rain had washed away all impurities. It was just like the night Angel Kingsley was murdered, Linton thought. The change in the weather was the last thing they needed.

"Linton? You all right?" She pulled her head back in. It was Hooper, arriving with another mug of tea. "Where's Brown?" he asked, "I've made him one as well."

"Gone to get a snack from the canteen."

She thanked him, sat back down and picked up the local paper from her desk, speed-reading the first five pages which were devoted to 'the serial killer in our midst.' She had a quick flick through the rest of the paper, to see if there was anything else of interest and found an article about Glastonbury's appeal.

If Simon Talbot hadn't written it, she wouldn't have read it, but despite everything, she was curious. There were interviews with several people in the town: the mayor, a vicar; a shopkeeper who insisted Glastonbury held a particular appeal to aliens because the Tor acted as a beacon for extra-terrestrial contact. She skimmed the article, part of her brain reluctantly admitting it was well written, another part of it nagging away at something.

When she reached the end of the article, she bristled once more at the sight of his name. Simon Talbot. *Otherwise known as Talbotski.*

God, she hated him.

As she stared at his name, thinking what a dick he was, something in her brain whirled and clicked, catching up with what she'd read in the article.

She now knew what had been nagging away at her.

"Shit," she said aloud. "Shit, shit, shit."

Her heart thudded uncomfortably in her chest. She grabbed at her computer mouse, her hand shaking. She found the notes on the Avebury cases and raced through the circumstances of Sadie Carter's death, stopping short when she got to the crucial part.

"Oh my God," she whispered. *Could it be him?* she thought, as a previous conversation with Brown came simultaneously flooding back.

"But better than being stuck with the names my brother and sister got."

"Why? What are they called?"

"Saturn and Venus."

"Anyway, I thought you said your brother was called Michael?"

"That's what he calls himself now."

She thought about the note her dad had written in the draft he'd sent to her.

"I've decided to change the DI's name from Summers to Stone. I think you'll agree it makes him sound much tougher, more resilient. Names are so important, don't you think?"

She needed one other piece of information. To be sure she was right. It took a few minutes to find the list of exhibitors.

Just as she expected, the name was there.

•••

Thanks to the officers who'd arrived only minutes before, the door to the flat on the High Street was open. They'd broken the window next to it, sending the smallest officer through to open the door from the inside. There wasn't much difference between the police and criminals when it came to forced entry. They both used the quickest and simplest way of getting in.

Linton tripped over the doormat as she followed Brown in, steadying herself against the wall of the badly lit hallway. Wells came out to greet them. "We must've missed them by minutes. The bed's still warm." They followed him into a small, stark room. The only furniture was a single bed pushed up against the far wall.

Despite the cold, the air was pungent, thick with the odour of the unwashed.

"It stinks," said Brown, jerking his head back as they moved closer to the bed, careful not to kick over the black bucket giving off the unmistakable stench of urine.

"Where are they now?" asked Brown.

"Fuck knows. We've got officers going up and down the street, banging on doors to see if anyone saw anything. It's gone eleven though. He obviously waited until everyone was in bed."

Brown had left the room before Wells had finished his last sentence. He was like an impatient estate agent, thought Linton.

"Have you seen this?" he shouted. "In here."

She followed the voice into a musty box room at the end of the dingy hallway. The floor was hidden under piles of tatty books and yellowing newspapers. An enormous map of Glastonbury hung from the wall, dominating the cramped space. It was covered with hundreds of red lines.

"Glastonbury's Ancient Landscape: Ley Alignments and Energy Centres," Brown said, reading aloud from the map. "The red lines on this map show the ley alignments between sacred sites. Descending the Tor, the most powerful ley lines pass precisely through other key sites in Glastonbury's sacred geography. Primary among these are the Chalice Well, Glastonbury Abbey and Wearyall Hill. . ." He stopped. "Shit."

"What?"

"He's used the map to decide where he's going to carry out his next sacrifice." He was out of the door before Linton had a chance to answer.

"Oi, Wells!" she heard him shout. "We need officers at Chalice Well, the Abbey and Wearyall Hill. And get a helicopter out. My money's on Wearyall Hill: it's the only one without security cameras."

•••

"Tonight's the night, Sam. We're finally going home."

She could smell rust. Or was it blood? Cold metal beneath her knees was digging into her skin. Up and down she bumped, wincing every time she went over a mound or lump. She'd come round only moments before, when he'd knocked into something. She was jerked forward and her head hit her raised knees. It took a moment to work out what was going on, until he started pushing her again. She was sitting in a wheelbarrow, her feet dangling over the front, like a bonfire guy brought to life.

The ground beneath was muddy and uneven. He must be finding it hard work because he was breathing heavily and kept stopping to rest. Now, as the rubber wheel hit something soft and squishy, she smelt something else. The sweet, tangy smell of a cowpat.

"We're nearly home," he said. "Not long to go now."

•••

Wearyall Hill. It was a high bank of land running for over a mile, almost reaching the outskirts of the neighbouring town of Street. From the top it gave a perfect overview of what was once the Isle of Avalon, its surrounding marshy levels making it an island in ancient times. From the top you could see the town and the Abbey and the other holy hills of Glastonbury: the Tor, Chalice Hill and St Edmund's Hill.

Linton had lived in Glastonbury for most of her life and had never set foot on it.

"You're joking!" said Brown, as they turned into Wearyall Lane, the steep road that would take them to the top of the ridge.

"I don't see what the big deal is," she said.

Brown cursed as a succession of speed humps forced him to slow down. As they neared the top of the hill, the road changed without warning from an ordinary-looking residential one into a narrow country lane with thatched-roof cottages either side. A second later, they pulled up at a farm gate behind two police cars, a police van and a white Nissan. Officers were still emptying out of their vehicles and bolting over the stile. Brown turned off his engine and pulled a torch from the glove compartment.

"Shouldn't we wait," Linton said, "let them do their job?"

"Fuck that. You can stay here if you like. I'm going."

"But how do we know where he is?"

"He'll be on the top of the ridge, I reckon. Follow me."

A second later they were out of the car, the frigid night air a shock after the festering warmth of Brown's car. Linton clambered over the stile behind him, skidding in the soft mud as she landed on the other side.

"Brown," she called out in a loud whisper, "slow down."

He stopped and turned to wait. As she ran to catch up, she slipped and crashed into him. She tried to grab his shoulders to steady herself, but he slid and lost his balance, staggering backwards. The next thing Linton knew he was on the ground and she was on top of him.

"Fuck," said Brown.

"Sorry," she hissed. She started to pull herself up, but Brown grabbed her arm and put his finger over her lips. From behind she heard a rustling. She lay still, trying not to breathe.

"A badger," said Brown, as it ran out of the hedge. Linton gasped at its size. Up close, it looked like an enormous dog. They watched him scurry off, both of them unmoving, as though caught in a trance.

As they lost sight of him, Linton was conscious of something hard pushing against her thigh. Embarrassed, she started to pull herself up, but Brown was already pushing her away.

"Let's go," he said gruffly, staggering to his feet.

Had adrenaline caused his obvious arousal? Linton wondered. But surely that had the opposite effect. It was part of the fight or flight thing. Wasn't it?

They began to move forwards. Once again Brown was out in front. Linton could just about make out his outline. He was going too fast. Probably as anxious to put some distance between them as he was to catch up with the rest of the force. Then, as he moved into some trees, she lost sight of him. From behind she heard a rustling sound.

She turned, expecting to see another badger and found herself staring into the piercing eyes of Simon Talbot.

•••

ONCE UPON A TIME

The Social Studies lesson was in J-block, in one of the portakabins. They were erected as a temporary measure when the school started running out of space, but lack of money had turned them into something permanent.

The teachers hated teaching in J-block. The rooms were sticky in the summer and stuffy in the winter thanks to the night-storage heaters, which couldn't be turned down.

Sam Jenkins could tell that Miss Edgar didn't just hate teaching in J-block, but that she hated it full stop. It was her first job since leaving training college and it hadn't taken the pupils long to smell easy prey.

"Okay, Samantha?" she now asked, smiling with what could've been encouragement, but looked more to Sam like a desperate plea for her to behave. "It's your turn to tell the class what you've discovered from looking at your family tree."

Sam stood up and strolled to the front of the classroom. Looking out across the sea of expectant faces, she smiled.

"What I've discovered from my family tree," she said, pausing for effect, "is that I'm adopted." She paused again, sensing the class straining forward with anticipation as they waited for her next sentence.

"I've always wondered why I was so different from everyone else in my family," she continued, with a smirk. "I don't even look like my parents. That's because they discovered me when I was a baby, in the field behind our house. They found me lying in a patch of burnt grass and glowing all over. They reckoned a space ship dropped me off and I was a superior being from another planet . . ."

"Samantha Jenkins," interrupted Miss Edgar, "that's enough. If you're not going to bother doing your homework, I'd appreciate you telling me up front instead of wasting mine and everybody else's time."

To the rest of the class it was just a funny thing to talk about on the way to the next lesson. It would all be forgotten by tomorrow. But for the boy in the corner of the classroom with the large, staring eyes, this was a realisation. An epiphany.

Samantha Jenkins was special too.

She was like him.

He wasn't alone.

•••

"What the hell are you doing?" Linton gasped.

"My job," said Talbot. "The same as you."

"It's your sister-in-law again, isn't it? She told you we were here. She's going to be in deep shit this time."

He laughed. "I don't know what you're on about. She's not even working tonight. I was in my flat and saw the police cars driving past, so I followed them."

"You're a liar. Don't you care that there could be three women's lives at stake? Go home. Now."

She started to move off, but he grabbed her arm.

"Three?" he said, pulling on her roughly. "Who's the other one?"

"Gail Chapman," she said, shaking free, hoping to shock him by giving him the name of someone he knew. She was taken aback when instead he laughed.

"It's serious," she said. "She's not answering her phone."

"He hasn't got her," he sneered.

"And how would you know?"

"Because I just left her in my flat. In bed. We spent the day there."

Linton's relief was brief. It was quickly replaced by scorn. "I thought you had a girlfriend," she spat.

"It didn't bother you the other night."

"That's because I didn't know she existed."

"And if you had, would it have stopped you?" He paused. "You know, thinking about it, maybe it wasn't the beer that caused our little problem. I've seemed to have been doing all right with Gail."

Linton stepped towards him and he put up his hand in mock defence.

"Calm down, dear. What is it? The time of the month?"

"No," she said, taking advantage of his raised hands and kneeing him as hard as she could in the groin. "It's time you learnt to treat women with some respect."

She turned and ran in the direction Brown had taken. She strained her ears, but it didn't sound as though Simon was following her. Hopefully he was doubled over in pain.

Shit, she thought suddenly. What if he reported her? But then she imagined the look on Gemma and Lisa's faces when she told them what she'd done and decided she didn't give a flying fuck.

•••

ONCE UPON A TIME

Sam couldn't believe he had the nerve to speak to her. She was coming out of K-block when he hurried over and said nervously, "You know what you said about being left behind in that field? Were you making it up?"

She looked at him blankly, trying to work out *why* he was talking to her, never mind *what* he was talking about. He was good-looking, she had to admit, but he was weird. And he had a temper. She'd seen it in action when one of the bullies had tried it on with him. He hadn't tried since. People were wary of him. She didn't speak to him; he didn't speak to her. So why now?

"In Social Education," he continued. "What you said about being from another planet."

"Oh. That." Out of the corner of her eye, she saw Karen walking towards her, raising her eyebrows as if to say, *"What the fuck?"* Oh my God, she definitely didn't want her to think she was talking to him. It was an unspoken competition between the two girls. Both jockeying for position of Queen Bee within the group of girls humming and buzzing around them. This could be ammunition.

"It's true," she replied pushing past him.

What exactly had she said? She couldn't even remember now. All she cared about was what her friend was going to say.

"What did he want?" asked Karen, nodding over her shoulder.

"Nothing," Sam replied.

"He must have said something. Is he your new secret boyfriend?"

"Get stuffed, Karen. He wanted to know when our English assignment's got to be in."

He walked away smiling. He'd overheard her lying to her friend. She obviously wanted to keep their conversation a secret.

The others had laughed. They hadn't believed her. But he knew now, it was true.

•••

Above Sam were the brightest lights she'd ever seen. She felt the air around her being whipped up, turning her hair to a rope that flapped and burnt against her cheeks. More bright lights, shining on the ground, coming towards her. Lots of shouting. Footsteps thudding. Men calling her name.

They were coming for her. Just like he said.

A dark shape crouched beside her and a gloved hand gripped her arm.

"We've got you now, Sam. You're safe."

She felt the tape being pulled back across from her mouth and heard the whimpering of a frightened animal. She realised the sound was coming from her.

"It's OK, Sam. You're going home." *No,* she tried to say. *Leave me alone.*

In the distance she could hear him shouting. "Get off me. You don't realise what you've done. They won't come back for me now. She was my only means of escape."

•••

By the time Linton reached Brown, it was over. A group of officers stood huddled round a dark figure. His head was bent down, his body shaking as though he was sobbing. She could see Sam Jenkins laid out on a stretcher, paramedics either side, being rushed towards the helicopter.

Brown ran towards Linton as soon as he saw her.

"Is she OK?" she yelled over the noise of the chopper's blades.

"She's alive," he shouted back.

"Where's Becki?"

"We don't know. He won't say."

"Was it him?"

"Yeah," he nodded. "You were right."

•••

Star Child. Formerly known as Richard Cooke. Dick to his friends.

The man Linton had seen in the queue at the doctor's surgery only that morning. The man who worked in the gem shop on the High Street. The nephew, otherwise known as Mr Child, who'd worked on a stand at the healing exhibition in Bristol. The same man who 'discovered' the body of Sadie Carter in Avebury when he was still known as Richard Cooke, before he'd changed his name to Star Child by deed poll.

The man Simon Talbot had interviewed for his piece in the local paper.

Star Child, formerly known as Richard Cooke, has lived in Glastonbury for most of his life . . .

The man with two names who was entered onto the murder enquiry database as two different people.

TWENTY-FOUR

"I want you so much, Linton."

They stumbled through her front door unable to wait any longer, grabbing and tugging at clothes as they kissed, their tongues urgent and probing, discovering one another's mouth for the first time. He grabbed her hips and pushed her up against the wall until her feet were a few inches shy of the floor. She kicked off her shoes and pointed her toes into the waistband of his underwear, pulling it down past his thighs and knees. They paused momentarily, looking into each other's eyes, their breathing short and ragged.

"God, you're beautiful," he said. And then he entered her, the sheer force of it causing her to gasp. She wrapped her legs around him and he began to move, slowly at first, murmuring her name, pushing himself deeper and deeper into her, faster and faster until he was moving in rhythm to the loud ringing noise. *What the hell was that loud ringing noise?*

She fumbled for the phone, knocking her alarm clock off the bedside table.

"Hello," she croaked. Her tongue felt thick and furry.

"Linton? It's me. I'm outside. Can I come in?"

Oh, my God. Brown. Hadn't they just been having sex?

"I'm in bed," she said, already clambering out of it, the lingering feeling of otherworldliness quickly disappearing with the movement. "Give me two minutes."

She stumbled into her bathroom and looked in the mirror. *Shit.* She splashed her face with cold water, gargled with mouthwash then looked down at the washed-out, oversized t-shirt she was wearing.

She staggered back into her bedroom, weak and sweaty with the effort of being up and about. Her hands trembled as she yanked on clean underwear, a pair of skinny jeans and a white t-shirt. She studied herself in her full-length mirror.

Fuck.

Rummaging around on the top of her chest of drawers, she managed to find a hairband. Ponytail in place, she rubbed some blusher on her cheeks and took another look.

Fuck, fuck, fuck.

Now he was ringing the doorbell.

"I thought you said two minutes," he shouted through the letterbox.

"I'm coming," she yelled, fumbling with the lid of her mascara and eventually giving up. She took one last look and felt like crying.

"You look awful," he said when she opened the door.

"Thanks," she said, feeling a flush creeping up her neck. Five minutes earlier she'd been having sex with him, up against this very wall.

"Is it Becki?" she asked quickly, trying to hide her embarrassment. "Have you found her?"

He shook his head. "He's denied abducting her. And, to be honest, I think he's telling the truth. Fuck knows where she is."

"So why are you here?"

"I thought you'd want to hear about Cooke. Star Child. Dick. Whatever you want to call him."

"Why didn't you phone?"

"I wish I had now. You're not exactly welcoming," he said, brushing past her, and through the door that led to her kitchen. "A cup of tea would be nice."

"No problem," she said, following him, unable to drag her eyes away from his backside, impossibly pert in his dark blue jeans. "Make yourself at home. Don't worry that I've got a temperature of 103 and feel like shit."

He sat down, flinging his battered briefcase onto the table. "Have you got any biscuits? I'm starving." He put his hands in the air in mock surrender as she shot him a poisonous look.

Flicking the switch on the kettle, she pulled herself up onto the kitchen counter so she was facing him.

"Go on then," she said. "Why did he do it?"

Brown cleared his throat, but didn't say anything.

"What?" she asked, puzzled by his reluctance.

He shook his head. "It's so fucking weird, I don't know where to start."

"Try."

"Well," he said, pausing, "you know he changed his name by deed poll to Star Child?" She nodded. "It's because he thinks that's what he is."

She jumped down from the worktop as the kettle came to the boil. "He thinks he's what?"

"He thinks he's from somewhere else. I mean not from Earth. An *actual* star child."

She laughed as she opened the cupboard and grabbed a couple of mugs. "You mean like an alien?" He was obviously winding her up.

"You think I'm joking, don't you?"

She put the mugs on the worktop and turned to him. "Well, you are, aren't you?"

He shook his head. "I told you it was weird. That's why I came round. It's easier to explain it in person."

•••

EXTRACT OF TRANSCRIPT FROM POLICE INTERVIEW WITH MR STAR CHILD (FORMERLY KNOWN AS MR RICHARD COOKE)

INTERVIEW TAKEN BY DCI HARGREAVES / ALSO IN ATTENDANCE DI BROWN

SC	I was fifteen when I first heard about them. There was a talk at the town hall. I'd seen a leaflet so I went along. The lady that did the talk, Cassandra, said how astral children were easy to recognise because they didn't fit in or follow the rules. They were the ones who found it hard to make friends and were always in trouble at school.
DCI	And did you feel like that?
SC	Yes.
DCI	So you thought you were one. An astral child.
SC	Yes. Except I didn't think, I knew.
DCI	It made it easier didn't it? A convenient way of

	excusing your behaviour.
SC	It wasn't like that. I could relate to what she was saying. It all fitted. Why I'd never got on with mum and why dad left home so easily. It was because I wasn't theirs. Afterwards she came up to me and said she saw an aura round me. She knew I was one.
DCI	You still haven't explained why you killed Hannah James and Angel Kingsley. Or left Sadie Carter to die in the cold.
SC	I didn't mean to.
DCI	So what did you mean to do?
SC	I wanted them to help me get home.
DCI	Home?
SC	Where I'm from. My star.
DCI	And how were they supposed to help?
SC	They were meant to attract my people.
DCI	Like a sacrifice?
SC	No! Why does everyone keep going on about sacrifices?
DCI	Sit down, Mr Child. You need to calm down.
SC	They'd all seen one. Either on Avebury Stones or the Tor.
DCI	What had they seen?
SC	My transport home. Call them UFOs if you like. I'd say they're more like taxis. It's because of the ley lines. They're like landing strips.
DCI	Landing strips?
SC	For astral beings. I've spent years looking but I've never seen one. The girls had though. They'd all seen UFOs. I thought if they were with me, they'd attract my people. And then I could ask them to take me home.
DCI	Why did you need the garden flares?
SC	So my people could see us. It was dark.
DCI	Tell us what happened with Hannah James.
SC	I met her when I was in Avebury one weekend. I've got a friend who lives there. He took me along to a

meeting about UFOs. Hannah was there. She
reckoned she'd been abducted by aliens. Afterwards
we got talking and I asked her to show me where it
happened. A couple of nights later I drove back to
Avebury and met up with her. She took me to the
stones but once we got there she said she'd made it
up.

DCI   I expect you frightened her.

SC   It wasn't like that.

DCI   But you got angry.

SC   In the end. But it wasn't my fault. She kept laughing
at me.

DCI   We all get angry, Mr Child, but don't all go round
killing people. But then you've always been a violent
person haven't you? That's why got you into trouble
at school, wasn't it? And we know what you did to
your mum. How you used to hit her around. Sit
down, Mr Child. For the record the suspect is
crying.

Interview terminated 13.15
Interview resumed 13.27

DCI   Tell us about Sadie.

[Silence]

DCI   Answer the question, Mr Child.

SC   It was a month later. I was staying in Avebury
looking after a friend's dog. I went to the
newsagents where she worked. I was buying a
magazine, about UFOs, and we got talking. She told
me she'd seen one near the stones on her way back
from the pub. I thought if I took her there it might
come back. But I knew she wouldn't go at night. Not
after what happened to Hannah. So I invited her
round to the flat.

DCI   And she came round, just like that?

SC	I think she fancied me.
DCI	Then you drugged her.
SC	The Doctor gave me Temazepam. For my insomnia. But I didn't like taking it, in case I got addicted. I had a whole packet left so I made her take some.
DCI	How?

[Silence]

DCI	How did you get her to take them?
SC	I'd already tied her up by then. I said if she didn't I'd have to kill her. I didn't mean it.
DCI	How did you get her to the stones?
SC	She's only small so I carried her. No one saw. And if even they had, they'd have thought she was drunk.
DCI	Why did you leave her there to die?
SC	That isn't what happened.
DCI	Well, tell me what did.
SC	I heard someone. They were walking through the field. It's a shortcut to get back from the pub. Anyway, I ran off. I went back in the morning but they'd already taken her.
DCI	Who?
SC	My people. They'd come for her and left her body behind.
DCI	Is that what you meant when the vicar heard you shouting, "It's not fair"?
SC	Well, it wasn't. They should have taken me instead.

•••

Linton made a second cup of tea. She also relented and opened a packet of shortcake fingers. Brown demolished them, leaving behind a sprinkling of crumbs and a reminder of why living alone had its good points.

"I never got round to telling you," she said, "but I saw him at the doctor's that day. Queuing up."

"Who?"

"Cooke. Richard. Star Child. Whatever you want to call him. He was picking up a repeat prescription."

"That was for the Temazepam. He'd run out."

"It's ironic. We were on the lookout for repeat prescriptions and there he was. Picking one up, under my very eyes."

Brown shrugged, "Except it wasn't for insulin."

"How's Sam?"

He folded his arms. "On the road to recovery."

They sat in silence for a few seconds, sipping their tea, lost in their own thoughts.

"There's one thing that doesn't make sense," Linton said suddenly.

"What's that?"

"The size fourteen prints they found at the second Avebury death."

"The body Cooke pretended to find?"

She nodded. "Why didn't the Dorset lot put two and two together? They should've known the prints belonged to him when they saw him wearing the Timberlands."

Brown took a slurp of tea. "He didn't have them on in the morning. He'd put his wellies on when he went back out because the grass was wet. They were a size fifteen."

"So you were right. About people not always wearing the right size shoe."

"And I was right about somebody sending the Timberlands from America. His dad lives there."

"But why wasn't Cooke ever a suspect? He found the body."

"He had an alibi," he explained. "The next-door neighbour. She'd heard him going up and down the stairs but it was probably his mate's dog. Besides he was only staying in Avebury temporarily. They had no reason to suspect he'd been there when Hannah was killed."

"What about Angel?"

"The night he killed her they got talking in the pub about UFOs. She told him she'd seen one once."

Linton nodded. "Her mum mentioned it."

"He followed her out of the pub and asked her if she wanted to go up the Tor and look again. They went to his flat first, to get the flares and walked back up the High Street which was when they passed our blind witness."

"So that *was* them."

"I've been thinking. She probably called him Dick, not dickhead. And when she told him not to get his hopes up, she wasn't talking about sex. She was on about seeing a UFO."

"But why did he kill her?"

"Because she didn't take him seriously. When they got up the Tor, she started joking around."

"But how did he manage to meet her off the bus?" she asked. "He didn't leave Bristol until after six."

Brown shook his head. "He left Bristol at four-thirty."

"But he and his uncle went to a café for the afternoon. We saw the receipt."

He shook his head. "His uncle went to his mate's house to score some drugs. He told his wife he'd stopped using. He was worried she'd ask what he'd been doing in Bristol on his own, so he asked Richard to lie and say they spent the afternoon together. He got the receipt from one of the other exhibitors in case his wife got suspicious. The paranoia of the drug-taker."

"But why wasn't his name entered onto the database properly after house-to-house spoke to him?" Linton said. "If they'd entered Richard Cooke, instead of Star Child, we'd have had a match against the Avebury cases."

"But his name *was* entered properly. He changed it by deed poll so it's on all his official documents. They entered him as Mr Star Child. Whoever did it thought Child was his surname."

"Surely someone must've questioned the name."

"Come on, Linton. This is Glastonbury. People call their kids all sorts. You of all people should know that. Look at what your parents called your brother and sister." He paused. "How is he by the way? Michael."

Linton shrugged. "The same."

They were silent for a moment. "Hargreaves must be pleased," she said eventually. "That he's got his man."

"He's not happy with me though."

"Why?"

"You obviously haven't seen the *Forum*," he said, yanking his briefcase towards him and unlocking it. He rummaged around for a few seconds and then pulled out an A4 booklet. "I think it's taken some of the shine off it."

"How d'you mean?"

"Page five," he said, handing it to her. She flicked through until she found a photo of a tanned and grinning Brown.

"It's your question and answer thing."

"Have a read."

She skimmed the first couple of answers stopping short when she got to the title of his favourite film: *Misadventures at Megaboob Manor.*

"Oh my God," she snorted, "I thought you were going to change the answers."

"I emailed them the wrong version, didn't I?"

She wasn't sure if it was the tension of the last two weeks being released or the thought of Hargreaves reading Brown's answers, but Linton laughed until there were tears running down her face.

"It's not that funny."

"It is," she spluttered. "I can't believe they printed it," she said, when she finally got herself under control again.

"I can. Sandra Wallace works on it. I had a thing with her a while back, more of a one-night stand. I think this was her way of telling me I should have phoned when I said."

"It makes you look like a womanising tosser."

"I *am* a womanising tosser, I've decided. There's no point in pretending to be anything else. Which reminds me. I'd better get going. I've got a date tonight, with PC Turley."

Linton felt her stomach tighten. "A date?"

Brown nodded. "She's going back to Devon tomorrow, so I thought I may as well have a go." He looked at his watch. "I better be off. Anyway Ben'll be home soon, won't he?"

"Ben?"

Brown cocked his head to one side. "I thought he'd moved back in."

"What made you think that?"

"I drove past here the other night," he said, shoving the *Forum* back into his briefcase and clicking it shut. "After you rang me about the shampoo. I needed to get some cigarettes from the Esso garage. For my flatmate. He wasn't sober enough to drive. Anyway, I saw Ben's car parked outside your house."

"We were talking. Well, arguing."

"Oh. Right."

After she'd let Brown out, Linton mentally tracked the car journey from his home to the garage. He had no reason to drive past her house. And besides, he was an ardent non-smoker in the way only a former twenty-a-day addict could be . . .

Crawling back into bed without even bothering to take off her clothes, she lay looking up at the ceiling, going over the events of the past few days, thinking about what Angel's mum had said:

Don't leave it too late. Tell people how you really feel about them.

She cleared her throat and picked up the phone from the bedside table and dialled. It's now or never, she thought.

"Hi, it's me. Look, I wanted to tell you something. Something I should've said before." She paused. "I think you're amazing. You're gorgeous and clever and kind and funny and I'm so lucky to have you in my life."

There. She'd said it. It wasn't so bad, was it?

"I love you," said the voice on the other end.

"I love you too, Michael. Thanks for being a great brother."

TWENTY-FIVE

"It's dreadful that the shop was forced to close down," said Rachel predictably, as they drove into the village. She said it every time they stayed at their house in Devon.

Andrew waited for the next part of her tirade, when she launched into her rant about the locals. He could quote her word for word he'd heard it so many times.

"They moan about us second home owners ruining the village, but they were all off shopping in Sainsbury's while we were in there, racked with guilt, buying soggy apples and frozen lasagne at three times what you'd pay anywhere else."

But as they pulled up outside Sunny Thatch, his wife was quiet. She was peering up at their cottage that was set back from the road, looking as though it was built into the side of the hill. It still gave him a thrill every time he saw it. It wasn't so much the house, but what it signified. Success.

"That's odd," she said.

"What?"

"Look. Our bedroom window's open at the top. And the curtains are open. I'm positive I left them closed. I always check before we leave. I remember doing it. Oh, my God! I think someone's broken in."

He was out of the car and running up the steps before she'd even finished her sentence. He unlocked the front door, pushing his hip so hard against the painted wood he fell into the hallway. From somewhere in the house, he heard the muffled sound of music.

"What's happened, Andrew?" It was Rachel rushing in behind him, breathing heavily. He heard a creak on the stairs and they both looked up.

"Will!" Rachel shrieked. "What the hell are you doing here? I thought you had seminars this week."

Their son was naked from the waist up, a lilac towel wrapped tightly around his hips.

"What about you?" he said indignantly. "You told me you weren't coming down for a few weeks."

"I had some time on my hands," said Andrew. "That's what happens when the subject of the book you're writing goes missing."

He heard a click to his right-hand side and turned to see the kitchen door slowly opening.

"Andrew?" The voice belonged to a pretty blonde wearing Rachel's floor-length, pink towelling dressing gown. A pretty blonde he'd seen only hours before staring at him from the front page of his newspaper.

"Becki?" he said. "What the hell are you doing here?"

•••

"Let me get this straight."

Rachel was standing at the kitchen sink, rubber-gloved hands plunged into the steaming water, scrubbing furiously. The dishwasher, which she'd insisted on loading ("I can't think straight with all this mess"), was whirring quietly to her right.

"Becki," she said tightly, "you're on the run from a famous man you had an affair with because you threatened to name him in your autobiography and now he wants to bump you off. Am I right so far?"

"Um, yes."

"And in order to put this man off your scent, you went to Glastonbury for the night. Then you got my son to drive you down here, so it looked as though you were abducted by the nutcase who murdered those other women in the hope the man who's after you would leave you alone."

"That's right."

Andrew looked over at Becki. She was nervously picking dried Weetabix off the table with her long fingernails.

"And what did you plan to do? Stay down here forever? There's a nationwide hunt going on for you, in case you hadn't noticed." Rachel turned round and glared at Becki. Soapy bubbles dripped off her gloves onto the charcoal floor tiles. "I don't understand why you don't just tell the police if you're so worried this man is after you."

Becki didn't look up, just carried on picking at the Weetabix.

"I was scared they wouldn't believe me."

"I'm not bloody surprised," said Rachel. "It's the most ludicrous story I've ever heard."

Becki didn't say anything, just carried on staring at the table.

"You're not on the run at all, are you?" said Rachel.

Becki shook her head.

"Perhaps you better tell us what's going on."

So she did.

•••

Linton sighed. It was five minutes since she'd last done it. Perhaps, if she listened again, it would make sense.

She reached for her phone, dialled 1571 and pressed two so she could hear the saved message once again. The one Brown had left last night while he was out on his date with PC Turley.

"Linton. It's me," he shouted over the pumping music in the background. "I tried your mobile but you're not answering. Are you there? I've been thinking, shit, hang on a sec. WHAT? Hold on. It's my flatmate. CAN'T YOU SEE I'M ON THE PHONE? Sorry. Gotta go. Maybe I'll see you tomorrow if you're in."

She put the phone down. If only she hadn't felt too ill to answer it last night.

She picked it up again, dialled 1571 and pressed two.

•••

Claire Jenkins looked at her watch. It was ten-past. Perfect. She'd made sure she was late so the meeting had already started. She didn't want to have to make small talk with the others. They were bound to ask about her sister and she didn't want to talk about it any more. Her emotions were all over the place, especially after Sam's confession.

"Dad was going on at me again. About not taking college seriously enough," she'd rasped, her throat hoarse with dehydration and exhaustion. "I took my hands off the wheel and stuck my fingers in my ears to wind him up. That's why we crashed. That's why he died."

She paused outside the door and ran her hand through her hair. She felt silly now, making all this effort. She hoped her make-up wouldn't look overdone under the harsh lights of the church hall and that her top wasn't too low-cut.

She took a deep breath and pushed open the door. Seven faces turned to look at her. One of them instantly lit up and broke into a broad grin. She couldn't help but smile back.

•••

INSIDE STORY MAGAZINE. DECEMBER 5TH

10 HOT STORIES EVERYONE'S TALKING ABOUT THIS WEEK

1. The reality-show star who lost touch with reality
One of the most bizarre stories to have hit the headlines this week is that of Becki Harvey.

Famous for appearing on *Working Girl* three years ago, the D-list celebrity has been charged with wasting police time after faking her own kidnapping. The charge carries up to nine months in prison and a possible £10,000 fine.

Becki disappeared from Glastonbury last Wednesday night amidst fears that the recently captured ley line strangler had abducted her.

She was discovered hiding in a house in Devon by the parents of a male friend. She'd told the friend she was on the run from the famous married man she was threatening to name in her forthcoming autobiography believing he'd put a 'hit' out on her.

However, in a further twist, it turns out *she'd invented* the famous man to make her autobiography more interesting. When publishers put pressure on her to name him, she 'disappeared' from Glastonbury so it would look as if she was abducted. Her plan was to 'escape' from the ley line strangler in the hope her publishers would forget about the invented married man and concentrate on her kidnapping and dramatic getaway instead.

"I've made a mess of everything," she's reported to have said.

Or has she?

The irony is that even without the revelation of an affair, with a possible jail sentence hanging over her head, Becki Harvey's book is predicted to be a bestseller.

BOOK 2 IN THE KATE LINTON SERIES

EENY MEENY MINY MOE

OUT MAY 2012

Eighty-year-old former model, Lauren Hampton, is found suffocated in the drawing room of her Glastonbury manor house. DS Kate Linton and DI Rob Brown investigate the case against the backdrop of a series of vicious sex attacks on local women.

It was a quarter to nine when Sheila arrived home. Silence greeted her and as always she rebuked its welcome by turning on the radio as loudly as she could bear. She needed noise. She worried if it ever got too quiet, she'd be able to hear him. When he was alive, he'd filled every corner of the house with his presence. Every wall, mirror and surface had seemed to scrutinise, criticise and chastise her.

"You'll never be good enough."

She'd see the words on the television screen as she rubbed at the children's handprints so they didn't interfere with the news; she'd smell them in the bleach as she scrubbed the toilet and taste them in the meals she cooked him every night.

Tonight though, the house felt different, lighter somehow, as though it had sensed her brighter mood.

And then her phone rang, its shrill tone making her jump.

"Sheila?" It was the unmistakable voice of Mark Hampton. She hesitated. There was only one reason for him ringing at this time of night. Too late now though.

"Yes?"

"I can't get hold of Lauren. I don't suppose you know where she is?"

"At home, I'd imagine," she said, snapping at each word as though they were dry twigs.

"I'm at the theatre and I can't find my wallet. I've been ringing throughout the interval to ask if she's seen it, but she's not answering. I can't understand where she is." He paused. "The thing is I'm just about to go back on stage."

"Oh," said Sheila. She knew what was coming next.

"I don't suppose you could nip up and see if everything's OK?"

She wondered why he bothered phrasing it as a question. They both knew she'd say yes. She had no choice.

"I'll leave now," she said. "I'll ring you when I get there."

Tonight, more than ever, Elmtree Manor seemed to sneer at Sheila as she completed the winding approach of gravelled driveway. It was a greedy house, she thought. Over the years, along with its owner, she'd felt the place consume her, until she was nothing but an empty carcass.

Lauren Hampton's silver Mercedes was parked in its usual spot. Sheila climbed out of her Polo and crunched her way towards the front entrance. She knocked loudly and waited, expecting to hear the clipped tones of her employer, "For God's sake, I'm coming." But there was nothing. She knocked again and waited. Still nothing. She'd try the old servants' entrance, she decided. It was normally left unlocked, as though personality alone could keep intruders at bay.

She unlatched the ornate metal gate and followed the path that led down the side of the house to a small wooden door.

"Hello?" she called as she edged it open. "Mrs Hampton? It's me. Sheila."

Nothing, only an ominous silence. She let herself into the narrow corridor, pushed the door shut behind her and turned left into the vast kitchen. "Mrs Hampton?" Still no answer. She glanced across at the kitchen worktop. It was a jumble of cereal packets, dirty plates, bowls, cups and glasses. *Lazy bitch.* It had only been a day. She shuddered to think what state the house would fall into if she were allowed to take more time off.

She crossed the room and stepped out into the gloomy hallway.

"Hello?" she called out. "It's Sheila." She stood for a moment, listening intently. The familiar sounds of the house seemed amplified; the rumble of the old boiler like distant thunder, the ticking of the grandfather clock like a loud, mocking clap. Still no answer from Lauren.

The garden. *Of course.* She was probably messing about with her roses again. No wonder she hadn't heard the phone. What a waste of her time.

It was quicker to reach the rose trellis through the French windows in the drawing room, so Sheila marched across the hallway and through the open door. The curtains were drawn, to protect the antique furniture from sunlight, so it took a moment to adjust to the half-light.

And then she saw her. Lauren Hampton. She was lying in a heap beside the leather armchair that faced the French windows and the stretch of lawn beyond. Next to her head lay a crumpled carrier bag. Sheila tried to focus on this oddity, but a perverse curiosity insisted on dragging her eyes back to the face instead. It looked twisted, bluish-grey and ugly, as though Lauren's true essence had seeped out through her skin and was now visible to the world.

She was dead. There was no doubting it. Sheila had seen a corpse before of course, but this time she was unprepared for it. Now, in contrast to the inanimate body before her, she was aware, more than ever, of how vital her own was. Her skin tingled, the hairs on her arms and neck rose up, her heart pounded uncomfortably and a rush of noise, a sort of gurgled roar, filled her head.

She tried to move. The phrase 'frozen to the spot' came to mind and along with it a memory of her daughter and grandson, when he was a year old. They were out shopping. Heather had given him a plastic bag to play with in the pushchair. He liked the noise it made when he scrunched it up.

"You can't give him that," she'd said. "It's dangerous."

"Oh, mum," her daughter had replied. "I'm watching him the whole time. I'll stop him if he starts to put it over his head. And anyway, how many people do you know who've been suffocated with a plastic bag?"

At least one, she'd now be able to say.

She felt herself stagger backwards. *The police*, she thought, trying to pull herself together. *I need to ring the police.*

Her legs had turned to jelly but somehow she managed to stagger out into the hallway.

"I need to phone the police," she said, as though saying it aloud would confirm her intention. She could hear and feel the shake and judder in her voice.

The telephone was on the sideboard, cradled in its black holder, a small green light flashing to show that Lauren had messages. *Messages she would never hear*. Sheila grabbed at it, but her fingers felt as though they didn't belong to her, as if they'd swollen up like sausages, except when she looked they were the same size as always. She managed to grasp the phone and as she did she noticed a white envelope, addressed in Lauren's handwriting, next to the dead woman's handbag. The name on the envelope was familiar. Michael Fenn.

How did Sheila know that name? She couldn't think straight, her heart was beating too fast. She felt sick, dizzy, as though she might faint at any moment. Michael Fenn. Michael Fenn. Michael Fenn.

Then it came to her. Of course. She'd seen his name so many times before; it was only because it was out of context, she couldn't place him straight away. She picked up the envelope and slipped it into her handbag.